THE MURDER RULE

"Matters culminate in a courtroom fireworks display worthy of Perry Mason in his prime. *The Murder Rule* holds one's interest from its cheeky opening pages through its final scene."

—*Wall Street Journal*

"Excellent.... McTiernan [is] an uncommonly fine mystery writer.... What a thrilling book this is." —*New York Times Book Review*

"Gripping and full of tension, with twist after unexpected twist. You won't just read *The Murder Rule,* you'll devour it."

—Karin Slaughter, *New York Times* bestselling author of *Girl, Forgotten*

"Dervla McTiernan is an extraordinary writer, and *The Murder Rule* is a brilliant, breathtaking, and irresistible thriller with unforgettable characters and twists on top of twists."

—T. J. Newman, *New York Times* bestselling author of *Falling*

"Dervla McTiernan has become one of my favorite writers, and if you read *The Murder Rule,* she will quickly become one of yours. This book is diabolically clever, highly compelling, and deeply moving. I loved *The Murder Rule* and did not want it to end."

—Don Winslow, *New York Times* bestselling author of *The Force* and *The Border*

"Extraordinary. Haunting. An incredible thriller. I could not put this book down. Dervla McTiernan is a gifted writer with a very special way of telling a story. This is a heart-stopping roller coaster of a tale."

—Adrian McKinty, *New York Times* bestselling author of *The Chain*

you can read them. The characters are excellently drawn and the plotting is pacy and intelligent. I totally enjoyed this gripping read."

—Patricia Gibney, author of *The Guilty Girl*

"Thrilling, compelling, and packed with twists, this is McTiernan at a whole other level. I can't get enough of this author."

—Jo Spain, author of *The Perfect Lie*

"Thoroughly addictive. . . . An absolute must-read."

—Anna Downes, author of *The Safe Place*

"It's a tough call when she has consistently set the bar so high, but *The Murder Rule* by Dervla McTiernan may be her best yet. Taut, gripping, and beautifully written, it also packs a devastating twist."

—Simon Lelic, author of *The Search Party*

"With a refreshing willingness to wade into uncomfortable gray areas, Dervla McTiernan's exceptional *The Murder Rule* has nailed something fundamentally true about being human: that none of us are quite who we pretend to be and that being the hero in your own story doesn't stop you from being the villain in someone else's. Grabs you from the first page and refuses to let go. Brilliant."

—Gabriel Bergmoser, author of *The Hunted*

"A serpentine tale of diverse motivations, unforeseeable surprises, heinous betrayals, and appalling brutality, *The Murder Rule* stuns and shines." —*Free Lance-Star* (Fredericksburg, Virginia)

"McTiernan keeps the suspense high." —*Publishers Weekly*

"Hannah's considerable ruthlessness and determination make her one of the most memorable characters in current crime fiction."

—*Los Angeles Review of Books*

THE
MURDER
RULE

ALSO BY DERVLA MCTIERNAN

The Rúin

The Scholar

The Good Turn

THE
MURDER
RULE

A Novel

Dervla McTiernan

WILLIAM MORROW
An Imprint of HarperCollinsPublishers

For Kenny, Freya, and Oisín. Always.

THE MURDER RULE. Copyright © 2022 by Dervla McTiernan. All rights reserved. Printed in the United States of America. No part of this book may be used or reproduced in any manner whatsoever without written permission except in the case of brief quotations embodied in critical articles and reviews. For information, address HarperCollins Publishers, 195 Broadway, New York, NY 10007.

HarperCollins books may be purchased for educational, business, or sales promotional use. For information, please email the Special Markets Department at SPsales@harpercollins.com.

A hardcover edition of this book was published in 2022 by William Morrow, an imprint of HarperCollins Publishers.

FIRST WILLIAM MORROW PAPERBACK EDITION PUBLISHED 2023.

Designed by Nancy Singer

Library of Congress Cataloging-in-Publication Data has been applied for.

ISBN 978-0-06-304221-6

23 24 25 26 27 LBC 5 4 3 2 1

From: Hannah.Rokeby1872@maine.edu
To: RobertMParekh@law.virginia.edu
Subject: Fall Semester 2019—Volunteer
Date: Sunday, August 18, 2019 4:33 P.M.

Dear Professor Parekh,

My name is Hannah Rokeby. I am a third-year law student at the University of Maine and I am transferring to UVA Law this coming semester. I apologize for emailing you directly, but I understand that the official application period for the Innocence Project program has closed. I am so eager to volunteer for the Project that I thought perhaps I should write and appeal to you personally. I am hoping you will make an exception in my case.

My mother has been ill with cancer for some time, and she is now enrolled in a medical trial at University Hospital. I will be attending UVA Law for the coming semester so that I can be close to my mother and reachable if she should need me.

I have a 3.9 GPA (please see my attached transcript). I'm third in my class and I have already completed sixty-eight credits so I am well on track to graduate. I would therefore be able to dedicate more days and hours than most students to my work at the Innocence Project. I passionately believe in the work you do with death row prisoners and others who have been wrongfully convicted, and I would be so grateful to be given the opportunity to work for a cause that is so close to my heart. I can be contacted by email or by phone at any time.

Sincerely,
Hannah Rokeby
207-555-0134

From: RobertMParekh@law.virginia.edu
To: Hannah.Rokeby1872@maine.edu
Subject: Re: Fall Semester 2019—Volunteer
Date: Monday, August 19, 2019, 10:46 A.M.

Dear Ms. Rokeby,

Volunteer positions for the coming academic year have been
allocated. The application process is highly competitive for the
Innocence Project clinic, and all positions are filled, following
rigorous interview, in the final semester of the preceding academic
year. For future reference, when assessing applications I look for
evidence of research skills and self-organization (e.g., knowledge of
application closing dates), as well as grades.

Robert M. Parekh
Associate Professor of Law, General Faculty
Director, Innocence Project Clinic

From: Hannah.Rokeby1872@maine.edu
To: RobertMParekh@law.virginia.edu
Subject: Re: Fall Semester 2019—Volunteer
Date: Monday, August 19, 2019, 10:52 A.M.

Dear Professor Parekh,

Thank you for your email. Perhaps I should have mentioned that I'm
very good friends with a former student of yours, Annabel Bancroft.
I expect that you remember Annabel, as I understand you worked
very closely together. Annabel told me in detail about the personal

mentoring you provided to her, which I found fascinating. I wonder if others would be as interested.

I sincerely hope that you might reconsider my application.

Hannah Rokeby
207-555-0134

From: RobertMParekh@law.virginia.edu
To: Hannah.Rokeby1872@maine.edu
Subject: Re: Fall Semester 2019—Volunteer
Date: Monday, August 19, 2019, 3:11 P.M.

Hannah,

Come and see me when you get here next week. We may be able to find a place for you.

Robert M. Parekh
Associate Professor of Law, General Faculty
Director, Innocence Project Clinic

Hannah

ONE

The night before she left for law school, Hannah Rokeby didn't sleep. She went to bed early and listened to the sounds her mother made as she moved about the house. Their home in Orono wasn't small, but it was old, and sound traveled. Hannah heard the clatter of dishes from the kitchen, the opening and closing of cupboard doors, Laura's footsteps as she moved into the living room, then silence. No television, but that made sense, because Laura would likely be reading. At eleven-thirty P.M., when the creak of floorboards signaled that Laura was finally climbing the stairs to go to bed, Hannah closed her eyes and concentrated on her breathing, making sure that it was slow and even. Her bedroom door opened. Laura entered the room, came over, and sat on the bed. Hannah could smell her mother's perfume—jasmine and cedar. She tried not to flinch as Laura stroked her forehead, once, twice, three times.

"My darling." Laura's voice was soft, not much more than a whisper. Hannah kept her eyes closed. Breathed in, and out. A minute passed. Laura was very still, so still that Hannah's mind started to play tricks on her. Could she still feel the weight of her mother's hand where it rested against her lower back, outside the blankets? Still feel the slight tilt in the mattress caused by Laura's position on the bed? Hannah resisted the urge to open her eyes. Laura liked to talk and Hannah couldn't bear that, not tonight. Another long moment passed before Laura sighed, and finally rose. She left the room, closing the door behind her, and Hannah opened her eyes. She reached for her phone and checked the time. She set a silent alarm, closed her eyes again, and tried, unsuccessfully, to sleep.

At four A.M. Hannah got out of bed, opened her closet, and took out her large backpack and her shoulder bag. The backpack was already packed. She filled her shoulder bag with those small essentials she hadn't been able to pack without prompting questions from Laura that she wasn't ready to answer. Her hairbrush, toothbrush, and her small bag of makeup and toiletries. The copy of *Vanity Fair,* hidden under her pillow, that had started all of this. A couple of textbooks—Charles O'Hara's book on criminal investigation, and another on forensic and criminal psychology. Legal pads and a few pens. Hannah hesitated. There was something she was forgetting, something important. Memory returned and she took two quick steps to her nightstand and drew out a small, battered notebook with a faded red cover. She held the notebook between her hands for a moment, drawing strength from it, then carefully tucked it between the textbooks in her shoulder bag. It would be safe there.

Hannah turned off her bedside lamp and left the room. The house was very dark. What light there was came from Laura's bedroom; her door was open. Hannah set her bags down gently and crept forward. A floorboard creaked and she flinched. She waited a moment, then leaned against the doorjamb of her mother's room and peered inside. Laura was sound asleep. She had left her blinds open and moonlight streamed in across her bed. She looked beautiful, but that was to be expected. Laura always looked beautiful. In her early forties, she was still slim and blond with fine features and an air of fragility that seemed to attract the wrong kinds of men. It was only in sleep that that fragility—expressed by a slight tightness in the set of her lips, a suggestion of strain in her eyes—faded away and she looked like she should. As if nothing had ever hurt her.

Hannah pulled the door slowly closed. There was no creak from the hinges, because she had oiled them the day before. She went downstairs, took a folded note from her backpack, and placed it so that it was held in place by the coffee machine. Okay. Almost there. Hannah went to the laundry room. There was an extra freezer there that they used to store frozen vegetables and ice cream. She opened the door and pushed aside the bags of frozen peas that covered her stash. For the past two weeks she had made extra portions of the meals she prepared for lunch and dinner, boxed and labeled them, and stored them here, where she could be sure Laura wouldn't find them. Using the light from her phone as a flashlight, Hannah chose a portion of quiche and another of shepherd's pie and carried them back to the kitchen fridge, where Laura would see them.

Everything was in place. It was time to go.

Except . . . damnit . . . should she search? One last time before she left? Hannah was torn—on the one hand, searching was a betrayal of Laura's trust (she had *promised*); on the other, it would be irresponsible not to, right? Hannah looked at her watch and grimaced. She had time, barely. And she could do it quickly, run through the usual places. First the water bottles in the fridge. Check the seals, make sure they haven't been opened. Then run a hand behind the books on the shelves in the living room. Next lift the couch cushions, then look inside the ficus planter in the corner, then the water tank in the downstairs bathroom. She found nothing. Hannah's spirits lifted. Where else? Laura's tennis bag—it was hanging on the end of the stairs and there was a plastic water bottle tucked in the outside pocket. Hannah opened the bottle and sniffed. Water. She was being silly. This was a delaying tactic because she was afraid to leave. *Pathetic.* Enough. Time to go.

Unlocking the front door meant undoing the chain and the dead bolt. There was no way to close them all again from the outside, but it was only a couple of hours to dawn now. Laura would be fine, Hannah told herself. *Laura would be fine.* The air was cool and clear, and there was an Uber idling out front, lights on. Hannah hurried down the drive, put her backpack in the trunk, and climbed into the car. The driver was a hulking shadow in the darkness.

"When I booked you, I left instructions to wait down the street," Hannah said.

He shrugged his indifference. His eyes met hers briefly in the rearview mirror. "The airport?"

"Yes."

The car pulled slowly away from the curb and Hannah looked back at the house.

"Wait."

"What?"

"Just give me a second." Hannah was out of the car before he'd come to a complete stop. She ran to the trash cans that were lined up neatly to one side of the garage. She opened the recycling can. It was full of empty milk cartons and yogurt containers, with cardboard packaging neatly folded on top. Hannah rummaged through everything, telling herself all the time that this was crazy, that she was being paranoid, and yet feeling nothing but a sense of inevitability when her hand closed around a bottle that wasn't empty at all. She drew out a full bottle of Grey Goose, then another. She searched again, but that was it. Goddamnit. What did this mean? The bottles were full. But . . . at least they hadn't been opened. That was a good sign. Laura might have bought them, but she hadn't had a drink. So far, at least, she had kept her promise. Hannah opened the bottles, poured the vodka into the lawn, and put the empty bottles back into the recycling can. Then she ran back to the cab.

"Everything okay?" the driver asked. She could see his eyes again in the rearview mirror, assessing, curious.

"Fine."

He drove on through dark and empty streets, and they didn't speak. Hannah looked out of the window, watched the houses as they passed, saw the occasional light come on as early risers started their day. She thought of Laura, waking alone to a dark house.

HANNAH'S FLIGHT LANDED AT DULLES AT TEN-THIRTY A.M. AT eleven-thirty she boarded a bus. She fell asleep almost before the bus left the station and slept on and off all the way to Virginia. The bus pulled into Charlottesville just before one P.M. and she got off, feeling groggy, headachy, and hungry. She hesitated, then turned on her phone. She had six missed calls from Laura and three text messages. Hannah ignored the calls and the messages and instead used her maps app for directions. The place she'd rented was less than a mile from the station. She grimaced as she thought about calling an Uber. She couldn't face small talk, and maybe some fresh air would make her feel better. Besides, a walk would give her a chance to check out a little bit of Charlottesville. She set off, and was just beginning to regret her decision when she reached the apartment building. Hannah checked out the three-story building and let out a sigh of relief. She'd expected a dump. When you book the very last rental available the week before classes start, that's almost what you deserve. But so far, so good. According to her maps app, the building was only a five-minute walk from the law school, as promised. The paint was clean and bright. There was even a little yard out front, pretty and well-maintained. Hannah made for the entrance and pressed the buzzer for apartment 5B. A few moments later a slightly distorted voice came through the speaker.

"Yes?"

"Yes, hi. I'm Hannah Rokeby. I'm looking for David Lee?"

There was a moment's silence. "Uh . . . yeah? This is David."

"I'm subletting Prisha Laghari's place this semester. She said you'd have the keys."

"Oh yeah, right. Sorry. I'll be right down. Just two minutes."

It was closer to seven minutes before David appeared. He was a good-looking guy, sloppily dressed in jeans and an oversize T-shirt. He pulled the front door open and gestured for Hannah to come inside. He had the smudged remains of eyeliner around his eyes.

"Sorry," he said. "It took me a minute to find them." He held up a key ring, a stainless-steel dolphin with two keys and a swipe card attached. "Prisha's place is on the third floor. I'll show you." He led the way toward the elevator. Hannah followed. She had her backpack on her back, her shoulder bag dangling from her right hand.

"You travel light," David said. "You should have seen me yesterday. My parents took my Mom's minivan, and I drove my car and we could barely fit in all my stuff. But I play keyboard, you know, and guitar. With my amps too it takes up a lot of space."

"Right," Hannah said.

"I'm in a band." He looked at Hannah with an air of expectation. It was clear that he wanted her to ask him about his music, his gigs; maybe even ask him for coffee to talk about it. Hannah stared back at him blankly. She wasn't there to make friends. They rode up in the elevator in an awkward silence, arrived on the fifth floor, and he led the way down the corridor. Inside, the building was bright and modern, the carpet very clean and the paintwork fresh.

David stopped outside apartment 5B and held out the keys.

"This is you," he said. "See you around."

"Thanks."

He left, and Hannah turned and unlocked the door to 5B. She walked inside, dropped her bag on the ground, and shut the door behind her. The apartment was . . . great. It was a studio. It had high ceilings and two large windows that let in a lot of light. There were bookshelves, still half-full, and a kitchenette built against the wall to the left. There was a double bed against one wall, its mattress bare. Suddenly everything felt strikingly unreal. Like she'd just taken a step into someone else's life. Hannah crossed the room and sat on the bed, then sank back, pulled a pillow toward her and pressed it to her face. What was she doing? Was this crazy?

Ever since she had stumbled across the *Vanity Fair* article two weeks ago and found out exactly what was happening at the University of Virginia, she'd been too caught up in the frantic forward momentum of her plan to have time to think. Except, no . . . that was bullshit. She'd had plenty of time to think, she just hadn't allowed herself to. And now she was in Charlottesville, at the point of no return. It wasn't too late. She could still leave, take her bags, head back to Maine. Except . . . she'd be going back to *what*? More of the same? No chance for change, for things to really, truly, get better?

No. No way. She was here for a reason and no way was she going to chicken out before she'd even gotten started.

Hannah

TWO

Hannah unpacked, showered, dressed, then grabbed her jacket and decided to explore the campus. The law school offices probably wouldn't be open, but she could figure out where everything was, save time later. And it was a beautiful day, better to be outside. The sun was shining and the sidewalks were busy with students. Classes started tomorrow, and most students had already moved in, but a few stragglers were still arriving. There were students out jogging, others lugging mattresses into apartment buildings, and more just walking with friends, coffee cups in hand. Hannah yawned widely. Coffee. That was an idea. She bought a cappuccino from a friendly girl at a café where the speakers played Tracy Chapman, and fought the urge to sit there for the day.

The offices of the Innocence Project were in the law school building, which was a five-minute walk from the apartment. The law school was set among trees, with a beautifully manicured lawn in the front. The building itself—built in redbrick and perfectly symmetrical—was modern and attractive and could not have been more different from the law school building at the University of Maine, which had been designed in the brutalist style, and had the dubious distinction of making an *Architectural Digest* list of the eight ugliest buildings in the United States. Hannah climbed the steps to the entrance hall and pushed open heavy double doors. She expected to find a security desk, an ID check at least, but there was nothing. Just a large, empty hall and wide corridors leading to the left and right. Hannah followed the sign that told her student services and clinics could be found in Slaughter Hall. This part of the building was older, a little more worn, a little more functional than the grand entrance hall.

She found the offices on the first floor after wandering for ten minutes. A simple door, with the words Innocence Project—Prof. R. Parekh stenciled on the glass. It was Sunday. The place was likely empty, the office locked up. Still, Hannah put her hand on the door and pushed gently. It opened. She stepped inside. The office was unremarkable, and Hannah let out a breath, feeling something between disappointment and relief. What had she been expecting, exactly? It looked just like any other midlevel corporate office. A large, open-plan space with a reception desk and behind that, multiple coworking desks and cubicles. There were three doors against the wall to the right that presumably led to other offices or meeting rooms. The place seemed deserted, except that the door to one of the private offices was open, and there was a light on inside.

"Hello?" Hannah said. A man emerged from the open office door. He was lean and handsome and she recognized him from the *Vanity Fair* article. Robert Parekh, Professor.

"Can I help you?" he said.

"I'm Hannah. Hannah Rokeby. You said to come and see you when I arrived on campus. I can come back tomorrow . . ."

"Grounds," he said.

"Sorry?"

"We call it grounds, here. Not campus." He shook his head. "It's not important. Come in, come in." He stepped forward and opened the little half-gate to the left of reception, ushering her inside. "I wasn't expecting to see you today, but actually, your timing is quite good." She followed him through to his office. His accent was British and very clipped. He sounded like one of the royal princes, which made sense, given his background.

The article in *Vanity Fair* had sold itself like a social justice piece, with multiple references to the Project's work on behalf of death row prisoners, but the article—which was four pages long— had included a full-page photograph of Parekh. He'd worn a navy silk shirt with the top two buttons undone and had stared straight into the camera with a look that suggested both deep thinking and a hint of impatience. The headline had read *Robert Parekh: The Next Caped Crusader?* Parekh was a very good-looking man. The journalist who'd interviewed him had clearly been impressed—the tone of the piece had been almost fawning and the article had included lots of unnecessary detail about Parekh's wealthy family, his years at Eton playing polo with royalty, and his relationships with beautiful, high-profile women.

Parekh took his seat behind his desk and Hannah sat too, folding her hands in her lap. For a long, disconcerting moment, he just looked at her. Hannah's stomach tightened. She tried to read his expression. Given the way he'd responded to her email, she'd assumed this meeting would start with tension and excuses or denial and recrimination. But he was so calm, so in control that it was hard to imagine that he was in any way worried about her not very veiled threat to share what she knew about his relationship with his former student Annabel Bancroft.

Annabel was a law student, a part-time model, and a friend of Hannah's friend Millie. Hannah and Millie had been undergrads together in Maine. When Hannah had called Millie—who had just graduated from UVA law—to ask a few discreet questions about Parekh, Millie had been happy to share the gossip about Annabel.

That she'd had a short-lived, wildly passionate affair with Parekh. Which meant a potential scandal, something that could be used, maybe. But Hannah didn't know Annabel personally, had never spoken to her, and Millie had said that the relationship was over and that Annabel only had good things to say about her ex. And now Parekh was so calm, so unbothered by Hannah's presence, so it looked like he wasn't worried. If that was the case, why had he agreed to see her? Maybe this wasn't an interview. Maybe he was about to give her a verbal kicking and throw her out of his office. Hannah clenched her fists. That absolutely couldn't happen.

Parekh picked up a thin file from his desk, opened it, and sorted through the papers within. "Yes. Here you are. Hannah Rokeby. University of Maine for undergraduate and law school. I assume that choice was driven by personal circumstances. Your transcript suggests you were capable of better."

His snobbery irritated her but she didn't allow it to show. "My mother needed me. It made sense for me to live at home while going to school."

He nodded, but waited, eyebrows raised, as if her answer had been incomplete.

"My mother has cancer. She's taking part in a clinical trial at University Hospital here in Charlottesville for the next three months. She's staying in special housing close to the hospital, so I can't live with her, but I thought coming to UVA for a semester would be a good way to stay close enough that she can call on me if she needs me. I can more easily spend weekends with her."

"Yes," he said. "That was in your email. And of course, it's an opportunity for you too. To get a taste of the kind of education that perhaps you should have had."

His eyes were sharp. Hannah suppressed the urge to defend her school and her professors.

"That's true." She cleared her throat, pressed forward. "I have excellent research skills. During my summers I volunteered at the Maine State Free Legal Advice Clinics, so I have experience working directly with clients. The clinics were very busy, so I got a lot of hands-on experience."

Parekh looked bored. His eyes dropped again to the application form. Hannah spoke more quickly, injected a bit more enthusiasm into her voice.

"A large part of the appeal in transferring here to the University of Virginia was the prospect of working for the Innocence Project. I've been reading all about your work with Michael Dandridge, and the approach you've taken with the case is really inspiring."

No reaction. Hannah hurried on. "I've been working on an accelerated timetable in Maine, so I'm ahead of where I need to be. I thought I might be helpful if some of your more experienced students are struggling with heavy class loads. I could pick up some of the slack."

"What about your mother?"

"I'm sorry?"

"Don't you have to spend time with your mother? Given her illness?"

"Mom's doing much better now. She's very independent." Hannah's throat tightened at the lie. "I'll need to see her at weekends for a few hours. To catch up. Otherwise I'll be free."

Her words appeared to be having little impact. His eyes were on the papers in front of him.

"Hannah. All of the kids here are bright, they're all hard workers, and they're all motivated. I'm looking for something more. Your email made me think you might have it."

"Oh . . . okay, well, I'm glad—"

He cut her off. "You tried to blackmail me."

Shit.

"I . . . I didn't mean . . ."

"Oh, yes, you did," Parekh said. He looked more amused than angry. "I'm not upset about it," he said. "I think you should have shown better judgment, and I think you should have done a little more research. I was not Annabel's professor when we started seeing each other. She had already dropped my class, in fact, and UVA policies only prohibit relationships between faculty and students where the faculty member has a teaching authority over the student. So."

"I'm sorry," Hannah said, as sincerely as she could manage.

"You should be," he said, still with that trace of amusement. "But here's the thing." He gestured broadly around the room. "Here at the Project, we are not the police and we are not the FBI. We have a very limited budget to pay investigators. I need students who are imaginative, inventive, and willing to be creative when it comes to pursuing our cases. Working here does not mean sitting behind a desk drafting motions—our staff attorneys take care of that. We need students to do the hard grind of investigating facts and tracking down *new* evidence. If you could be as dogged with that as you were with trying to get a place here, maybe you could be of use to me."

Hannah could feel the flush rising in her cheeks. She made herself hold his gaze. This was not the time to play the shy girl. Though . . . she had a feeling he wouldn't react well if she was too assertive either.

"I'd like to try," she said steadily.

"Why?" he asked.

"I'm sorry?"

"Tell me exactly why you want to work with us."

Hannah took a breath. "Because I believe that the system is broken. Too many innocent people are going to prison and I think that may get worse, not better, given the political situation. The Innocence Project is fighting back, trying to fix things, and it's doing it in all the right ways. Fighting individual cases, but also lobbying for systemic change. It's actually making a difference, and there aren't very many organizations that can say that these days. I want to be part of that." She had practiced her speech in front of the mirror a hundred times. She knew exactly what she looked like as she delivered it—frank, painfully sincere, maybe a little embarrassed by her own intensity. But Parekh looked Hannah right in the eye as she delivered her monologue . . . and he didn't believe her. She could see it. She tried desperately to think of something else she could say to convince him. Nothing came to her. After a minute his eyes flicked away from hers. He hesitated.

"You'd be starting at the bottom," he said. "I appreciate that you have some experience, but there are other students who were with us last year. They know our cases, and we've had an opportunity to supervise them directly."

"I'm happy to do whatever is needed." It was a start. She was in. Hannah felt a nauseating lurch of relief.

Parekh stood. "Tomorrow is the first day back. Be here at nine A.M. We'll get you started." It was clearly a dismissal. Hannah hesitated. Should she offer a handshake? No. That would be awkward. Trying too hard. "Thank you," she said, as she stood and picked up her bag. "I'm excited to begin."

Parekh didn't smile and there was no sign of his earlier amusement when he replied. "It's a big commitment. Our students are expected to work a minimum of fifteen hours per week, and frankly there are times where the workload is far in excess of that. When you're a little more settled, and assuming things work out, you'll be assigned to work with a group of three or four other students on a case. You'll find that most of our best students routinely work much longer hours. It's difficult to set limits when you're working to prove someone's innocence. In some cases, to save a life."

"Of course." Hannah nodded energetically, hoping that she was coming across as enthusiastic and not sycophantic. Parekh was very difficult to read. His tone was so dry. But what he had said was true; the Project did save lives. The debate, of course, was whether all of those lives deserved to be saved.

"Do you have a car?" Parekh asked, walking her to the door. "It can be useful, if you're independent, for research and interviews."

"Yes," Hannah didn't hesitate to lie. "I have a car." After everything else, getting a car would be easy.

"Excellent," said Parekh. "I'll look forward to seeing you tomorrow then."

Hannah found her way out through the maze-like layout of the administration building. She walked outside, looked around until she found a quiet place, a bench set in trees to the side of the pretty lawn at the front of the building, then took out her phone and called her mother. Laura answered immediately.

"Are you all right?"

"You got my note?"

"I can't believe you're in Virginia. The whole idea is crazy. You should come home—"

Hannah cut across her mother. "Let's not do this. Please. You have to trust that I know what I'm doing."

There was silence on the other end of the phone.

Hannah sighed. "You know I had no choice, Mom." Her voice was as gentle as she could make it. "I couldn't sit back and do nothing. That just . . . it wasn't an option."

Still silence.

"Mom?"

"I wish you'd never found my diary. If I'd known it would lead to this, I would never have written it. Or I'd have burned it before you read it."

"You would have had to tell me the truth eventually," Hannah said.

"Never. I *never* would have," Laura said. "Some things are better left in the past." Her voice was tight with anxiety. But she was sober. She hadn't been drinking. Hannah could always tell. Did she know yet that Hannah had found her stash? Maybe. It didn't necessarily mean anything that she hadn't mentioned it yet. Sometimes she held things back, let things build.

"I met the lawyer, Mom. I met Robert Parekh."

"You did?"

"I'm in. At least, I'm not on the case, not yet, but I have a trial with the Project, at least. It's a start."

"There isn't much time."

"I know."

There was another silence. Then Laura said, "I'm proud of you. I wish you weren't there. I think this is a bad idea. But you're very brave, Hannah. I wish I had your confidence."

Relief made Hannah babble. "If you need help, don't forget Jan is going to call in three times a week. She'll help with shopping, with cooking and cleaning. Whatever you need. And she'll take you to your meetings. And you can call me, any time you need to talk. You're going to be okay. I promise. We'll get through this."

After the call Hannah walked back to the apartment. The conversation could have gone much worse. She shifted the weight of her bag on her shoulder, resisting the urge to check again that the diary was safely inside. She knew it was there. She never left it behind. Of course, she should never have read it in the first place, that went without saying. But Hannah had been fourteen years old and in the teary, sorry-for-herself aftermath of a fight with Laura

when she'd come across the notebook, and therefore not very inclined to respect boundaries. And, of course, the fact that the diary
was Laura's *old* journal, written when she wasn't much older than
fourteen-year-old Hannah, had made it all the more fascinating.
Hannah had read that notebook cover to cover and then a second
time, then a third. She'd read it at least ten times before she confessed her sin to her mother. Laura had been much more forgiving
than she'd expected or deserved.

It was too late now for any regrets, and Hannah felt none. The
diary had brought them closer together at a difficult time, bonded
them forever in understanding. Because of the diary, Hannah knew
exactly what had happened to Laura, and she knew exactly who was
to blame.

LAURA

DIARY ENTRY #1

Saturday, July 9, 1994, 9:00 p.m.

It's a weird feeling, starting a diary. I feel kind of embarrassed. Maybe I have diary prejudice, but I feel like writing in a diary is something you do in junior high, when you first discover boys and/or masturbation and you just HAVE TO TALK ABOUT IT ALL THE TIME!! Writing in a diary is a habit you're supposed to grow out of. Starting one now, at nineteen . . . I'm like the girl who brings her My Little Pony collection to her college dorm.

Except now that I've said how uncool this is, I'm free to continue doing it, and now it's in a cool, ironic kind of way. Right? Also no one's going to read this and I'm going to burn it when I'm done so . . . Just, if you're reading this at some time in the future (because, I don't know, I'm suddenly paralyzed and therefore fail to destroy it as planned), don't waste your time. Nothing exciting lies ahead. I'm not writing this because I'm such a great writer or because I have something important to say or something cool to talk about, but just because I'm bored and lonely and broke and this is one way to entertain myself.

Right now I'm working as a cleaner. (See? Exciting stuff.) I work at a fancy hotel near Seal Harbor (which, if you don't know, is on Mount Des-

ert Island, which is in Maine). The job's fine. It could be better. I took it because I wanted to get out of Boston for the summer. It's so depressing being there, when all my friends go home and spend their vacation time with their families, and I'm still stuck working my shitty dead-end job. I figured, better to work a shitty dead-end job somewhere pretty. Somewhere with rich tourists who leave big tips so I can save up and maybe, maybe, get to college myself someday.

It's not like I plan on working as a cleaner my entire life. I'm trying to save. I've saved almost three thousand dollars, but it's really slow. Every time I feel like I'm getting somewhere there's some great disaster and everything goes to shit. Like, last year, I got kicked out of my apartment because the building wasn't up to code or some crap, so then I had to find a new place which meant $$$ for a new deposit and everything. Good luck getting your old deposit back from a landlord of a building that's just been condemned. Ha-ha.

It's actually really nice here. The island is beautiful. Lots of walking trails and hiking and climbing and swimming. My job comes with a room (which is just as well—rentals here are $$$$$—rich people only need apply) and I share with a girl called Marta. She's all right. Kind of. She's crazy about some guy she left behind in her hometown and she mostly wants to just hang out in our room and play Mariah Carey on repeat and cry into her pillow. Fun.

So. I haven't really made any friends here.

However . . .

I met a guy today. Not a guy guy. Not like a crush or anything. I'm not saying he wasn't cute, because he was. It's just that it wasn't that kind of situation. I was working, cleaning his house, which isn't exactly an ideal way to meet someone. Background—I've been making some extra cash by taking extra shifts cleaning private houses on the hotel. Most of the girls at the hotel do it. Rosa, the housekeeper, sets everything up. I don't know *if hotel management knows about it, or if they'd care if they did, but we all keep it on the downlow because that extra work is the only way any of us are going to see any real money this summer.*

Anyway, today Rosa picked up me and Marta after our hotel shift and dropped us off at the job she'd set up for us. And the whole thing was kind of off from the beginning. For starters, the house was out in the middle of nowhere (most places I've been to up to now have been in town—awesome houses with ocean views). But today Rosa drove until we were way deep in the woods, taking a series of turns until I was completely lost. In the end she took a turn up a long gravel driveway and dropped us off in front of this house that was pretty much hidden. It was tucked back in the trees, and all we could see was stone steps leading up and glimpses of more wood and stone. It was spooky as hell and when I'm nervous I try to be funny.

"Seriously?"

"What's the problem?" Rosa has zero time for other people's problems. And honestly, I'm not a whiner. But I hadn't been expecting a gloomy dump stuck in the middle of the woods.

"Come on, Rosa. It's like a scene from a horror movie. You'll drive away and Marta and I will go innocently into that house in our little maids' uniforms and an hour from now we'll be running through the woods, fleeing for our lives." (We wear little gray dresses that are cut to fit and go barely to our knees—my theory is that the ocean isn't the only view the guests at the hotel pay for.)

Rosa just rolled her eyes at me and kicked us out of the van. "You have four hours. Six bedrooms. No time for horror movies. And don't bother the family." She left us with the cleaning cart, but I don't know how she expected us to get it up the steps. In the end we abandoned it in the driveway and took what we needed. It was a while before the door opened. A guy . . . the guy (tall, dark blond floppy hair, blue eyes) stood there. He blinked at us like he'd just woken up from an afternoon nap. He said hey and I said hey back, like he was my buddy. I don't know why. Maybe because he looked about our age. Maybe because he was wearing ratty shorts and a gray Nirvana T-shirt that looked like it had already been washed and worn a hundred times. I knew right away he was cooler than me. (Note—I've never listened to a Nirvana song in my life, and I've got the tape of The Bodyguard *sound track stuck in my Walkman.) Marta was her usual happy self.*

"We're here to clean," she said, flatly.

"Really?" He looked confused. I don't think he'd been expecting us. But then he shook our hands, so formally that I wanted to laugh, and introduced himself as Tom Spencer. He showed us in through a big entry hall into the kitchen, then disappeared back into the house. Which was way nicer than I'd been expecting, by the way. I mean, you could tell that whoever owned the place had lots of money.

Marta did the kitchen and I did the upstairs. Everything was fine until I got to one room that was pretty gross. Empty beer bottles, dirty clothes and dishes all over the floor, and a nasty smell. Like, none of that is new, but the rest of the house was pretty tidy so I wasn't really expecting it. My interest in cute Tom in the Nirvana T-shirt diminished quickly. I cleaned everything up, took the dirty stuff downstairs, came back to dust and strip the bed.

The drawer in one of the bedside tables was open. There were two little baggies of coke inside and a small silver spoon. And the last of my interest in Tom died. (I'm not into coke and everyone I've ever met who is is an asshole.)

I stripped the bed and I found some porn magazines under one of the pillows—a copy of Hustler, *and a* Playboy *featuring Ronald Reagan's daughter Patti Davis. I put the* Hustler *back under the pillow (ick), but the* Playboy *promised an interview with Bill Gates, so I ended up sort of half-sitting, half-kneeling on the floor on the window side of the bed, flicking through the article. It wasn't as interesting as I'd thought it might be—there was a lot of blah about the information highway and democracy*

*and washing machines—and, look, porn's REALLY not my thing, but I
was kind of curious about the Patti Davis pictures, so I turned the pages
and had a look . . . and it was <u>exactly</u> at that moment that I heard footsteps approaching the bedroom. I swear, if I'd been doing anything else I
would have reacted differently. But . . . you know what it's like when you
know you're doing something you shouldn't and you're just about to be
discovered. You don't think, you panic. I ducked down behind the bed,
sliding my body halfway under. As soon as I did it, I knew I was acting
crazy. I almost sat back up, but there was no time. The footsteps entered
the room, the door was slammed closed, and the bedsprings creaked as
someone sat down. I heard the sound of a phone handset being picked up
and a number being dialed.*

*I should have stood up then and let him know I was there. I could
have shoved the magazine far under the bed, and pretended I was dusting, or something. Instead I shuffled sideways until I was fully under the
bed and just lay there. I breathed as quietly as possible, staring up at the
bed slats and the underside of the mattress, and listening to one side of
what sounded like a very angry phone conversation. Right away I knew I
wasn't listening to Tom Spencer. This guy sounded completely different.
His voice was higher pitched, and angry. His first word was a barked out
"Well?" followed by a pause and then an angrier "Just tell me." After that
I was distracted, because just above my head, between the mattress and
the bed slats, was a gun. It was a handgun, a semiautomatic pistol. It was
big and black and nasty and it sat there, just above my eyeline, while the
conversation above my head escalated into an argument.*

*Eventually I figured out that the guy was talking to his mom—only
because he said the word* mom, *like, five times. But honestly, otherwise
I wouldn't have guessed it. I'm not saying I never fought with my mother
(who doesn't?) but with him there was this* tone. *If she'd been there in the
room and he was talking to her like that, in person, I think he might have
hit her. I was freaking out the whole time I was there, sure that at any mo-*

ment he was going to realize that he wasn't the only person in the room. *That maybe he'd suddenly go looking for his missing* Playboy, *which I was still holding (why? why?) clutched in one hand. So I wasn't really all that focused on the one-sided conversation going on above me, until he started to get really angry.*

"How could he have been so fucking stupid? I could have told him that guy was a crook. But he never fucking listens to me, does he?"

I couldn't hear what his mother was saying to him, but whatever it was he got angrier and angrier. He never raised his voice above a loud hiss, but the tone of it got really vicious.

"No. You tell him to keep his mouth shut, you hear me, Mom? No one is to know about this. No one. I'm working on fixing this goddamn mess. You need to leave it to me. Do you hear me?"

He told her to have his father call him, immediately. Then he slammed down the phone and let fly with a stream of swear words so ugly that I swear I blushed. He stood up and he kicked the closet door, once . . . then again. The third time he kicked it I heard the door splinter and give way. I heard a muttered fuck, *and then another voice, Tom's voice, coming from outside the room, from somewhere down the corridor—*

"Mike? You okay?"

There was the smallest, infinitesimal pause, and then I heard my stranger—Mike, obviously—open his bedroom door and say, in a cheery, upbeat, laughing voice that gave absolutely no hint that he'd just screamed at his mom and kicked the shit out of his closet—"I'll be down in a minute."

He closed the door and stood in absolute silence for a long moment. He gave the closet one last, vicious kick. Then he opened the bedroom door and disappeared down the corridor. As soon as I heard his footsteps on the stairs, I slithered out from under the bed, so fast that I bumped my head and scraped my forehead. I shoved the Playboy *under his pillow, gathered up the dirty sheets, and got out of there. Then I went and stood for a while in one of the empty bedrooms, until I had calmed down and pulled my-self together. It wasn't the coke or the gun or the argument that scared me. Honestly. It was the combination of all three, how close I came to get-ting caught, but mostly how nasty Mike had been on the phone. I knew I couldn't stay upstairs forever, but I didn't want to go downstairs with those sheets under my arm. In the end I waited about ten minutes, before deciding that it looked more suspicious to be standing there alone in an empty room than it did to get on with my job.*

One of the good things about wearing a maid's uniform is that it makes you almost invisible. You wouldn't believe the things people have done, right in front of me. Drugs and porn are the least of it. Husbands smuggling their mistresses into the house; a wife getting it on with her best friend in the pool house. One time this incredibly beautiful woman—you know, the ex-model trophy-wife type—sat for at least half an hour at her kitchen table flicking through a magazine while I cleaned her filthy kitchen. And for the entire time she picked her nose and wiped her finger on the linen tablecloth. I reminded myself of all of this as I went down-stairs with the dirty sheets. I'd left the laundry bags in the laundry room and I had to go through the kitchen to get to them. There were two guys in the kitchen as I went through: Tom Spencer, and a shorter dark-haired guy I figured was the angry Mike from upstairs. They were deep in con-versation. I ignored them and they ignored me. I went into the laundry room and stuffed the linens into a bag. The door to the kitchen was open and I could hear what they were saying pretty clearly. Mike was trying to convince Tom Spencer to take a trip north with him, to Canada. He was doing a good job of sounding chirpy and lighthearted, but Tom was unen-thusiastic. He changed the subject.

"Did you talk to your mom?"

Mike didn't even hesitate. "Sure. She said to say hi."

I tied the laundry bag and started back through the kitchen, just as

Tom said—"You're so lucky. I really envy what you've got with your parents."

Tom turned to look at me as I came into the room, so he didn't see Mike's response to his statement. I saw it though. And—I swear I am NOT exaggerating—it was a look of such naked, murderous rage that I actually took a step back. The look was gone as quickly as it had arrived, disappearing behind a bland smile.

"Did you find everything you need?" Tom was asking me. I guess he must have picked up on some of my reaction to Mike because he gave me this reassuring smile. I mumbled a yes and a thank you and got the hell out of there. I dropped the laundry at the front door and fought the urge to keep walking. I was feeling pretty freaked out by then. But what was I going to do, abandon Marta and walk back to the hotel? I could just see myself explaining to Rosa that I walked out because I overheard a guy having a fight with his mom. So I went back to work, helped Marta vacuum and mop the floors, and we finished early. Tom Spencer came to find me and Marta before we went home, to see how we were doing. He wasn't checking up on us, I don't think. Just being friendly. He even offered us coffee. We didn't accept—offers like that from people like him are not meant to be accepted. Still, he really does seem like a nice guy.

It's not unusual for a nice guy to be friends with an asshole. Hell, sometimes it feels like it's almost obligatory. But this wasn't that. This is one person thinking that everything's rosy while the other carries around some giant secret drama and a whole lot of anger. It's like Tom is living with an unexploded bomb and he has no clue. I feel guilty that I know this and he doesn't. Like it's my responsibility to do something. I keep telling myself that the whole situation has nothing to do with me. It's none of my business. Getting caught up in rich person drama is a recipe for disaster. I need to get on with my summer and forget that today ever happened.

So that's exactly what I'm going to do.

Hannah

THREE

MONDAY, AUGUST 26, 2019

Hannah arrived ten minutes early to the Innocence Project the following day and the place was already humming. There was a woman sitting at the reception desk, head bent and fingers busy on a keyboard, and most of the desks in the open-plan area were occupied by students, busy at their own screens. There was a buzz of quiet conversation, a couple of people were on the phone, a few others were wearing headphones to block out the noise.

"Can I help you?" The woman behind reception was in her fifties, blond and very polished, her hair cut in a sleek bob to just below her ears. She was wearing a dark gray cashmere sweater, and a ring on her wedding finger.

Hannah took a step forward. "I'm Hannah Rokeby," she said. "I met with Professor Parekh ..."

"Oh yes. Rob told me to expect you." The woman offered her hand. "Marianne Stephenson. I'm the office manager."

"Hello." Hannah took her hand and they shook, briefly.

"Come on through." Marianne stood, motioned for Hannah to follow, and wove her way through the cubicles to an unoccupied desk at the back of the room. "We thought we'd put you here, to begin with." A girl sitting at the neighboring desk looked up at their arrival and Marianne introduced her. "This is Rachel Mears. Rachel is back with us for a second year, so she knows her way around the system. Rob asked Rachel to show you the ropes."

Hannah smiled at Rachel, who smiled briefly in return. She was a rather severe-looking girl with intense eyes. Her dark hair was tied back in a tight ponytail.

"Thanks so much, Rachel," Hannah said. "I'll try not to take up too much of your time."

Rachel shrugged. "It's really not a problem. We're all here to help."

"Great," said Marianne briskly. "I'll let you get started."

Hannah took her backpack off and slid into her chair.

"Let's get you logged in," Rachel said. She leaned across Hannah's desk and switched the computer on. "Do you have your student ID? You just need your name and ID number to set up access, and then you create a password."

Hannah leaned down and fished her new ID card from her backpack. She handed it to Rachel.

"How did you manage to get a decent photo?" Rachel asked. "I swear I've never seen a good one on a UVA ID."

"Just lucky, I guess."

They waited for the computer to boot up.

"Okay," Rachel said. "So you're going to be working on assessing the applications that come in from prisoners. You know our criteria for accepting an application?"

"I think so."

Rachel counted the criteria off on one hand. "The inmate must have been convicted of a crime in Virginia. The conviction must be final, meaning that no further criminal proceedings or appeals are ongoing, and lastly the inmate must be claiming to be actually innocent of the crime for which he or she was convicted, and by that I mean factually innocent, not trying to get off on a technicality."

"When you say no appeals are ongoing, you mean no direct appeals?"

"Yeah, exactly. The convicted person has to have exhausted their direct appeals and then we'll look at post-conviction motions addressing issues like new DNA evidence, or prosecutorial misconduct, or ineffective assistance of counsel, to name a few. I mean, it isn't possible for the Project to get involved prior to conviction or the number of applications we get would just skyrocket."

"Got it," Hannah said.

"Our first job is to go through the applications and cut out everything that fails to meet those conditions. That takes time, but it's fairly straightforward. The next step is the hard part. We have to make a recommendation about which cases deserve further consideration." Rachel put her hand to her chest. "We, the students, have to make an assessment about the likelihood of being able to prove innocence, what legal remedies are available, and"—here Rachel paused for effect—"our current caseload. It's an enormous responsibility."

"Caseload is a constraint?"

"We have a backlog of eight hundred applicants right now." Rachel grimaced. She gestured around the room. "Most of us are running at least four cases at a time, investigating, trying to build up the file to the point where we can get something going. There are finite resources and a lot of need."

"I see," Hannah said. She put her hand on her mouse. "I thought . . . I suppose I just assumed that most of the Project's time would be taken up with death row cases."

Rachel shot her a look, gave a tight little laugh. "Death row cases get all the headlines," she said. "But they're only part of the work we do here."

"Of course," Hannah said. There was an awkward moment of silence and Hannah wondered if Rachel had ever worked a death row case. Probably not. That might be the reason for the spikiness. She should move on, to avoid provoking the other girl, but she needed to know how things worked.

"But students do get to work on death row cases from time to time? The Dandridge case, for example. I'd imagine that's going to suck up a lot of resources. When does it go to trial?" Hannah worried briefly if she was being too obvious, but she figured anyone volunteering for the Project would know about and be interested in Michael Dandridge. His case had been widely reported in left-leaning newspapers, not just the *Vanity Fair* profile where she had first read about it. The *Vanity Fair* article had been published before charges had been refiled against Dandridge, but there'd been other reporting since.

"Preliminary hearing for the Dandridge case is next week," Rachel said shortly. "And Professor Parekh's keeping the team pretty tight. There are three spots for student assistants and they're all taken." She turned back to Hannah's computer. "Let's get started," she said.

Rachel showed Hannah where to access the applications that came in through the website. How to open a digital file and save the application. "The next step is to write to the inmate and request a copy of their appellant's opening brief. Ideally we get that digitally, but a lot of the time it still comes in on paper. We have to scan the original paper brief into the system and return the brief to the inmate with this letter." Rachel pointed to a template letter sitting in the workflow. "This just basically tells them that we're assessing their case and we'll get back to them as soon as possible. And it asks them not to contact us until we get in touch, unless absolutely necessary." Rachel rolled her eyes. "We still get phone calls, of course, but Marianne deals with most of those."

"Right," Hannah said.

"So then you need to analyze the brief, and you need to write an evaluation for every application, including analysis of the facts, history of the case, evidence collected, and whether or not there's a possibility of DNA or other forensic evidence that might prove innocence. Let's look at a few examples."

The next hour passed very quickly. The process was fascinating, though it was a little shocking, the degree to which students here were doing such pivotal work, making recommendations that could end an inmate's hopes for freedom. But as Rachel worked through some examples, it became clear that many applications failed to fulfill the basic criteria. And as the afternoon wore on and Rachel insisted on explaining in laborious detail the logic of her analysis on her cases, Hannah began to question Rachel's judgment. Some of the cases that Rachel had worked on seemed to be so lacking in any kind of potential that they surely weren't worth the time she had given them. She wrote voluminous, repetitive notes on every application, regardless of their merits, and rejected all of them. When Rachel opened the sixth file, and launched into yet another detailed explanation as to how and why she had approached the file in a particular way, Hannah interrupted.

"Thank you so much, Rachel," she said. "I'm sorry for taking up so much of your time this morning. If it's okay with you, I'd like to give it a shot, and then I can put together some questions to ask you later."

"Oh. Well. Fine, if you're sure," Rachel said. She turned back to her own desk, clearly a little taken aback and not altogether happy about Hannah's sudden bid for independence. But after a single reproachful glance, she took Hannah at her word and left her alone. Thanks to Rachel's careful instruction, Hannah found she could navigate the system easily. She waited until she was sure that Rachel was fully engaged in her own work, and then she clicked through various options to see if there were restrictions on the files she could access. There weren't. Once you were in the system you essentially had free rein. Okay. It was too soon to do any real digging. It was possible that her movements through the system could be flagged, and she didn't want to set off any alarm bells this soon. Right now, she needed to do something to get noticed for the right reasons. She couldn't afford to be a Rachel Mears, languishing unseen off to the side. She needed to be right in the heart of the action.

She would start by checking out some case reviews prepared by other students. Hannah had a theory that the style and substance of the approach to reviewing inmate applications differed dramatically depending on which student reviewed them. Some reviews, like Rachel's, were verbose, going into unnecessary detail and circular arguments about why a file shouldn't be carried forward. It struck Hannah as completely redundant, particularly in cases where it was clear, for example, that the inmate hadn't claimed factual innocence in his previous defense. Many of the students wrote as if they were completing an assignment—reciting basic case law that would surely be known to the attorney they were briefing and including an irrelevant back story, as if to prove they had read the entire file. Other reviews were much sparer, much more clearly written. The best of them had been written by someone called Sean Warner. There was a confidence about his writing that made it stand out.

Time went by quickly. Lunchtime came and went. Rachel asked if she would like to go to student services, eat together. Hannah demurred. She had brought a sandwich. The afternoon wore on. Hannah worked her way through applications. If she wanted to be noticed, she had to do something worthy of attention, something that would make her stand out from the crowd. Her approach would be ruthless. She would seek out low-hanging fruit, those applications that clearly failed the base criteria and cull as many as possible. She was aiming for volume. From what she had seen, Rachel barely got through two applications a week. Hannah saw no reason why she couldn't clear ten or more by the end of the day, if she put her mind to it. If an application backlog was an issue for the Project, she would be the most efficient backlog clearer Robert Parekh had ever seen. And as she worked, she would keep an eye out for applications with real potential.

At one point late into the afternoon, Hannah looked up, blinking, from her screen. Rachel was staring at a small group standing outside Parekh's office—Robert Parekh himself, and three students. A very pretty Hispanic girl wearing jeans and a black sweater that hugged her curves; a blond girl, expensively dressed but with a pinched look about her; and a tall boy with tousled dark brown hair, wearing a blue shirt with the sleeves rolled up. They were deep in conversation with Parekh and after a moment or two they disappeared into his office and shut the door behind them. Rachel stared after them with a look of such naked longing and frustration that Hannah looked away fast.

"You asked about death row cases. We only have the Dandridge case right now, and only the A team will get to work on it: Camila Martinez, Hazel Ellison, and Sean Warner. As far as Parekh is concerned, they're the best of us. Even though Hazel's virtually the only student who didn't get a job offer after her summer internship, so what does *that* tell you?"

"I don't know." Hannah said it flatly. She didn't have a job lined up, not yet. But then Maine Law wasn't a top ten school . . . and she'd had other priorities.

Rachel shrugged and looked back down at her keyboard. "I'm

just saying, maybe they aren't the best. Maybe there are other reasons they've been selected."

"Why do you think they were chosen?"

Rachel rolled her eyes. "Well, Camila's Hispanic and he's gay, obviously. It's just tokenism. A diversity effort."

Hannah took a breath. She didn't want to make enemies this early. She didn't want to make enemies at all. She couldn't afford them. But Rachel was a pain in the ass. "I've read some of Sean Warner's recommendations," she said. "They're sharp. He seems like a smart guy."

Rachel flushed. "What are you doing reading his stuff?"

Hannah shrugged. "Learning," she said.

Rachel's blush deepened. "Whatever." She turned back to her computer and ten minutes later packed up and left without another word to Hannah.

Hannah kept her eye on Rob Parekh's office door. She waited for the so-called A team to emerge and settle back at their desks. They worked, it seemed, at three desks pushed together at a corner by the window. Hannah stood up, took a breath, and walked over as casually as she could manage. Only one of them—Camila—looked up at her approach.

"Can I help you?"

"I wanted to say hi," Hannah said, smiling warmly. "I'm Hannah. I just started here."

"Camila," Camila said. She nodded toward the others by way of introduction. "Sean. Hazel."

"Nice to meet you," Hannah said. Sean smiled back at her. He was tall, in shape, and very handsome. As well as the artfully tousled hair, he was working scruffy stubble and deep blue eyes. Hazel barely glanced up before returning her attention to papers spread out on the table in front of them. "Uh, I just wondered if you guys wanted to get a coffee some time?" Hannah had to work to maintain her light and breezy tone in the face of Camila's flat stare and Hazel's indifference. "I've got so much to learn, and I'm told you guys are the experts."

"Who told you we were experts? Rachel?" Camila said. Her tone was disbelieving.

"I . . . yes," Hannah said. Shit. She'd handled this all wrong.

Camila stared her down for a long moment. Sean seemed bemused and now even Hazel was looking at her. Hannah felt her cheeks redden.

"I could use a coffee," Camila said eventually. "There's a place down at the corner that's pretty good. I'll have a large cappuccino, two sugars. Hazel?"

"Same," Hazel said promptly.

"Sean?" Camila said.

He frowned. "Camila, come on—"

"It's fine," Hannah said quickly. "I'm happy to grab them. It looks like you guys have work to do." She let her eyes drop to the papers on the desk. They weren't pleadings. They looked like photocopied witness statements. From the Dandridge case? Hannah's heart beat faster.

"Yeah, Sean. She's fine to get them," Camila said.

Sean took a little more persuading, but when Hannah insisted, he asked for a black coffee. She smiled at him, got her coat, and went to find the coffee shop. The place on the corner was a ten-minute walk. Hannah ordered the coffees. She'd screwed up. It was obvious she wasn't going to charm her way into the inner circle. When she got back to the office, she should drop the coffees off quickly and retreat. Find another way in. Shit. She had so little time. She may need to do something drastic.

HANNAH WORKED THROUGH THE AFTERNOON AND INTO THE LATE evening. Completely focused on what she was doing, she barely noticed as the room emptied out and she was interrupted by Marianne Stephenson at eight o'clock.

Marianne cleared her throat. "Don't you have a home to go to?" she said, but there was warmth in her tone and a definite suggestion of approval.

"I'm so sorry," Hannah said. "Have I been keeping you? I lost track of the time."

"You're the last one here, but I always work late on Mondays."

Hannah started to pack up. "I'll be ready in just a minute," she said. Marianne nodded. She went idly to the window and looked out into the darkness while Hannah packed away her notebook and pens and water bottle.

"I guess you're not kidding around," Marianne said, over her shoulder.

"I'm sorry?"

"We get a mix of students here," she said, still not looking at Hannah. "Most of them appear to have a genuine interest in helping people, but scrape the surface and they're here for the course credit. Still, we get at least one true believer every year. They're usually the ones I see here late, burning the midnight oil."

"Right," Hannah said.

"True believers are great." Marianne turned around to face Hannah and leaned back against the window. "But they're not always that effective. It's easy to get disillusioned. Not all of our clients are easy to work with, and the system doesn't reward a heroic charge. Success here is more about hard work and the occasional dirty trick." She smiled and it took the sting out of her words. "What I like to see around here are the pragmatists. Are you a pragmatist, Hannah?"

"I . . . yes. I think I am," Hannah said. Her backpack was packed and zipped and she rested her hands on top of it. "I mean, I believe in getting results, if that's what you're asking." This was not a lie. She was a pragmatist and a realist. She saw the world for what it really was, which was more than could be said for most people. But it surprised her to hear Marianne talking of pragmatism, when Marianne worked for the Innocence Project, an organization that was so guilty of romanticized bullshit. But then . . . okay . . . maybe she shouldn't be surprised at all. Just because the Innocence Project sold the tale of the perfect innocent, caught up in and crushed by the system, didn't mean they actually believed it. They must know that at least some of the time, the picture was a lot more complicated than that. They just *chose* to sell the fairy tale because it was good for public relations and their larger policy agenda. Hannah felt a wave of fury so sudden and unexpected that she swayed slightly on her feet.

"Not everyone who comes here knows how to get results," Marianne was saying. "I put that down to inexperience, in some cases, personality, in others. But every now and again a student comes along who has that special something. Some people are just born knowing how to operate in the world." She looked at Hannah expectantly. Hannah swallowed her anger.

"I don't know if I was born with any kind of special skill. I don't think I was. But my mother was sick for a lot of my childhood, and there's just the two of us. So I never had the luxury of sitting back and trusting someone else to look out for me. For us. I had to figure things out. To make the system work for us, not against us."

"What does that mean, make the system work for you?"

Hannah's mouth was dry. "I suppose I'm talking about getting the best out of people, from social workers to school principals. You have to understand how to approach people to get what you need. I think I understand how to do that. And I think maybe those skills might be useful here."

Marianne nodded, as if she was reserving judgment but willing, so far, to give Hannah the benefit of the doubt. "Well, keep it up," she said. "Today was a good start."

HANNAH WALKED HOME IN THE DARK. SHE WAS SHAKY FROM THE residue of her anger. Her legs felt weak, the world a little off balance. Along the way she stopped at the grocery store and picked up some basics for her kitchen. What would Camila, Sean, and Hazel be doing tonight? They'd seemed like they were friends. Maybe they'd gone for a bite together, talked about the case. Or maybe to the library, to keep up with their class work. Or home to chill out with their roommates. Watch Netflix.

The streets were busy, but the apartment complex was quiet when Hannah got in. She let herself into the little studio and locked the door behind her, reaching automatically for a dead bolt that wasn't there. She paused, laying her hand flat against the door for a moment and waiting for the little spike of anxiety, the urge to double-check the door or call the locksmith in the morning. It never came. She felt only gratitude for the silence and privacy the apartment offered. How quickly this place had become a refuge. Hannah put away her groceries and made herself some toast, then sat down on her bed, took her laptop out of her backpack, and started a very different kind of research from what she had been absorbed in all day. She had no time to waste. She had to get on the Michael Dandridge defense team. And that meant not waiting around for her chances, but creating them, if she had to.

LAURA

Sunday, July 17, 1994, 9:00 a.m.

I went back to the house in the woods yesterday. Alone this time, which is actually all Rosa's fault. I like Rosa. She's fun to be around because she's so confident and because she so clearly doesn't give a shit about rich people. She's perfected this blank-faced stare that is beautifully polite on the outside, like, she gives them nothing to object to . . . but at the same time there's something in her eyes that is a perfect fuck-you. She can be a dragon though—that fuck-you look isn't so much fun when she turns it on you.

Anyway, Marta told Rosa that there wasn't much to do at the house, and Rosa decided one cleaner would be enough and then she put the squeeze on me to take the job. Marta had an excuse (period pain—she gets it bad, or at least she says she does), so she was out, and Rosa likes to send the same girls back to the same places. I guess the customers are happier if they don't see new faces every week. I said okay. I didn't want to, but I'm usually first in line for every job (money money money) and Rosa was giving me a hard time about it and I didn't want to bring up the gun or the coke or the argument (I was pretty sure she'd be more pissed at me than anything . . . plus it would have seemed strange that I hadn't mentioned it for a full week) so before I knew it, I was nodding yes and Rosa was dropping me off.

I was nervous when I climbed the steps to the front door and knocked. At the hotel, in the real world, it was a warm, sunny day. In the woods it was gloomy, chilly, and there were too many shadows. But when Tom opened the door, he was wearing the same ratty shorts, a different Nirvana T-shirt, and he had a big grin on his face. This time, it seemed like he'd been expecting me.

"Hi. Come in. Can I get you anything? Coffee?"

I told him I had to get my work done first and he said, "Sure sure," and led the way to the kitchen. It was actually pretty tidy. The surfaces were all clear, and the floor looked like it had just been vacuumed and mopped. Tom sat down at the kitchen table. He had obviously been eating breakfast and drinking coffee and reading a book before I showed up, and he seemed happy to get back to it while I worked. I started emptying the dishwasher. He talked with his mouth half full.

"I didn't hire you guys."

"I'm sorry?"

"I guess it was my mom who arranged it. The cleaning, I mean. That's the kind of thing she does."

I was standing there, feeling like an asshole, a glass in each hand. "Do you . . . do you want me to leave?"

He looked anxious, suddenly, and blurted out, "God, no. I didn't mean it like that."

I said okay and put the glasses away, feeling really awkward.

"Sorry, I just didn't want you to think I was like that. Like, the kind of guy who would ask someone to clean up after him."

I laughed. I couldn't help it. I was absolutely sure that he'd had people cleaning up after him his entire life. Maybe in his parents' home it had felt less about him, and I was close to his age, so that made things weird for him. He flushed, looked down at his book, and took another bite of toast. I got on with emptying the dishwasher. When I finished I wiped down countertops that didn't need wiping and looked around at floors that already looked really clean.

"I think it's pretty good in here. I'll do the bedrooms now."

"Oh, no," he said. "No, I mean, there's no need." I guess I just looked at him, and he explained that his room was fine, and that Mike was away.

"Where'd he go?" I asked. I couldn't help myself.

"He took the boat north, to see some friends."

"Boat?"

"Uh . . . a sailboat? Like a yacht? It's my father's. We sailed it here from Virginia. That's why we're here actually. It was Mike's idea. Get away for a couple of weeks before college starts."

I nodded. Silence descended again. I moved to the door. "I guess I'll do the other floors, and some dusting. Unless there's something in particular . . . ?"

He shook his head. "It's fine, really." I mumbled something about it being my job and he looked even more awkward for a second and then blurted out, "I just thought . . . you know, we could hang out."

I stared at him. I'm pretty sure my mouth dropped open.

"No one needs to know. Well . . . that sounds weird. I just meant, it's so hot today. I don't have anything to do. I thought we could swim, if you like. Just chill." His expression changed; he started to look worried. "Not that you have to, I mean, of course, if you'd like to go home I can give you a ride. Or if that gets you into trouble you could just wait in the library and read, or something. I mean . . ."

"You cleaned the house so that we could hang out and swim?" I said.

"I didn't mean to offend you, I—"

"Okay," I cut across him.

"Okay?"

"Yes."

I said yes to Tom's invitation because, first of all, only an idiot would have said no. Who wouldn't want to spend an afternoon swimming, instead of scrubbing toilets or listening to Mariah Carey on repeat? And second, he seemed really lonely.

I'm not stupid. The whole sweet/awkward thing might be an act. I mean, on paper it wouldn't make sense for a guy like him—completely loaded, and a college student—to try to make friends with his house-cleaner. If I told my friends about this, they'd say he's just trying to get in my pants. I don't think that's it but I think you'd have to be here to get it. I mean, for starters, anybody stuck in a big old house with his toxic friend Mike would probably go looking for other friends. And also, we spent the whole afternoon together and he didn't make a move once.

First he showed me the pool. It was so beautiful—wide and deep and tucked away in a grassy little dell protected from the wind by sheltering trees. There was a small pool house with a changing room, a stack of towels, and some spare bathing suits. I borrowed one and we swam, a few lengths first to warm up then sort of aimlessly. Conversation started and stopped and I thought about going home. But I didn't. I was—I still am—curious about him. He is insanely loaded. I asked Rosa and she told me that the family is worth hundreds of millions, his dad is from the South, his mom (she's his dad's second wife) is some New York City socialite. She knew a lot about them—I guess Rosa likes to read the society pages. Who knew? Tom has one stepbrother and one sister. Is it weird that I know so much about him? He knows nothing about me. So I stayed, because I was curious, and maybe because I've been lonely. It was nice to have company, to be social, even if things were a bit awkward in the beginning, and after a while we both started to relax and talk and he was pretty good company.

When we'd had enough of swimming, we got out of the pool and dried off and he asked if I wanted to see the beach. I said sure, so we got dressed and he led me away from the pool and down a stone path that meandered for a little while, then broke out of the trees again to the most incredible view over the water. It is so weird, by the way, that that house is built way back in the trees when the property line goes right down to the water. The owners could have had views out over the ocean if they had wanted. I asked Tom about it but he didn't know anything about the architect or the history of the house or anything.

"If your father rented the place, how come he's not here?"

Tom gave me a sideways smile and told me that his dad had rented the house because their vacation home was being remodeled. And then his mom hadn't wanted to come (the island wasn't nice enough or cool enough or something), so they went to Europe instead.

I rolled my eyes. I couldn't help it. I'm one hundred percent sure he saw me too, but he didn't react, just kept walking. The land dropped away in front of us, sloping down toward the water. There was no sand, just a pebble beach and a rocky outcropping, a quiet bay with navy-blue water, and a single timber jetty that extended maybe fifty feet into the water. That's where they moor the boat, when Mike hasn't taken it off somewhere. We sat on the jetty for a while.

"You're not what I expected," I said, at one point.

"What were you expecting?"

I shrugged.

"A spoiled brat? Someone who doesn't care about other people? Someone who doesn't appreciate what they have?"

It was a weird moment. I could tell he was kind of upset and I already liked him so it was hard not to feel a little sympathetic. But there was a definite hint of self-righteousness about him too. And, you know, he was standing there on his private beach complaining that the world didn't understand him. So I said, "What do you care?" and he mumbled some-

thing about people thinking they knew something about his life but not really having a clue. I smirked, kind of. I wasn't trying to be mean . . . but PLEASE!! Anyway he obviously saw the smirk and then he frowned at me, so then I started to feel a bit pissed so I said a few things.

"Maybe they do have a clue. Maybe it's just that the stuff that matters to them doesn't seem that important to you."

"Like what?"

I started out easy. "Ever had a job?"

He flushed. "No."

"Do you have a credit card that you don't pay for? Are your parents paying your tuition? What about your friends? Do they all have money?" I was on a roll, so I kept going.

"Ever been homeless?"

"No, I—"

"Ever gone to bed hungry because you couldn't afford food? Ever known anyone who's had to go hungry?" He didn't answer either of those, just looked at me sadly like he suddenly saw who I was, and I wanted to push him into the water. Instead of pushing him I kept talking. "That stuff—access to good food and a safe happy home life, a doctor when you need one. That seems like nothing to you because you've always had it. That and a hell of a lot more." I had a sudden image of Tom at Thanksgiving, sitting in a fancy living room in a tastefully decorated mansion, surrounded by his siblings and his loving parents. That hurt. That he'd had all that and didn't even really see it.

But then he told me that he had nannies when he was very small. That, when he was eight, his parents sent him to boarding school. When he was eleven, three other boys beat him up so badly that he had to go to the hospital. His parents didn't visit. Just made a concerned phone call to the school principal. He wasn't lying. I know a liar when I see one.

"Your mom?"

He shrugged. He had this small, slightly embarrassed smile on his face, and I thought maybe he regretted saying anything. "She is who she is. She's not a bad person. She's just . . . being a mother doesn't come naturally to her. I'm pretty sure she had us because it satisfied a condition in the prenup."

I asked him why he'd told me. He laughed and shook his head. "I don't know. Maybe because you pissed me off."

We went back to the house and he made sandwiches and we sat at the counter and talked about books (he likes Iain M. Banks, I like Terry Brooks, we both love Pratchett). I tried to find out more about Mike, without being too obvious. But I didn't get much, other than the impression that maybe Mike's family isn't as uber-rich as the Spencers (they don't have a yacht of their own, boohoo) and Tom hinted that Mike's parents are going through a rocky patch, which was one of the reasons Mike wanted to get away from Virginia for a while. Tom said that their fathers are good friends but that he and Mike weren't, particularly, before this trip. They hang out in college together, as part of a larger group of friends. It was Mike's idea to come, to take the new boat up the coast and spend a week or two in Maine before heading back.

Mostly I was just happy that Mike wasn't there and I didn't have to see him or worry about anything bad happening to Tom, who genuinely seems to be a decent person, even if he is a bit sheltered.

When I got back to the hotel, I found out that I'd missed some drama. Marta's sister called while I was out and delivered the news that Marta's precious boyfriend had cheated on her. Instead of calling the asshole and dumping him over the phone, Marta handed in her notice, forfeiting her end-of-season bonus, and packed her stuff, determined to run home and win him back. Why God, why?? Didn't she read any Judy Blume when she was younger?? Forever is never really forever. I did try to talk to her, but she just looked at me in a pitying you'll never know love kind of way that made me want to slap her, so I let her go. Now I have the room to myself, *and while it's lonelier than ever, I can't pretend I'm sorry. It's so nice to have silence.*

Tom invited me back and I think I'm going to go. No more fake cleaning shifts though. That's just weird. We've agreed that I'm not going to take any more jobs at the Spencer house, and if I come over it'll just be as friends. I'm hoping Rosa'll give me work at one of the other houses, so that I won't miss out. And I'm looking forward to seeing Tom again. He's interesting, he's kind, and he's funny. I like him, but . . . I don't know. Can you ever be friends with someone when they're rich and you're broke? I guess, maybe, we'll find out.

Hannah

FOUR

By Tuesday morning Hannah had a plan. Rachel had given her a starting point, with her little jibe about Hazel Ellison failing to secure a job offer after her summer internship. On Monday night Hannah trawled through selected social media. She found that Sean had his social media accounts locked down on fully private settings, but Camila's were public and she posted a few times a week. Hazel was even more prolific. Between social media and the student newspaper, Hannah got all of the information she needed. Sean and Camila were both in their final year at UVA Law, and both had already accepted job offers from major law firms. Hazel was in her third year too, and had had a summer internship at McKnight Babbage in New York, but at the end of the summer there'd been no offer for her.

And there lay an opportunity.

By eight A.M. on Wednesday morning Hannah was ready. She made a call to Hazel Ellison, first routing her number through a website so that a 212 area code would come up on Hazel's phone, rather than Hannah's own cell number.

"Hello?" Hazel sounded distracted, a little confused.

Hannah tried to tighten her voice, make it a little nasal sounding. "Am I speaking with Hazel Ellison?"

"Yes. Yes, that's me."

"I'm calling from Gabriel Ryan's office at McKnight Babbage," Hannah said. According to Hazel's social media posts, she had worked on Ryan's team during her internship.

There was silence from the other end of the phone. Hannah waited for Hazel to fill it, but she said nothing.

"I'm getting in touch because McKnight Babbage is looking again at staffing requirements and we have a number of first-year associate positions available. Mr. Ryan has recommended that we consider you for one of those positions."

"I . . . Gabe recommended me?"

"Yes. Certainly." Hannah concentrated on sounding professional and no nonsense. "Mr. Ryan's team is growing, with four major acquisitions kicking off simultaneously next quarter." According to the McKnight Babbage website, Gabriel Ryan was a senior partner on the mergers and acquisitions team. "We do need to fill out his team quickly, however, so this position would require you to be available for an interview immediately. We would need you in the New York office next Monday at nine A.M. The interview process takes place over three days and includes an aptitude test and two rounds of interviews."

"I . . . I do have some commitments. I work for the Innocence Project at UVA. There's a trial . . . Would it be possible to reschedule my interview?"

"No. I'm sorry. Mr. Ryan and the other partners have very full schedules. Next week is the only time we were able to clear for the process. But of course, if you aren't available, we do understand given the late notice. And we would wish you luck with your other opportunities."

"No. No, I'm not saying I'm not available," Hazel said. "If it has to be next week then I can make some arrangements."

"Excellent. I'm sure Mr. Ryan will be pleased. Please arrive at the main desk in the ground-floor lobby by nine A.M. on Monday and ask for Margo Dowling. You'll be escorted to the interview suite and guided through the process from there." Margo Dowling was another name Hannah had plucked from the firm's website. It was a risk, giving Hazel the name of a real HR manager at the firm. There was always a chance she would call Margo Dowling to ask a question. But Hannah thought it was worth the risk. You always need to add that extra something for authenticity.

"Thank you," said Hazel. "That's fine. So this position would be with the mergers and acquisitions team?"

"Yes. That's right," Hannah said.

"Working . . . uh, working directly with Mr. Ryan?"

Shit. Hazel sounded wary. "Not directly, based on the organizational chart I've been provided," Hannah said.

"That's fine. I mean, of course, I would be happy to work with the entire team."

"Mmm-hmm. Then we'll see you at the office on Monday." Hannah hung up the phone. She took a long slow breath and let it out, then lay back on her bed and thought about her next move.

HANNAH WENT FOR A RUN BEFORE WORK. SHE NEEDED IT TO FOCUS her mind for the day ahead. She got to the Project offices at ten A.M. Marianne Stephenson gave her a nod and a smile but otherwise her arrival went largely unnoticed. Robert Parekh's office door was open and Hannah could see him in there, sitting on the edge of his desk, feet on a chair and phone pressed to his ear. He saw her pass and nodded to her. Rachel was already at her computer, as were Sean, Camila, and Hazel. Hannah put her head down and kept walking. She made her way to her desk, said hello to Rachel, and started work. Today her approach would be different. Monday had been all about metrics and efficiency. Today she wanted to show that she could dig deeper. She had been working quietly for a couple of hours when Robert Parekh dropped by her desk.

"Hannah," he said.

Hannah looked up, aware of Rachel's small jump of surprise next to her.

"Hello," Hannah said.

"Marianne talked to me this morning," Parekh said. "She keeps an eye on all of our new recruits. I've had a look at the work you have done so far and I read your recommendations so far. Good work. Very good work."

"Thank you," Hannah said.

"I guess they give you good training up there at the Bangor legal aid clinic," he said.

Hannah smiled. "The best," she said, and he started to move away. "Sorry, Professor Parekh?"

He stopped. "It's Rob, please."

"I've come across one application here that I think has a lot of potential. The applicant's sister sent in her appellant's brief over-night, and I think . . . well, you'll be the judge of course, but I think there's a case here. The applicant's been in prison for more than twenty-four years and she has eleven years left to run. I'm hoping to finish my analysis today, and I was just wondering who I should send my recommendation to for review?"

"You can send it to me." Parekh glanced at his watch. "You know what? I've got a few minutes. Why don't you come by now and run through what you have so far?"

"Great," Hannah said. "I'll just print out my notes."

Parekh left for his office and Hannah printed her document. She was conscious of Rachel, sitting to her right, quivering in outrage. Rachel's head was still bent to her work, but she had two spots of color high in her cheeks and her hand was clenched around her pen.

"You're a fast mover, aren't you?" she said in a sharp whisper.

Hannah said nothing.

"I told you yesterday that our recommendations go to the staff attorneys for review," Rachel said.

"This is a good case," Hannah said. "I don't want it to get lost."

"Sure," Rachel said. "You're just thinking about the applicant, right?"

"That's what I'm here for." Hannah picked up her notebook and pen and made for Parekh's office, stopping only to collect her notes from the printer. She paused as she entered his office.

"Door open, or closed?" she asked.

"Open is fine," he said. "Take a seat."

Hannah sat in one of the seats in front of his desk and, conscious that they could be interrupted at any time, launched into her pitch without any preamble.

"The applicant's name is Nia Jones. In 1994 she was twenty-two years old and living in a trailer in a park outside Richmond with her children—a six-month-old baby boy named Andre, and a two-year-old little girl named Carly-Anne. At approximately ten-thirty P.M. on a Friday night in October, the trailer caught fire. The fire started in the kitchen area. Nia was asleep in the bedroom with the baby, and Carly-Anne was asleep too." Hannah looked up. "Carly-Anne slept in the living room. The couch there converted into a bed at night, but that meant that she was caught on the other side of the fire from Nia and Andre." Parekh nodded, and Hannah looked back at her notes.

"Nia managed to get outside with the baby, and witnesses say that she went straight around to the side of the home and broke the window. The window was high up off the ground . . ." Hannah put her papers down and demonstrated with her hands. "It would have been above head height for Nia, who is only five foot two. But she broke the window and managed to climb halfway inside before the fire drove her back. She had deep lacerations to both hands and second-degree burns to her face and upper body."

"The little girl didn't make it," Parekh said.

Hannah shook her head.

"And Nia was charged."

"Yes. With arson and felony murder. I've looked at the reporting around the case. There's a strong streak of prejudice running through everything. Lots of talk about how she was a single mother of two. Lots of references to previous arrests for drug offenses at the trailer park, though there's nothing to suggest that Nia had any drug history. Her sister tells me that she had no history with the police at all, that she was a good mother who loved her children and was doing her best. No drugs, no alcohol abuse."

Hannah would never deny that there were innocent people in prison. She had, however, been a little taken aback by how easy it had been to find a case that seemed to be such an obvious case of wrongful conviction. Was that just luck? Or were they really stacked up, ten deep?

"You said felony murder?" Parekh asked, brow furrowed.

"Yes."

"Anything in that we can use?"

Hannah shook her head. "I don't think so." Felony murder charges could be controversial. It was a basic legal principle that to be convicted of a crime an offender must have both committed the crime and had the intention of committing it. The felony murder rule was an exception to that principle, and it had, on more than one occasion, resulted in convictions that most people would consider to be unjust. Under the murder rule, when an offender accidentally kills someone while in the process of committing another serious crime, like arson, rape, or burglary, the offender can be charged with first-degree murder. But it goes further than that. In some circumstances, the killer's *accomplices* in the original crime can be found guilty of murder too, even if they weren't physically present when the death took place. Hannah had read about a case where a burglar was already in handcuffs in a police car when her accomplice in an earlier burglary shot a police officer. The burglar in handcuffs was found guilty of felony murder. There was another case where a twenty-year-old loaned a car to a friend. The friend used that car to travel to commit a burglary, and during the burglary, he beat a young woman to death. The twenty-year-old was convicted of felony murder and sentenced to life without parole. The prosecution had argued that the twenty-year-old knew that his friend was planning a burglary, but it didn't seem likely that he could have known that the murder, which had been spontaneous, would take place.

Hannah could see that the murder rule was problematic, but she wasn't sure she agreed with critics who said it should be removed entirely. For her, it was a question of moderation, rather than complete removal. Virginia had added a requirement that the murder result directly from the offender's own acts, rather than those of an accomplice, and that felt like a reasonable approach. If Nia Jones *had* intentionally set fire to her own trailer and her baby's death had been the accidental result, Hannah would have wanted to see Nia punished. So Hannah's problem with Nia's conviction wasn't that it resulted from a charge of felony murder. The problem was, as far as Hannah could see, that there was no evidence that she had committed any crime at all.

"You made contact with the sister?"

Hannah nodded. "Her number was on the application. I thought calling her might be the quickest way to get what we needed. She had the brief and she was able to send it through overnight."

Parekh nodded. "Okay," he said. "Let's talk about the evidence."

"Right," Hannah said. "Well, the arson investigation found evidence of accelerant in the living room. Two arson investigators testified with confidence that the fire had been started deliberately, that someone had poured kerosene in a line across the living room floor and set the whole home on fire. They specified that the accelerant was the reason the fire had burned so quickly and so fiercely. Nia had no explanation for the accelerant found in the trailer. She said she had never poured or spilled kerosene or anything similar in her home. She had a small kerosene heater, but the arson investigators had already discounted that as the source of the blaze. At her trial Nia said that the trailer wasn't hers. She'd been renting for two years, so she suggested that the kerosene could have been spilled by the owner or a previous tenant, but the arson experts said no way."

"What was the motive?" Parekh asked.

"They said she intended to make an insurance policy claim."

"Okay," Parekh said. Raised voices came from somewhere outside and Parekh looked over Hannah's shoulder, squinting a little as if to try to make out who was speaking. "Talk to me about the evidence," Parekh said.

Hannah had read about nothing but exoneration cases for the past week, which was why Nia's case had jumped out at her. In her reading about death row cases she had come across more than one case where arson evidence had later been overturned. She hadn't just been searching social media feeds the night before. She'd also spent several hours looking for specific case law where new scientific evidence had been effectively introduced. She'd worked until three A.M. but it hadn't been in vain.

"The National Registry of Exonerations shows that at least seventeen arson convictions have been overturned in the past twenty-four years, including that of David Lee Gavitt, who had been imprisoned for twenty-six years for the murder of his wife and two baby girls by fire. Investigators in Gavitt's case, and others, pointed to charred patterns in the shape of puddles and other signs to argue that the fire had been intentionally set. They used almost word for word the same language used by the arson investigators in Nia's case."

He was listening to her, she definitely had his attention, but the raised voices from outside the office weren't going away. What had started out as a lively discussion sounded like it was degenerating into an argument. Parekh stood.

"All of the evidence has since been debunked. There is no scientific basis for it," Hannah said. "The only real evidence against Nia was the evidence of the arson investigators and I think it's unreliable. If we could get the right expert . . ." But she had lost him. He went to the door of his office, leaned out.

"What's going on?" he said.

The argument outside stopped as soon as he spoke. Hannah turned in her chair, craning her neck to try to peer around the door, but Parekh was blocking her view. There was a mumbled response, and then Parekh said—"My office, please. Right now." Hannah stood up, hovered, unsure if she should stay or go. Parekh came back inside, closely followed by Camila and Hazel. Both girls looked flushed and unhappy.

"I'm sorry, Hannah. We'll have to pick this up later," Parekh said.

"No problem." Hannah turned to leave.

"I think you have something there. Stay on it. Finish your recommendation, send it to me, and let's set a time to talk again," Parekh said.

Hannah nodded and left, closing the door behind her. She went back to her desk. The atmosphere in the office was strained for the next few hours. Rachel treated Hannah to an icy look and silence on her return to her desk. Rob Parekh's office door stayed closed for half an hour, and when Camila and Hazel finally emerged it was clear that their argument was far from over. Hazel went straight to her desk and started packing up, emptying drawers into her backpack. Camila stood beside her, talking at her, and though she kept her voice low it was clear from her expression and her body language that she was angry.

"Leave me alone, Camila," Hazel said, loudly enough that everyone in the open plan area who wasn't already watching the drama raised their heads.

"You never cared about the Project at all," Camila said, raising her voice now too. "It's all about you, isn't it?"

Hazel just shook her head, lips tight. She shoved the last of her belongings into her bag, slung it over her shoulder, and walked out without another word to anyone. Hannah saw the anger on Camila's face crumble to something else and for an awful moment it looked like she was going to burst into tears in front of everyone; moments later Sean Warner had ushered her outside and they were gone for at least an hour. When they came back they went quietly to their desks, and the morning wore on with no more drama, though it was hard not to be distracted by small movements around the office.

HANNAH WORKED UNTIL LUNCH, THEN WENT OUTSIDE INTO THE sunshine to eat a sandwich. She was back at her desk by two P.M. Rachel was gone, finished for the day by the look of her organized desk. Robert Parekh came by ten minutes later.

"No classes today?" he asked.

Hannah shrugged. "None today, one tomorrow. I have a very light class load this semester."

He nodded, looked at her carefully. "Think you can keep up long hours here? Full-time hours, even?"

"Absolutely," she said firmly.

"Okay. Look, we've got an issue. One of the students I had put on the Dandridge case has had to drop out unexpectedly. We've got the preliminary hearing next week and we're not as prepared as we should be. I need all hands on deck, but I don't want anyone I have to carry. I need someone who is committed. Someone who can pull their weight without hand-holding. I would be giving this to a student with more experience than you, but"—he gave an almost imperceptible grimace in the direction of Rachel's desk—"we don't have the right fit right now. I'm thinking about bringing you on." He paused and Hannah held her breath, trying hard to look cool and calm and not desperately eager.

"Look, Hannah, I'll give you a trial. Join us for the case conference at three o'clock today. Let's see how things go."

"Thank you," Hannah said. "Thanks for the opportunity."

"Let's see if you make the grade before you thank me," Parekh said. And he disappeared back into his office.

AT THREE O'CLOCK THE STAFF ATTORNEYS AND SEAN AND CAMILA filed into Parekh's office, and Hannah followed in their wake. She was the last to enter the room and she shut the door behind her. Robert Parekh crossed to the front of his desk and leaned back against it. Everyone else spread themselves around the room.

"Say hello to our new teammate, Hannah Rokeby," Parekh said. He waved in Hannah's direction. "Hannah, this is everyone." He gestured to a slim dark-haired man with a close-cut beard. "Hannah, this is Jim Lehane. Jim is our senior staff attorney and he's supervising the Dandridge case. You'll get to know everyone else in time, but after me, Jim is the boss. Got it?"

Hannah nodded. She was conscious of the surprise in the room at her sudden inclusion in the group, and of Sean and Camila's reactions in particular, but she kept her eyes firmly on Parekh.

"Right," said Parekh. "Some of you are new to the Dandridge case, so the purpose of this meeting is to get everyone up to speed and assign tasks. Jim's going to start with a basic rundown of the facts of the case. After this meeting, Sean, Camila, perhaps you'd be kind enough to take Hannah out? Feed her—as far as I can see, she doesn't leave her desk—and fill her in on everything she needs to know about how we work. She'll be taking over anything that Hazel was working on. Oh yes, for those who don't know, Hazel will not be available for the Dandridge case. A job interview, next week, apparently. As Hazel's commitment to the Project is less than what I expect of our students, I've asked that she not return."

A murmur passed around the room, but the reaction was fairly muted. Most people, it seemed, already knew.

"Okay, I'm going to give you a very quick rundown of the case history so far, then Jim's going to brief you about the facts around the murder itself. After that we'll assign tasks and then we get to work.

"I'm going to assume you're all aware of the basics—Sarah Fitzhugh was murdered in June 2007, and our client, Michael Dandridge, was convicted of her murder and sentenced to death in April 2008. From prison Michael made contact with a law firm called Lovell McCain, who agreed to act pro-bono for him. Jake Lovell made any number of appeals for Michael right up until October 2018, all of which were either procedurally barred or ultimately rejected on their merits. In November 2018 Michael had exhausted his direct appeals, Jake Lovell walked away, and Michael filed an application with our office." Parekh smiled at them all, and his charm was so thick it was almost uncomfortable.

"It didn't take long for the application to make its way to me, and I interviewed our new client in December of last year. Michael was able to convince me pretty quickly that he had been the victim of a gross miscarriage of justice."

Hannah swallowed hard. The self-righteousness was nauseating.

"Michael told me that Sheriff Jerome Pierce beat the living daylights out of him in custody," Parekh continued. "Got him in an interview room and beat him up, threatened him, until he confessed. Michael says he told this to both his original attorney and to Jake Lovell, but neither Lovell nor the original defense attorney ever raised this in Michael's defense. Why do you think that is? I mean, granted, Jake Lovell did not have a great deal of experience with wrongful conviction cases. Let's just say that he was more enthusiastic than he was skilled. But still." He looked around the room. "Anyone? Ideas?"

Camila half raised her hand, as if she was in the classroom. "Were they concerned about believability? Do we have photographs of Michael's injuries? Does Pierce have a record of complaints made against him?"

"No photographs," said Parekh. "Michael was too afraid to talk until he saw the prison doctor at Sussex I prison after his conviction more than a year later. And Pierce's discipline record is good. Two complaints from his rookie days, nothing for twenty years."

Camila grimaced. "Maybe he's just gotten better at covering his tracks."

Parekh pointed at her. "Maybe. But let's bring it back to the attorneys. Why didn't they raise Michael's allegations of coercion at his trial or on appeal? Yes, there would be challenges to overcome, but to not even make an attempt?" He shook his head. "Something smells here. Something feels off to me. Let's bear that in mind as we move forward.

"I filed an appeal with the fourth circuit in January arguing actual innocence. By its nature that appeal was limited to the facts and arguments that had been put before the original trial court. I wasn't permitted to put forward new evidence at that time, my arguments had to focus essentially on the failures in the original case. The fourth circuit ruled in our favor and referred the case for an evidentiary hearing, which was held over the summer break. I worked that case along with Jim and Mary Calvas. Jim, do you want to take us through what happened next?"

Jim Lehane gave a brisk nod. "We received a copy of Michael's original attorney's file. We took up everything we could get on discovery. We did the usual cross-referencing and double-checking. And we found that the numbers on the evidence dockets from the crime scene weren't sequential. One docket seemed to be missing. So we went direct to the forensics lab—well, we found the cash for an investigator and he went directly to the forensics lab—and discovered that evidence that corresponded to that missing docket had existed, but had never been disclosed to the original defense attorney. Crime scene officers found a single hair on Sarah Fitzhugh's body. It was tested and compared to samples taken from Michael and there was no match. The hair evidence was then hidden from the defense, because it suggested that someone other than Michael committed the crime. Michael's original attorney never knew a hair had been found. The DA's office buried the evidence. On purpose."

This information had been publicly reported in the various articles written about the case. Presumably everyone in the room already knew about it, but there was still a murmur of discontent from the group. Hannah had to hold back an eye roll. Not that she was all right with prosecutors hiding evidence. That wasn't okay, ever. But assuming that a single hair on Sarah Fitzhugh's poor body meant Dandridge was innocent was taking rose-tinted to an extreme. Sarah could have picked that hair up from anywhere. And all this holier-than-thou shock at the prosecutor's cheating was painful. According to their biographies on the Innocence Project website, Parekh, and the other staff attorneys like Jim Lehane and Mary Calvas, had all worked as criminal defense attorneys outside the Project, which meant that they had routinely defended guilty clients. Everyone knew how that game was played. The convenient fictions that were maintained, the blind eyes that were turned, all so that they could put forward the best possible defense for clients they knew in their hearts were guilty as sin, without tripping over ethical rules that could get them disbarred. Now these same people were shocked and appalled that a prosecutor was willing to cheat to put a murdering rapist in jail? *Please.*

Parekh continued—"So the federal judge ruled that the county attorney's office failed to fulfill its constitutional duty to disclose evidence favorable to the defendant and had that evidence been disclosed it likely would have affected the jury's verdict. Hence the vacated conviction. In a fair world that would mean that Michael would be out and free right now. Unfortunately the judge gave the state the option to either retry our client or release him uncondi- tionally within one hundred and twenty days. That period was due to expire on the fifteenth of October and we assumed that Engle and his pals were going to keep Michael in prison right up until the last minute of the last hour of the very last day. We understood . . . we were *led to believe* that the delay in releasing him was petty re- venge and no more than that. But that was not the case, because as we all know, eleven days ago, on the sixteenth of August, Jackson Engle refiled charges against Michael and we are now going to trial all over again." There was a collective groan from everyone in the room. "Until eleven days ago we thought this case was done. The state was running down the clock and we thought, *we hoped,* that they would quietly let things slide rather than risk the publicity of a retrial."

Jim Lehane nodded. "Right. Unfortunately it has become very clear that they intend to try the case again and there's every indication that they are as eager as ever to convict our client."

"We have a lot of work to do," Parekh said. "We never expected to take this case to trial. We filed our appeal, we won our evidentiary hearing because of the buried evidence, and for six weeks or so we thought we were just running down the clock. So now we find ourselves in new territory. The legal arguments that won our appeal, the buried evidence, none of that will help us in a new trial. Now, everything resets. And we can't rely on any of the information gathered by Michael's previous attorneys. I don't trust the standard of their work. So we can't take anything for granted. We have to look at everything afresh."

"Why are they doing this?" Sean asked. "I mean, it seems like a crazy choice for the DA. The case is going to attract more media attention. Michael is obviously innocent. They set him up first time around. They can't think they're going to get away with that again. Isn't it going to look really bad for them when they lose?"

Jim Lehane was shaking his head. "Michael was convicted eleven years ago. Jackson Engle prosecuted him. Jerome Pierce was in charge of the investigation. Pierce and Engle are still in place in Yorktown today. There's been too much media coverage already for their liking. They can't let it go now. They don't want egg all over their faces when it comes to reelection. And if they're willing to go back into court, they obviously think they can win this case. They have resources we don't have. We can't afford to be overconfident. We're coming from behind here."

Parekh stood up. "Here's what I have to say about that. I don't care. I don't care about anyone's motivation but ours. And here's our motivation. It's pretty simple, as mission statements go—we're in it to win it. We are not going to lose this case. Does everyone understand that? I don't care if they've got us on the back foot. I don't care that we have no resources, no investigators, and no money. We're still ahead in this game. Would you like to know why?" He held up a hand, started to count down on his fingers. "Because they're full of shit. They hid evidence. They beat our client up to get a confession. There's one eyewitness statement from a child who was too young to know better. That's it. That's what they have. I know with the talent in this room, we are more than good enough to tear this case apart. So let's get to it."

LAURA

DIARY ENTRY #3

Saturday, July 30, 1994, 8:30 a.m.

When I started high school, I was kind of young for my age. I wasn't really ready for dating. Guys asked me out and I said yes because I didn't want to seem like a loser, but I honestly hated making out. Everything always got hot and heavy way too fast. Like, dating = a burger and a milkshake + awkward conversation + sloppy making out + a sweaty hand burrowing under my bra. Excuse me for not swooning. I say that now, but at the time I was convinced I was frigid and I was TERRIFIED that anyone would find out so I always acted like I was into it. Which was surprisingly easy to pull off. Why is it that guys always believe you when you act like you're into them, and never believe you when you say you aren't?

Whatever. All that was history when I made out with Vinny Thomas in my junior year. Vinny was unbelievably hot (Luke Perry in 90210 except with darker eyes) and he was way out of my league, but we made out at a party once. That's when I figured out that I wasn't frigid at all. But I've never really had a serious boyfriend. Life got pretty messed up after mom died. I didn't think about dating or anything like that for a long time. And now that I'm not in school it's harder to meet someone. When I'm in Boston I feel like I'm the odd one out, like all Jenna's friends are going somewhere and I'm just this loser girl she's kind to. Mostly, these days, I don't date at all and I'm cool with that. I mean, I'm really lonely sometimes, but I don't think dating's any solution to that. With Tom, it's been pretty clear from the beginning that he wants a friend, not a girlfriend. I get zero romantic vibes from him. He just seems to like me, like spending time with me. Honestly? I think maybe he has a girlfriend in Virginia, or something. Or maybe (shock of all shocks) I'm just not his type. The second time we hung out we went for a swim and afterward we went for dinner in Seal Harbor. I say dinner—we bought a pizza and a couple of beers and sat by the water and talked. I asked him about Mike, where he was, what he was up to.

"Still sailing," Tom said. He picked chorizo off the last slice of pizza and ate it.

"Again?"

"He's gone for a few days. Taken the boat three hours north to a place called Blacks Harbour, over the border in Canada. He has some friends there."

"You don't mind?" I was thinking about how much the yacht was worth—probably a lot. "It's safe for him to go by himself?"

Tom made a face and said something about the boat being state of the art, and safe to take out alone for a few hours. And then he said that it was probably a good thing for them to have a break from each other. So I asked if they weren't getting along, but he shrugged it off.

I couldn't tell if he really thought everything was fine between them or if he didn't want to talk about it with me. I kind of wanted to bring up the cocaine and the gun—I still do—but I'm afraid he'll think I've been snooping. I've probably waited too long. Anyway, Tom changed the subject pretty quickly after that. We stayed late at Seal Harbor, drinking beer and watching the sun go down and talking. I told him a lot about myself. More than I've told anyone but Jenna. I don't usually talk about that stuff, but he was so honest with me about his own family that I felt guilty holding back. And I miss Jenna a lot. So I told him a little, then a bit more, and before I knew it I had told him almost everything. And he was great *about it all. Understanding without being too sympathetic. He's a good listener. He's a good friend.*

Mike was gone for almost a week and Tom and I have fallen into a routine. Every day after I finish work he picks me up, we swim or hike or just hang out. And it's been really nice. Mike's back now, of course. At first he was actually okay to be around—smiling and joking all the time—but it didn't last. He started dropping hints about how they should head back to Virginia early, get ready for school, and when Tom didn't jump at the idea right away, nice Mike disappeared. For the last couple of days he's been smiling on the surface but tense and angry underneath. I've tried to bring it up with Tom, but he thinks I'm reading too much into things. We've stopped hanging out at the house as much though. We just go hiking instead. I think we've done every trail in Acadia at least once. Anyway, tonight I complained about my sore legs and Tom said we should go sailing tomorrow instead. !! I'm kind of excited. I've swapped my shift with Liza. We're going to pick up some food and go out on the boat for the whole day. Slightly nervous . . . am I going to get seasick?? That would be embarrassing.

Sunday, July 31, 1994

We were on the water by ten a.m. And oh my God was it beautiful. The blue sky, the wind, the cool sparkling water. For the first time in my life I felt like I got it—the reason so many people will do anything to be rich. It's a completely different way of living, filled with experiences. Poor people don't have experiences because we're too busy trying to eat. I'm not proud of this, but for just a second I almost hated him . . . because he's so free and I'm not. It was a shitty feeling but it didn't last. Thing is, it's impossible to resent Tom. He's always so nice to me. He acts like I'm the most important person in every room, like I'm his best and oldest friend. It makes me happy and sad at the same time. Happy for the obvious reasons, and sad because he's going. This is all temporary. And sad because he's making me realize that no one has ever been that nice to me before, not even Jenna. Not even my mom, if I'm honest. How fucking pathetic.

Tom taught me a bit about sailing and I pretended to help, but really he did almost everything. Late in the afternoon he sailed us into a little sheltered bay and dropped the anchor. Tom wanted to swim and I wasn't so sure so he gave me this big grin, pulled off his shirt, and dived into the water. I stripped down to my bikini and followed. Oh my God . . . it was so cold I swear I couldn't breathe for a second. And it was kind of scary, swimming in such deep water. I climbed out pretty quickly and sat on the boat in the sunshine to dry off, trying to hide the fact that I'd chickened out. Tom sat beside me, close enough that I could feel the warmth from his skin. He handed me a towel. When I took the towel I noticed that he had a thick, silvery scar that ran right across the palm of his left hand. I asked him about it and he held his hand out flat and we both looked at it.

"I'm not actually sure what happened. I think I was five. My mother says I fell and put my hand through a window. My aunt thinks I cut it on a broken bottle."

"Wouldn't your mother know?"

"She was away at the time. Traveling. And the nanny we had then left soon afterward. The story just seems to have gotten confused over the years."

I figured they'd probably fired the nanny, and I told him so.

He looked surprised. "You're probably right. I never thought of that. Just that it was strange to have a mark like that and not really know how you got it."

I reached out and ran my finger down the scar. His skin was softer than I expected. Warm. He closed his hand around mine. He looked straight into my eyes and kissed me. I guess maybe some part of me knew it was coming but there was still that moment when I wasn't sure and then he did and . . .

and...

anything I say about it is going to sound so cheesy, or over the top, but the truth is, it was so, so different. He kissed me really gently to begin with, and then he kind of leaned back and looked at me, like he was checking I was okay. And then he kissed me again, except deeper, and everything about it was perfect. His skin was warm and he smelled so good, of the sea and himself and everything was perfect. His body is so beautiful. Oh man, I know, I know this is so over the top and I'm blushing like crazy as I write this but I've never wanted anything so much as I wanted him. The funny thing is, there's a little cabin on the boat and we could have gone there, but I never thought of it and he didn't suggest it. We just sat on the deck and made out until my chin was raw from his stubble and the sun started to set. He said we should sail home. I stood with him at the tiller and we kept trying and failing to have a conversation. All I could think about was how happy I was, and . . . at the same time how scared I was that this was going to screw everything up. But we touched all the time—his hand on my shoulder, mine on his back. I think we both knew that we were going straight to his bedroom the moment we docked. But then . . . we turned into the quiet little bay and sailed toward the jetty and there were two people there, waiting. Both men, one of them standing still and the other pacing. We were too far away to make out their faces. I looked at Tom but he shook his head. He had no clue who they were either. We had to sail a lot closer before we could see that it was Mike, and someone else. An older man. Heavyset, dark haired, with a beard.

I thought it might be Mike's dad, but Tom shook his head again, said he didn't recognize the guy. He got on with taking down sails and bringing the boat in to dock, so I stayed on deck and watched Mike and the stranger and their vibe was really off. I can't put my finger on what it was. Maybe it was the way they were standing—stiff and still—or the way they never spoke to each other the whole time we were docking. Mike caught the rope

Tom threw him and tied it up, and when he finally spoke there was an edge to his voice.

"You took the boat out. You never said anything. I came looking for it and found it was missing."

Tom gave him a look and said something like, "I wasn't aware I had to ask permission to use my own boat." Which sounds snarky now, when I write it down, but he didn't say it in a snarky way. Tom was more cold than anything, and something about the way he said it made him seem older, suddenly. Mike saw it too. He gave one of his fake laughs, acting like he thought Tom was kidding around, but I could see he was nervous. He was sweating, even though the sun had nearly set and the evening had cooled.

"Who's this?" Tom said, nodding toward the stranger.

"Sorry, sorry, this is my friend Dom. He's thinking of buying a yacht, same model as yours, so I offered to show him around. Is that okay?" Mike's tone was so exaggeratedly apologetic that it bordered on sarcasm. Maybe he thought he'd embarrass Tom, but he was wrong. Tom said it would be fine, but in a disinterested kind of way, and then he started gathering up our things. He took his time, not hurrying. I helped. Dom just stood there watching, saying nothing, with a tight smile on his face. He was wearing jeans, white sneakers, and a T-shirt that was a size too small. The clothes were really young for him. He should have looked ridiculous, but actually, he was just scary. Intimidating. He had this look on his face all the time, like he was holding himself back from saying what he really wanted to, but only by the thinnest of threads. And he was completely silent the whole time we were getting ready. I kept thinking that there was something familiar about him and it was only later that I realized what it was. He had the same vibe as a debt collector for a loan shark. There was violence shimmering just under the surface.

When we were ready, Tom slung our bag over his shoulder and helped me off the boat, and we walked up the path toward the trees and the house. I stopped at the top of the hill and looked back. Mike had already disap-

peared below deck, but Dom was still standing on the jetty, and he was watching us. I shivered. Tom took my hand.

"You okay?"

I told him I was fine, but I wasn't. I had that horrible feeling again, like something bad was going to happen. Tom was frowning, looking back over my shoulder toward the boat.

"Come on. I'll take you home. I don't know what that was all about, but I'll talk to Mike when I get back."

I thought about suggesting that I stay. Not for romantic reasons. Just to provide support. But Tom drew me quickly through the house to the car and I followed. And a few minutes later, when he was driving and we had the windows down and music playing, I started to feel a lot better. He held my hand and I ran my thumb along his scar. And the whole mood changed again and everything started to build. By the time we got to the hotel we had both forgotten about the whole Mike thing.

Tom parked the car and leaned over and kissed me. I pulled away, looking into his eyes. His expression was so serious when he looked at me and it made me want him so much more. It was my turn to take him by the hand and lead. My room is pretty basic—just a single bed, a desk, and a tiny bathroom—but with Marta gone it's private. I closed the door behind us. Neither of us turned the light on. The sun had set but the moon was bright and there was enough light coming in through the window that we could see each other, just. I took off my T-shirt. He untied my bikini top and dropped it on the floor. He kissed me and we fell onto the bed. And everything was perfect. Until afterward, when I suddenly felt afraid. I don't know why, but I suddenly had this horrible feeling that I was about to lose him. Maybe everyone feels like that when they find someone special.

"Stay," I said, clinging to him.

He turned over and kissed me. Told me he wasn't going anywhere. Five minutes later he was asleep. And I've been lying here, staring at the ceiling, since.

Hannah

FIVE

When Robert Parekh finished his pep talk, Jim Lehane took center stage and started to run through the details of the Sarah Fitzhugh case. He didn't have Parekh's natural magnetism. He was lower key, less intense, but he had no trouble keeping the attention of the room.

"Here are the basic facts. In 2007 a young mother by the name of Sarah Fitzhugh was alone in her apartment with her children—she had two, Samuel, age seven, and Rosie, who was a baby, just over six months old. Sarah and Samuel had dinner—pizza, I think—and Sarah fed the baby. Then—we don't know for sure but we're assuming she followed her usual routine—she put the children to bed. Probably no later than seven-thirty. After that, she watched TV for a while. Her husband, Saul, was a midshipman in the Navy, and he was halfway through a six-month tour. By all accounts their relationship was good. Sarah's parents lived two blocks over so they were able to help her when Saul was away, and that made things a little bit easier. Anyway, Sarah's parents had nothing but good things to say about Saul, and as he was three thousand miles offshore at the time of the murder, it's safe to say that Saul had nothing to do with her death.

"At nine-thirty Sarah turned off the TV, put her dishes in the sink, and climbed the stairs to bed. We know about the TV and timings because Sarah was living in a small apartment in Yorktown, and it seems the walls were paper thin. The neighbors could overhear each other's conversations." Jim looked down at his notes. "Rita and Thomas Stamford gave evidence that they heard Sarah's television going until about nine-thirty, and they heard nothing at all after that. Sarah went upstairs, took a shower, changed out of her jeans and T-shirt, and put on a nightgown. It's probable that Sarah fed the baby again later, before returning her to her crib. At some point in the night a man entered Sarah's bedroom and raped and strangled her in her own bed." Jim cleared his throat.

"It seems that Sarah did not scream or make any loud sounds during the attack, which the pathologist later said likely went on for some time, given the nature of her injuries. She may have been unable to scream—she was strangled—or she may have been keeping quiet for other reasons. The prosecution suggested in the original trial that her attacker may have threatened to hurt the children if she cried out. According to the prosecution, her little boy, Samuel, slept through the attack, and only woke when the baby started crying. At approximately one-thirty A.M.—but please bear in mind the evidence about the time line is shaky at this point—Sarah's attacker finally killed her through strangulation, and left the house."

Hannah was listening intently. So much of this she already knew, had gleaned from microscopic examination of every newspaper article written about the case, but it was different hearing it spoken about here, in this manner. Jim was to the point, straightforward, but he was also respectful, unlike many of the newspaper articles, which lingered over titillating details and ignored others.

"The prosecution's case was that Samuel Fitzhugh, then age seven, woken by his sister's crying, came to the door of his bedroom and watched, unseen, as the attacker left the house. Samuel later identified our client from a photographic lineup, but we all know how unreliable eyewitness testimony is at the best of times. And we're talking about a traumatized seven-year-old here. Not exactly the gold standard. Anyway, Samuel ran to his mother and found her unresponsive. He was very distressed, but somehow he managed to get his sister out of her crib and he carried her next door to the Stamford apartment. At two A.M. Thomas Stamford called the police, who showed up twelve minutes later."

Jim looked around at everyone, making sure that he still had their attention. He had nothing to worry about. The room was completely still. No one fidgeted or looked at their phones. They were all completely focused. "That's it, really, in terms of the facts of the attack. We know that police effectively had no leads. The killer was extraordinarily careful. He used a condom and presumably gloves. As we now know, a single hair was found but no match to that hair has been found in the system to date. Police canvassed the neighborhood and interviewed neighbors, family, and friends. Three weeks after the murder they had no meaningful leads, and no arrests. That was when they went looking for our client."

"Why?" Hannah asked.

Everyone turned and looked at her and she felt her face reddening.

"Sorry, I'm just wondering what brought the police to question Dandridge in the first place." She already knew the answer, but she wanted to make some small counterpoint to the innocent victim narrative they were so eager to run with.

"An anonymous call," Rob Parekh said. He held up one finger. "That was the first link. Police claim that an anonymous caller told them that Michael had murdered Sarah Fitzhugh. For that reason they brought him in for questioning. Forty-eight hours later they had their confession." Parekh held up a second finger, then a third.

"Then they had seven-year-old Samuel Fitzhugh pull Michael out of a photo lineup." Rob Parekh turned his hand around to face them, all fingers extended like he was offering them a high five. "That's it. An anonymous call, a forced confession, and a lineup with a traumatized, highly suggestible seven-year-old. That's what it took to convict our client of murder." Parekh exchanged glances with Jim Lehane.

Jim leaned forward. "The case goes to a preliminary hearing on Monday. A preliminary hearing is usually a nonevent." His eyes swept over Hannah, Camila, and Sean. "The point of a preliminary hearing is for the prosecution to lay out enough information to convince the judge that there is probable cause to hold the defendant for indictment and prosecution. Generally speaking, the judge will not even consider defense evidence. A preliminary hearing is not a trial. After the preliminary hearing the case goes to a grand jury and then, eventually, to a full trial."

"That's how it usually works," Parekh interrupted. His eyes were bright; his expression said he was fully switched on. "But not this time, if we can help it. I want to kill this thing before it gets off the ground at the preliminary hearing. I want to knock down everything they put up, convince the judge that there's no evidence to support the case moving forward. We have one week. Jim and I will be hard at work on the motions needed to exclude Michael's coerced confession and Samuel Fitzhugh's evidence. If we win those motions we might win the case there and then. I'm confident we'll exclude the confession, less confident about the lineup." Parekh nodded at Sean, Camila, and Hannah. "I want you guys working every angle you can think of. We need new facts, anything that wasn't explored or presented at the first trial. Anything we can use to disprove core evidence the prosecution is likely to present at the hearing.

Dandridge's alibi. This so-called anonymous caller. Look for any police who might have retired or moved out of the county. Is anyone willing to break ranks about what happened in the original case? I don't want to go into court with a dry case based solely on technical argument. I want a narrative, a story to tell. Understood?"

There were murmurs of agreement, and Rob Parekh stood up. "Right," he said. "That's it. We'll meet as frequently as developments demand—Jim will send you all a schedule, but let's stay flexible, people—don't be afraid to come to me or Jim immediately if you feel that something warrants attention. Remember, we're working against the clock. And one more thing—public perception will be a big part of this case. The outcome may come down to public or political pressure. Be careful about what you say and who you say it to. The prosecution isn't above playing dirty tricks."

HANNAH WENT BACK TO HER DESK WHEN THE MEETING BROKE UP and Camila and Sean followed her there.

"Well," Camila said. "Welcome to the team, I guess." She looked pissed.

"Thank you," Hannah said. She had to force herself not to say anything else, not to rush in with explanations and apologies for her sudden introduction to their little group.

"Yes," said Sean. "Welcome." His welcome was warmer, more sincere. He had an open, expressive face and he looked at her with interest. Hannah suppressed an inward shiver. Which was the bigger threat to her plans? Camila's irritation or Sean's curiosity?

"I suppose . . . should we get to work?" Hannah said.

"Parekh said to feed you. Let's go to the bar."

They took her to a little bar on Main Street that had comfortable booths and soft lighting. Sean and Camila ordered beers and burgers so Hannah did too.

"Fucking Hazel," Camila said, as soon as the waiter left the table. "Can you believe this? I mean, can you actually believe this?"

Sean shook his head.

"What? You think it's okay that she just walked?"

"I'm not saying it's okay. I'm just saying that I understand it."

Camila shook her head. "Well, I don't. What's the rush? She made a commitment to the Project. She made a commitment to us, for that matter. It's bullshit."

"What happened?" Hannah asked. She should show interest. Surely sitting there in silence would seem odd? "Why did she go?"

"She got an interview," Camila said. "Like, literally this morning. Nine A.M. this morning she gets a phone call from a New York firm telling her they want to see her next week, and by ten she's in the office telling Parekh she's out."

"Come on, Camila," Sean said. "You would have gone too. You wouldn't hesitate."

Camila had just taken a swig of beer. She widened her eyes at Sean, and swallowed. "I would not. Take it back."

"Of course you would. So would I, if I didn't already have a job lined up. So would anyone. We all need to work when this is over. Right? We're all going to have bills to pay. So Hazel had to miss a few days next week. And the timing is bad. But Rob could have given her a break, right? He didn't have to throw his toys out of the stroller and kick her off the project."

"She knew before she even went to talk to him that that would happen. She knows what he's like. We all do."

"Sure," said Sean. "She knew. That doesn't make it her fault."

"Hazel didn't *have* to take the interview, Sean. She's not like you and me. She has a rich daddy, so she doesn't have to worry about paying her bills, does she?"

Sean put his head to one side, looking at Camila and smiling as if to say *We both know you're talking shit, but keep going if it makes you feel better.* "So you're saying that because she could live off her father that she should?"

Camila was quiet for a moment. Then she picked up a beer mat and threw it at him. "Whatever."

He laughed at her. He turned to Hannah. "Okay, Hannah, spill. What's your story?"

"My story?" Hannah said.

"Your story," Sean nodded. He drank from his beer, swallowed, and gestured with his right hand. "I mean, where you came from, how you managed to get on the team. I don't think I've ever heard of anyone getting into the Project without jumping through all of the hoops. Camila and I applied midway through our first year and we had to sit for an interview and all of the rest of it."

"Right," Hannah said. "Well, I'm only here for a semester. My mother is getting medical treatment in Richmond for the next few months. Cancer. She's in a clinical trial at the hospital. We'll both be going back to Maine when the trial is over. I just wanted to be as close as possible to her while she's in Virginia."

Sean's interested expression turned to one of quick sympathy. "Oh, I'm really sorry," he said. "Is your mother going to be okay? How is she doing?"

Hannah looked at Sean with all the frankness she could muster up. "For now," she said. She cleared her throat. Sean's expression had changed completely, his dark blue eyes were regarding her with real empathy. She needed to change the subject.

"Can you tell me more about the case?" she asked. "The Dandridge case, I mean. I know next to nothing about it. I didn't expect to be working on it, so I feel like I'm coming from behind." Hannah winced inwardly. That had been an unnecessary lie. She could have said she'd read some of the reporting about the case; there would have been nothing unusual about that. She put her beer down on the table, pushed it away a little. She needed to be more careful.

Sean ran his hand through his hair. "I feel like I'm just getting up to speed myself. I mean, I read all the public stuff over the break, because I knew the case was one of ours, but I didn't work on it last year. None of the students did, so I haven't seen the case file or anything."

"I read through some of it today," Camila said. "I started a good facts/bad facts list."

Hannah's confusion must have shown on her face because Camila started to explain.

"It's something Parekh likes to do when we work on a case. He has one of us start a good fact/bad fact list on a white board. You know, we list the facts in the case that would help our client with a jury, and the facts that would hurt us."

"Okay," Hannah said. "That's interesting."

"So what did you come up with?" Sean asked.

"Well, okay. Here's an obvious bad fact—the eyewitness. Sam Fitzhugh. He was a little boy. His mom was murdered. He's always going to be an incredibly sympathetic figure to a jury, right? If he's convincing on the stand that could be the whole case, right there."

"True," Sean said, nodding. "Okay, some good facts. Dandridge didn't know the victim. He'd never been to her apartment. There's no DNA placing him there."

"Yes," said Camila. "And he had a job. That's a good fact. But he also played around with drugs, smoked a lot of weed. That's a bad fact. He was estranged from his family at least partially because of his drug use. And here's something that didn't come up in the briefing today—Dandridge claimed to have an alibi but the guy disappeared. I don't know if that's a good fact or a bad fact. How do you categorize that one?"

"What do you mean, disappeared?" Hannah asked.

Camila leaned forward. She had abandoned her earlier standoff-ishness. Her face was alive now with interest. "Dandridge says in his statement that he spent the night of the murder hanging out with a guy called Neil Prosper. They were drinking, smoking, listening to music. Earlier in the night they ordered takeout, which was confirmed by the pizza company, although because the pizza had been ordered and delivered hours before the murder, this wasn't much help."

"But you said . . . he disappeared? Neil Prosper?"

Camila shrugged. "He was never called in the original trial. The original defense attorney couldn't find him. There's no public record of his death, and his family claim not to have heard from him for years—not since shortly after Dandridge's arrest, in fact."

"That's strange," Hannah said. To her it only made Dandridge look more guilty. Why would his only alibi disappear shortly after his arrest? Didn't it seem likely that this Prosper guy didn't want to be found? Which suggested an obvious conclusion—that he had been involved in some way in the murder and didn't want to be caught.

Sean looked at his watch. "Shit," he said. "I have to go. I'm sorry, guys. I have a paper due tomorrow, and it's getting late." He stood, zipped up his backpack. "Can I give either of you a ride?" he asked.

Camila shrugged. "I'm good," she said. "I think I'll stay and finish my beer. Catch up with Hannah here, if she's not in a rush."

"All right then. I'd better go and get this done if I'm going to be in the office with you guys all day tomorrow. Don't stay out carousing all night." He gave them a final wave.

"He's had enough of me," Camila said, watching him leave. "I can't blame him. I should have let it go, but Hazel's always managed to get under my skin."

Hannah gave her a sympathetic smile. "I get that," she said. "It's hard when you have to work closely with someone you don't click with."

"Get you another one?" Camila asked. Her beer was empty. She shuffled her way out of the booth seating.

"That would be great. But just one. I'd better have a clear head tonight if I'm going to get up to speed."

Camila came back from the bar balancing the drinks and a basket of fries. She slid the fries into the center of the table. "That's why I like this place. Free fries. Help yourself." She took one herself, and after blowing on it for a moment, popped it neatly into her mouth. Her outward manner was relaxed, but her eyes were sharp. "Tell me more about you," she said.

"Not that much to tell," Hannah said. "I'd rather hear your story."

Camila shrugged. "Undergrad at Yale—scholarship kid all the way. Family live in Richmond so wanted to get closer to home for grad school. Law school is costing me a fortune even with financial aid, so I work my ass off and keep my grades up. Fourth in the class at the moment, and I intend on keeping it that way or bettering it. Love the Project, totally down with the calling, but I want a job in a big law firm for big money because I've got sisters coming up behind me."

Hannah laughed. At least Camila was honest. She could respect that much.

"So how does your mom feel about you volunteering your time for the Project?" Camila asked. "I would have thought she would have wanted you with her, when she's not well."

"She's doing much better, actually. She just has to be close to the hospital for testing and monitoring. And she's always been insistent on me living my life. She gets uptight if she feels like I'm being too . . ." Hannah let her voice trail off. She couldn't find a way to finish the sentence. The idea of Laura pushing her to be more independent just struck her suddenly as simultaneously so unlikely and so attractive that she was struck dumb.

"Oh, I get it," Camila said. "My mother's not like that—she's always nagging us to get home for dinner more—but Sean's mom is just the same. She really wants him to live his own life. I think she gets scared that he'll keep trying to look after her and end up really tied down, you know?"

"Mmm-hmm." Hannah nodded and sipped her beer. It wasn't Laura's fault that she needed to keep Hannah close. There were very good reasons for that.

"My mom's Catholic, so she's really against the death penalty. Now my dad, he's weird about it. He's against the death penalty, intellectually speaking, and on one level he's fine with me doing this work, but then, he hates it when I visit our clients in prison. It's like some part of him just can't get past the idea that if they're in prison they must be bad people even though he *knows* they're innocent."

"Right." Hannah wanted to point out that bias worked both ways, that it was, clearly, just as easy to put someone on a pedestal of innocence and blind yourself to their faults. She was seeing that happen right in front of her. How could two smart, educated people like Camila and Sean take a fact—like, for example, a missing alibi witness—and read into that only evidence that confirmed their belief that Dandridge was innocent? It was like the truth was right in their faces and they kept looking around and behind it.

"What about your dad? Is he in the picture?" Camila asked.

"He died before I was born."

"Oh, man. I'm so sorry. That's awful."

Hannah shrugged. "I never knew him."

"And your mom didn't remarry? You didn't end up with a step-dad along the way?"

"Ha. God no."

Camila looked bemused. "Is that a crazy question?"

Hannah shook her head, smiling a little. "Not crazy. My mom, she's had boyfriends, on and off, over the years, but no one she'd ever bring home. She'd never let anyone into our lives that way."

"Well . . . now you're going to have to tell me why."

Hannah rolled her eyes. She was tired and feeling the effect of the beers. She didn't drink at all at home, couldn't, around Laura, and she wasn't used to it. "I guess she just has a whole theory about men."

"Your mom has?"

"Yeah."

Camila leaned forward. "Tell me."

"Oh, God. Okay. This might sound extreme, I don't know. She thinks that men are shallow. Ego driven, mostly. So that when they fail—which is bound to happen at *some* stage in their lives—they either collapse inward or they lash out and hurt someone. Whereas she thinks women get used to failing from early on in life . . . basically because men make it impossible for us to succeed, so we're better at it."

Camila put her head to one side, smiling slightly. "Right. Well, maybe there's some truth there, but—"

"Oh look, I know it's over the top. I'm not saying I agree with her." Except . . . maybe she did. Dating always seemed like it was more hassle than it was worth. If you couldn't trust a guy, if you knew they would ultimately let you down, then was any of it worth the effort?

"There are some men who fit within that category, but obviously not all," Camila was saying. "Why do you think your mom feels that way?"

"She had some really bad experiences when she was younger. And that hurt her, I guess. This is just the way she makes sense of the world now." Hannah realized that Camila was observing her closely, and she flushed. Shit. She replayed the conversation quickly in her head. No, it was okay. She hadn't said anything dangerous.

"Sounds like you guys are really close, huh?"

That didn't come close to describing the bond they shared.

"Yeah, we're pretty good friends."

"So this cancer trial, it sounds really interesting. Did you say your mom's in remission? That's unusual, isn't it? To be enrolled in a cancer trial when you're well?"

Camila's tone and manner were casual, but her eyes were sharp. Hannah stared back at the other girl. Where had that come from? Was Camila suspicious? Or was she just naturally spiky?

"Yeah, it's something she was participating in when we were in Maine, but they want her closer for the next few months, for monitoring." Hannah looked at her watch. "I'd better think about heading home, Camila. I have so much work to catch up on."

"Sure." Camila smiled. "It was great to get to know you a little. I'll walk out with you."

Hannah walked home. She was mad with herself. She had been stupid. Camila was smart and she asked tricky questions because that was the kind of person she was. Smart, questioning, and naturally suspicious. From now on Hannah would have to be much more careful. She would keep her distance from the others. A good working relationship was essential. Anything more than that could be dangerous.

LAURA

DIARY ENTRY #4

Sunday, August 14, 1994, 10:00 a.m.

It's been two weeks since Tom and I first slept together, and since then we haven't spent a night apart. Despite the fact that he has that big house and about five bedrooms to choose from, we mostly stay in my little single bed. I don't like being at the house with Mike, so I avoid it as much as possible. He won't leave us alone, won't give us any space; he's always there, with his fake bright smile and his barbed comments. He wants to go home to Virginia, but Tom is dragging things out, staying until the last possible minute, and the longer it goes on, the meaner Mike becomes. He just about keeps a lid on things when Tom is in the room, but if Tom leaves me for a minute, even to go to the bathroom, Mike steps things up. The other night he got aggressive, stood too close to me, breathed in my face until I stepped back. I tried to laugh it off and Tom came back before anything else could happen, but I swear I felt like Mike would have hit me, if we'd been alone. There's something really off about that guy. He scares me. We're staying in the house tonight, though, and I think for once Mike will be happy. He's got nothing to be angry about anymore. They're leaving for Virginia tomorrow.

It's not like Tom and I have a future. I'm not stupid. But this is so much harder than I was expecting.

Sunday, August 14, 1994, 9:00 p.m.

I'm back. At the hotel I mean. It's still Sunday but I'm back and so much has happened that I have to write about it right now. I biked up to the house right after work and let myself in. I had to take my bike because I was going to need it—Tom was going to leave tomorrow on the boat, and we were planning to say goodbye at the house. The front door is never locked and I just didn't think about it. I opened the door and called out a hello and no one answered me. They were too busy fighting to hear me.

If I close my eyes I'm back there, standing in the main hallway, kind of frozen in place. I don't know whether I should let them know I'm there, or just sneak out, or what. I can hear Mike—loud and angry—and Tom, he's quieter, but I can still hear every word he says. They're fighting about the fact that Tom doesn't want to go back to Virginia. He's going to stay for another two weeks. Mike is raging because it's move-in day at UVA in just over a week, which gives them just enough time to sail back. When I realize that Tom wants to stay I nearly explode in excitement, but then Mike keeps arguing and arguing and I think that Tom will just give in. But he doesn't! He's cool as anything.

"I've spoken to my father and he's arranged for a crew to pick up the boat next week."

"I can take the boat back alone, as I've said. It's perfectly safe to sail solo. I took it to Blacks Harbour, for God's sake."

"That was probably not such a good idea," Tom says. "And the sail home is much longer. Too long for one person."

"Christ, Tom. Can you try not to be so . . . Look, there's no need, that's all I'm saying. I'm happy to sail the boat myself."

Tom says no. He says it's not safe to sail solo overnight. He says his classes start on the thirtieth and he's planning on flying back the day before, but he's happy to arrange a flight for Mike now, if he wants to get back.

"I'll call a friend," Mike sounds almost desperate. "How about that? I'll call a friend to sail back with me so that there're two guys for the journey. Someone with lots of experience."

There's a moment's silence. And then Tom says, "No. I'm sorry, Mike. But the answer's no."

A moment later Mike blasts past me through the hall. I have been feeling almost sorry for him, but the look he gives me is so full of anger and violence that I take a step back. He hisses at me, "I hope you're satisfied, you dumb bitch. You don't know what you've done." And then he is gone.

Tom finds me. He takes me by the hand and leads me to the front of the house where he hugs me and tells me everything is going to be okay.

I hug him back and say, "I know that, stupid," and what was all this about him staying. I half-expect Tom to flush and stutter and ask if I am okay with it but there is none of that. He just looks at me steadily and said he isn't ready to walk away from us. That he thinks there is something real here, and he'd like to spend more time together. I am the one who flushes and stammers, like a fool. I am the one who gets tears in my eyes. And then he tells me he loves me and I tell him I love him too and then I start crying and for some reason it's really hard to stop. He just hugs me. He doesn't want me staying in the house when Mike is so pissed, so he drove me straight back to the hotel. He's going to pick me up tomorrow once Mike's gone to the airport. I'm so glad Mike's going. He's toxic to be around. And now Tom and I get two full weeks together. I'm going to beg Rosa to give me some time off. I can't really afford to take time off work, but I'll figure something out.

I trust Tom more than I've trusted anyone since my mother died. And I know he's a good person. I love him. I think I can be better with him. That's a lot to start with, right? And now he's going to stay so we can find out what else there could be. And I'm so, so happy.

Hannah

SIX

On Wednesday morning Hannah called Jan and got an update on how things were going in Maine. In Hannah's absence, Jan had committed to coming in every day, doing a little work about the house, and keeping an eye on Laura. Laura didn't have a job. That just wasn't possible for her because of her PTSD and extreme anxiety. Her attempts to work had always ended in disaster—alcohol abuse and a shame spiral that was very difficult to turn around. What worked best for Laura was sticking to a routine. Monday to Saturday, she and Hannah walked together in the morning. Sunday was for sleeping in. While Hannah was at school, Laura read or visited the library or, if she was feeling well, her yoga class. They ate dinner together at five P.M. every day, almost without exception. It was a very rigid schedule, but it was what worked. The predictability of the routine soothed Laura's frayed nerves, and she was happier and much more comfortable when they kept things simple. Leaving her alone like this would be like setting off a bomb in the middle of her fragile stability.

Hannah had worried and worried about the decision to come to Charlottesville, had weighed the risks of going versus the risks of doing nothing and ultimately decided that she had no choice. But it was one thing to accept that she had to go when the risks were still hypothetical, now she had to face the real-world consequences of that decision. According to Jan, Laura was eating all right (which meant she was probably eating almost nothing) but she was agitated. She was wandering in the garden, spending time on her computer, not settling down with a book. When pushed, Jan—the gentlest of women—had admitted that Laura was snappish and easily irritated. To most people this might seem like nothing to worry about, but anyone who knew Laura well would recognize signs of an imminent implosion. Knowing that the effort was completely inadequate, but needing to do *something,* Hannah got on the phone again, called a local bakery, and placed an order for muffins to be delivered to the house. She thought about calling Laura, but they had already planned a call for the evening, and it would be better to stick to their arrangement. She should press on with her work. At least that way, she might have some progress to report.

Hannah got to the office at eight A.M. and tried to shake off a nagging sense of disquiet. It was better, at least, to sit at her desk, hot coffee in hand, without the disapproving presence of Rachel Mears sitting to her right. Better still to have the freedom to search through the Dandridge files in the system without anyone looking over her shoulder. Important too, not to be so distracted by Laura and by her own activities that she forgot she was still on trial. If Robert Parekh felt like she wasn't making a meaningful contribution, he would remove her from the team just as quickly as he had added her to it. She'd have to have something to show him if he came looking. He had asked them to look for ways to attack the pillars of the prosecution's case—the anonymous caller, the confession, and the eyewitness lineup. There was no way she was going to do anything that might *help* Dandridge, but she needed to look like she was working hard and being productive. Hannah sipped her coffee and thought things through. Parekh was right about one thing—the evidence against Dandridge was weak. But that sheriff . . . Pierce? He'd worked very hard to put Dandridge away. He must have been convinced of Dandridge's guilt and he must have had a good reason. Men who rape and murder women rarely strike once. Maybe Dandridge had done it before and gotten away with it and Pierce had somehow known about it. That would explain Sheriff Pierce's determined effort to put Dandridge away.

Hannah ran a search online for any newspaper reporting about rapes and murders in the years around the Fitzhugh murder. It felt amateurish, to her, to be reading the bits and scraps of reporting she could glean from search engine results and online newspapers. But she wasn't a cop. She didn't have access to police or federal databases. After fifteen minutes she had managed to find only one rape with a shooting in Richmond, and one attempted rape with a break-in in Victory Hill. Victory Hill was very close to Yorktown, and the attack had taken place about ten months after the Fitzhugh murder. Hannah searched again; read every article she could find. The attacker had worn a black balaclava and had climbed in through an open window. The victim had been at home with her baby. The attacker took the victim to her bedroom, threatening to hurt the child if she didn't comply, but the victim's husband came home unexpectedly and the attacker had climbed out of the window and fled. According to the police, he'd left no DNA.

Hannah sat and thought. The husband had been on a business trip that had been cut short unexpectedly. Could Dandridge have known the family? Known that the husband had intended to be away that night? It felt like the Sarah Fitzhugh case. Sarah's husband had been away on a tour of duty. Dandridge had a job working on pleasure cruises; Sarah Fitzhugh's husband had been a sailor. Maybe there was some connection between them that had led to Dandridge finding out that Sarah's husband was away. It was frustrating not to know more about the Victory Hill case. Maybe the husband there had some sort of work connection with Dandridge too? It took her a minute to see the problem—the Victory Hill attack had been ten months *after* the Fitzhugh murder. Dandridge would already have been in prison. Hannah shook herself and turned back to the case file, started to read again. She had to know the Dandridge case as well as any of them. Better.

An hour later, Camila dropped into the seat beside her, cheeks flushed from exertion. She put a coffee cup down on the table and unwound a brightly colored scarf from around her neck.

"So," she said. "After I left you last night I started thinking about Neil Prosper. The guy Michael spent the evening of the murder with, the man who should have been his alibi. I started thinking about what else we could do to try to track him down."

Hannah was very conscious that her notes were on her desk where Camila could see them. Had she written anything that would look out of place? She couldn't look at them to check without drawing attention to what she had written. Sean arrived, and when Camila turned to greet him Hannah turned her notepad over. Better safe than sorry.

"It occurred to me that Prosper was an alum of Yorktown High School," Camila continued. "And every single yearbook for Yorktown High is online. So I trawled through them and I found the name of the girl Prosper was dating when he went to school there. Sweet couple. They were voted most likely to break up."

"Nice," Sean said.

"Well, I did manage to track her down. She's on Facebook, so it wasn't exactly a challenge. I messaged her last night, asked her if she was still in touch with Neil since high school. She isn't, but—"

"She knows someone who is?" Sean asked.

"No," Camila said. "But she does know who he was dating around the time of the murder. And she gave me the woman's number. Angela Meyer. Angie Meyer. She still lives in Yorktown. She runs her parents' B and B."

"Have you spoken to her?" Hannah asked.

"Not yet. I was thinking maybe we should go down there."

"What, to Yorktown?" Sean said.

"Maybe. She runs this B and B. Couldn't we stay there? Try to figure out what kind of person she is. Choose the right moment to ask some questions?"

Sean considered.

"Think about it," Camila said. "This is an actual solid lead. Someone who not only knew and spent time with Neil Prosper, but who probably knew Michael too. Maybe she knows where Neil is, maybe she doesn't, but it's possible she might have other information. I mean, what if she called Neil at home that night, and she could confirm the alibi, or something. Or she might know something else, something we wouldn't even think to ask."

"I suppose that makes sense," Sean said. "Maybe we should take it to Rob."

Camila nodded enthusiastically. "He's in his office," she said. "Let's go and talk to him now."

Parekh was willing to be convinced. He was happy for Camila and Hannah to take an overnight trip to Yorktown on the Project's dollar, but he wanted Sean in the office. Afterward, Camila was prickly. It was pretty obvious she'd wanted to go to Yorktown with Sean, not Hannah. Camila didn't trust her, not yet. She needed to work on that.

"Do you drive, Camila?" Hannah asked.

"I can, but I don't have a car."

"I do. I can drive, if you like." After lying to Rob about having a car, she'd booked a rental. The company had agreed to deliver the car to her apartment building and it had been parked outside when she woke up that morning. They agreed to take an hour to pack overnight bags. Hannah picked Camila up outside her place just after ten A.M.

"There's coffee, if you want it," Hannah said, gesturing to one of two Starbucks cups sitting in the car's cup holders. "Cappuccino, two sugars, right?" She gave Camila a sideways glance. The other girl paused in the act of putting on her seat belt and looked at Hannah. She laughed.

"Okay, my bad. Forgiven?"

"Forgiven."

They drove out of Charlottesville in the direction of Yorktown.

"So what do we say to her?" Camila said.

"What do you mean?"

"I mean, do we lay it all out on the table? That we're representing Michael Dandridge, that we're there about the case? Or do we just try to . . . I don't know. Finesse it in some way."

Hannah thought about it for a minute. "Honestly, I can't think of any way we could just casually bring it up without seeming like crazy people or journalists. And I think if I was the ex-girlfriend of the friend of someone convicted of a crime like that, there's no way I'd want to talk to a journalist. Who wants to be publicly connected to something like this?"

"Yes," Camila said. "Although, you know, people are crazy. Some people will do anything for attention. There's a reason *The Jerry Springer Show* was around for so long."

"I guess we could wait and see what she's like," Hannah said.

Camila thought about it. "You're right, direct is best. It's not like we can pretend we're journalists, right?"

"I guess not."

The drive to Yorktown was very pretty, the highway lined with mature oak and sycamore trees, which broke up every now and again to reveal glimpses of manicured farmland. When they turned off the highway for Yorktown itself they found a picture-postcard of small-town America, with wide, open streets and beautifully maintained heritage homes, American flags fluttering.

"I'd like to go to where it happened," Hannah said quietly. "Is that all right?"

"You mean the murder?" Camila said.

Hannah nodded.

"Yes. Okay."

Camila entered the address on her phone and they set out. Conversation died to almost nothing. It was only a ten-minute drive on the Old Williamsburg Road. Camila's Waze app called out directions, and Hannah followed them, pulling in eventually outside a small apartment building. It was a two-story building, made with white-painted weatherboard and pale yellow brick. The first floor had an external balcony, so that each apartment had a door that opened directly outside. Hannah and Camila sat in the car and stared up at the first floor.

"Have you seen the pictures yet?" Camila asked.

Hannah turned to her. "No. No, I haven't seen them."

Camila looked pale, her usual energy leached away. "Maybe don't look," she said. "I don't know that anyone needs to see that, if they can avoid it."

Hannah turned to look back at the apartments. "I see now what Professor Parekh meant about everything being so close together, about people overhearing." The building looked cheap, poorly built. The walls were probably paper thin.

"It's military housing," Camila said. "You know, looking at this, it makes even less sense that Dandridge would have been the killer. I mean, he'd never been on base, never had any interaction with Sarah Fitzhugh or any of her neighbors. Why would he choose her apartment?" Camila pointed at the building. "It's the one right in the middle, by the way, that one on the first floor. Why would he choose that apartment to break into? How could he have known what he would find? I mean, there's nothing about this building that even shouts families, in particular. He could have been breaking into an apartment filled with servicemen."

"I don't know, Camila. But there's so much we don't know. And to play devil's advocate for a moment, the prosecution could easily argue that Dandridge saw Sarah somewhere. Maybe in a supermarket checkout. That he followed her home." There were a hundred ways it could have happened.

"Yes, but how could he have known she would be alone that night?"

Hannah shrugged. "He could have done what we're doing. Parked outside. Watched her for a while."

Camila looked around. The street was very quiet. The apartment building had off-street parking. There were no parked cars on the street other than theirs. "I think it's a stretch," she said. "I mean, this is military housing. If I were a murdering rapist, I think I would choose more obvious victims."

Hannah started the car again, pulled away, and drove back in the direction of Yorktown. "Maybe that's something we should look at," Hannah said. "See if we can find other crimes where the perpetrator specifically targeted military wives or girlfriends. It could be a thing."

"That's a good idea," Camila said.

They drove to the B and B, pulled in, and parked. "Are you nervous?" Camila asked.

"A bit," Hannah said. "But you've done this before, right?"

"I've met witnesses," Camila said. "Asked some questions. And inmates, of course. But this feels important, you know? I don't want to screw it up."

They walked side by side to the front door. The inn was a very pretty, Colonial-style, two-and-a-half story redbrick, with tall chimneys and dormer windows. There was a generous porch at the front of the building with tables and chairs and umbrellas set up, so that visitors could choose to eat breakfast or take tea outside perhaps, and look over the river. Hannah knocked on the door. It was opened a few minutes later by a dark-haired woman, in her forties, and dressed in slacks and a pristine white shirt. She had an open, welcoming smile.

"Can I help you?" she asked.

"Angie?" Camila said. "Angie Meyer?"

"Well, I'm Angie McKenzie now, but yes."

"I'm Camila Martinez, and this is my classmate Hannah Rokeby." Camila smiled. "We're law students at the University of Virginia, and we volunteer for the Innocence Project. We were wondering if you'd be willing to talk to us about your relationship with Neil Prosper, and in particular, anything you might know about Neil's movements on the night of the Fitzhugh murder."

Angie seemed speechless for a long moment. But she didn't walk away, didn't close the door in their faces. She held on to the doorjamb and put one hand to her chest.

"I haven't thought about or talked about Neil for years."

"We understand if you'd prefer not to talk to us," Hannah said. She was conscious of Camila giving her a look, but she kept her eyes on Angie.

"Well, I didn't say that," Angie said. She hesitated. "Look, why don't you come in? Let's have a sweet tea, and maybe we can talk a bit." She led the way into the house, then stopped again. "I was going to bring you to the sitting room, but it feels a bit formal. Why don't you join me in the kitchen?"

They followed her through a formal hall and sitting room furnished with antiques and overstuffed chairs to the kitchen, which was a much brighter, more inviting space. There was a generous kitchen table and a bright modern kitchen and large windows with sunlight streaming in. Angie gestured toward the table.

"Take a seat," she said. "I've just been baking for the afternoon tea. I'll be with you in a minute." She bustled about, making tea, and cutting slices of cake. She asked them questions while she worked, small talk about the university and their drive to Yorktown and whether or not they'd always wanted to study law. She didn't appear to be nervous about what they were going to ask her.

"Cake?" she offered, as she joined them.

"Yes, please," Hannah said, and Camila nodded. It was honey cake, perfectly constructed in tiny layers with the thinnest scraping of icing between each layer. It was still a little bit warm and it tasted like perfection. "Oh my God," Camila said, between mouthfuls. "This is amazing."

Angie laughed. "These days everyone expects something a little bit special. Apple pie just doesn't quite cut it. You need something your guests can put on their Instagram."

"Well, this definitely fits the bill," Camila said. She sipped her tea. "And thanks so much for taking the time to sit down with us. I'm sure it must have been a bit surprising when we showed up at your door."

"A bit," said Angie. "I suppose I wasn't entirely truthful when I said I haven't thought about Neil in years. I've read about the case, of course, and I know that there's some chance that Michael will be set free, all these years later."

"Yes," Camila said. "We hope so. His conviction has actually been vacated, but he hasn't been released from prison because the Commonwealth is still pressing charges. There's going to be a new trial."

"They're going to try him again?" Angie said. She seemed genuinely shocked, and Camila and Hannah exchanged glances.

"I . . . uh, I hope you don't mind me just asking straight out. But do you think Michael is guilty? Do you think he murdered Sarah Fitzhugh?" Hannah asked.

Angie let out a sigh. "I don't know," she said. "Look, you know, every time . . . or almost every time, some high-profile man gets called out publicly about sexual assault, or whatever, it feels like he has three or four female friends lined up to say what a great guy he's always been to them. I don't want to be that fool, you know? I mean, I knew Michael. We hung out a few times, with Neil too of course. If you'd asked me then if Mike was capable of raping and murdering anyone I would have laughed in your face. But could he have done it? Sure. I mean, I wasn't there. And how well did I know him, really?"

Hannah wanted to cheer—finally someone with some goddamn sense—but Camila didn't hide her disappointment. Her face fell, and she put down her fork. She opened her mouth as if she were about to ask a question, then subsided.

"Do you know anything about Michael's movements that night that would lead you to think that he could have gone to the Fitzhugh house?" Hannah asked.

Camila shot a dagger look at her.

"God no," Angie said. "I'm not saying that. I just mean that I can't know, can I? I didn't know Mike that well. He never struck me as the violent type and he could be very charming. But there's no way to know, is there, what he was like with other people? He might have been very good at hiding his true personality."

Hannah nodded.

"Angie, could I ask you to go back a bit?" Camila said. "Can you tell us a little bit about your relationship with Neil Prosper? How did you meet? And anything you can tell us about Michael's friend-ship with Neil could be helpful too. Do you know if they were close? If they'd been friends for long?"

"Oh God," Angie rolled her eyes. "Me and Neil. It really wasn't any great romance. We were in high school together, but Neil was four years ahead. He was good-looking, really confident. You know, he wasn't a jock and he wasn't any kind of academic star, but he still had all the girls chasing him. He was in a band for a while, and I guess he was a charmer too, in his own way. He never noticed me in school. It was years later when we got together. I was in college, but I was home for Thanksgiving, I think, and we connected one night at a bar. Needless to say, my parents were *thrilled*." She laughed a lit-tle. "I don't really know much of anything about his friendship with Mike. They knew each other awhile, for sure. Mike was a lot older than Neil—I guess Neil would have been about twenty-six whereas Mike was in his thirties—but they sure liked each other's company. We never got into the history of their friendship, or anything. They talked about sailing sometimes. Maybe that was how they met?" She paused, then seemed to feel like she might have disappointed them. "Honestly, Neil was a bit of a slacker and he smoked too much weed, but he was pretty harmless."

"The papers said he was using heroin that night, the night of the murder," Hannah put in. There had been pro-prosecution coverage in the media that focused on the fact that Dandridge's story had been that he spent the night of the murder hanging out with Neil Prosper and using drugs, and that he had fallen asleep on Prosper's couch. The articles focused strongly on the drug use, saying that Prosper was Dandridge's drug dealer and that Dandridge's only defense was that he had been shooting up and was so strung out he couldn't have committed the murder. The tone of the articles was consistently skeptical, and had not been the defense used at Dandridge's trial. Hannah had supposed that his attorney had realized that heroin use was not the most sympathetic of excuses.

Angie made a face. "No way," she said. "I never saw Neil touch anything harder than an E tab. Besides, I was there that night."

Hannah caught her breath. Camila sat up straighter in her chair. "You were with Neil and Michael on the night of the murder?" Hannah asked.

"Yes," Angie said, simply. "Well, I was with them from about seven P.M. until just after ten. Then I went home."

"And you're sure about the date?" Camila asked.

"Yes. I was supposed to go back to school the next day, and I wanted to spend the night with Neil. I wasn't exactly thrilled to find Mike there when I got over. They were smoking and they were pretty well baked. I hung out with them for a while. They ordered pizza. I finally figured out that Mike wasn't going anywhere and Neil wasn't going to make him, so I went home in a huff."

"So you think you left at ten?" Hannah asked. How had Angie's presence not come to light before now? Why wouldn't Dandridge have mentioned her to his attorneys? Or maybe he had, and they'd decided her evidence wouldn't help.

Angie nodded. "I'm pretty sure."

"Well, the time line suggests that the murder happened a couple of hours later," Hannah said. "Can you think of anything that would suggest Michael might have left later? Did you ever talk to Neil about it?"

Angie raised her shoulders in a gentle shrug. "Honestly? I would have been surprised if Mike had gone anywhere that night. He often slept over on the couch at Neil's. I think he was lonely. He didn't seem to have many friends. And they really weren't in any shape to go anywhere that night. Apart from the weed, they were splitting a bottle of whiskey, listening to music. You know, they were settled in."

This was all just opinion. It wasn't proof of any kind. Whatever Angie said, there was nothing at all to stop Dandridge leaving the house as soon as Neil passed out. By her own admission Angie had been distracted by her boyfriend. It would have been easy for Dandridge to go with the flow, make it seem like he was drinking and smoking heavily while all the time letting Neil take the lion's share.

"Did you ever confirm that with Neil?" Camila was asking. "Did he ever tell you how the night ended?"

Angie shook her head. "I went back to school the following morning. And I was so pissed at Neil for not making an effort on my last night that I didn't call him for a few days. I kept waiting for him to call me, and then when he didn't, my pride wouldn't let me make the first move, you know? Three weeks later, when Mike was arrested, I called Neil then. I called him maybe four or five times. But I never reached him. Next time I came home to Yorktown, I went over to his place. You know, I had the excuse of wanting to pick up my stuff—I had left a few books, a couple of sweatshirts at his place—but really I just wanted to have a good argument. Get a bit of closure. But Neil wasn't there. His landlord lived in the place upstairs and he told me that Neil just bounced. He didn't even give notice, but because he'd paid a couple of months in advance, the landlord wasn't complaining."

"And that's it?" Hannah asked. "You never heard from him again?"

"Never," Angie said.

"What about his friends? His family?" Camila asked.

"Other than Mike, I never really got to know his friends. There were other guys they hung out with, of course, but I only saw them if we all met up at a bar. And Neil had a sister. She's older . . . I think they were close, but I never met her. It wouldn't really have occurred to me to reach out to anyone to try to get in touch with him. I guess I just figured if he didn't want me, that was that."

"You didn't think it was strange, that he never called you after that night?"

Angie shook her head. She sipped her tea. "I was snippy with him, when I left. And then I went back to college. And I guess I figured that he'd decided he didn't need the drama. He just moved on. And, honestly, I did too."

They were quiet for a moment.

"You said you ordered pizza," Camila said. "Maybe we could talk to the pizza guy. He could at least corroborate the early part of the night."

"No, I'm sorry," Angie said, screwing up her nose. "That was Derek Rawlings. The delivery guy, I mean. I knew Derek a little because his brother Claude was in my year in high school. Anyway, Derek died years ago. In a car accident, I think. But he really wouldn't have been much help to you. He just dropped the pizza off, got paid, and left."

Camila nodded. She looked a little disappointed. She must have known it would probably have been a dead end, but it was hard to have another possible lead, however slight, shut down. She leaned forward. "You know, Angie, no one heard from Neil after that night. He disappeared." There was a touch of drama to her voice and Angie made another face.

"I don't think that's right," she said.

"Oh?" Camila said.

"When I spoke to his landlord, he'd only been gone a few days. So that means he was still in his place for a couple of weeks after the murder. And I don't think it's right to say that he just disappeared. I mean, I think I heard he was living in North Carolina."

"Do you know where?" Camila asked quickly. But Angie shrugged helplessly.

"God, I don't know. I can't even remember who told me that. But I'm sure I heard it from someone."

"Do you know where we could get in touch with his sister?" Camila asked.

Angie thought for a moment. "I don't, but I probably know someone who does. I have a friend who has a sister who was in her class, I think. If you give me your number, I can try to find out for you."

Camila and Hannah looked at each other. "We're just here for the day," Hannah said, carefully, feeling again the need to appear to make a genuine effort. "Is there any way you'd be able to call her now? We don't want to push."

Angie stood up, looked around for her phone. "No, it's okay," she said. "She'll be at work, so she might not answer. I can give it a shot." But she had better luck than she'd anticipated. Her friend answered the phone and seemed interested in helping out. A couple of minutes later she called Angie back with a phone number for Sophia Prosper.

Camila and Hannah stood up, and Hannah offered her hand for a shake. "Thank you so much, Angie," she said. "We're so grateful."

Angie walked them out. She stood in the doorway, leaning against the doorjamb to wave them off. She looked sad.

"It all feels like a thousand years ago now," she said. "I got married. I have two children." She nodded back toward the inn. "When my parents retired I took over this place, which I can tell you was never in my plans when I was twenty-two. But I've lived a life. It might not be perfect, or what I thought my life would be, but I've lived a whole life. Michael though, all this time, he's just been in prison. If he didn't do it, can you imagine what that must be like?"

Hannah nodded gravely and thanked Angie again and said goodbye and all the while she thought about what Dandridge had done, all the pain he had caused, the lives taken, all the lives destroyed. No prison term would be long enough.

LAURA

DIARY ENTRY #5

Monday, August 15, 1994, 11:00 a.m.

I'm way too excited right now! I have the day off, and right about now Tom will be driving Mike to the airport, which means he's going to be with me by lunchtime. I keep telling myself to calm down. Just because he's going to stay on the island for another couple of weeks, that doesn't really mean anything has changed. He's still going to go back to college in Virginia. And I'm . . . what? Going to go back to Boston? To live on the fringes as my friends get on with their lives? I have to find a way to get enough money to go to college myself. I have to build my own life. If I were in school, maybe the gap between me and Tom wouldn't be so wide.

Monday, August 15, 1994, 2.00 p.m.

He's late. I wonder if the traffic was bad? It shouldn't be, not on a Monday morning. But maybe something happened on the bridge to the mainland. If there was an accident, that could slow things right down, or stop it entirely. I guess I'll eat something, and read, maybe, and just wait.

I fell asleep. I feel super groggy. Tom hasn't come. Should I be worried? I think I'll go and call him.

Monday, August 15, 1994, 8:00 p.m.

Everything's over. Everything's done. Tom is dead.

Monday, August 15, 1994, 11:30 p.m.

I'm in my room. In my bed. The sheets still smell like him. Why can't I cry? What's wrong with me?

I called the house, but there was no answer. I thought about biking over there but then Rosa came to find me. She'd heard about it from someone. I don't know who. A cop friend, maybe? The island grapevine? They're saying that Tom died because he got drunk, that he fell and hit his head on the jetty and just slipped into the water. They're saying all of this happened last night, after he drove me home, but that they didn't find him until this morning. It must have been Mike who found him, Mike who called the police. Last night when I lay sleeping, today when I was working and daydreaming about him, when I was waiting for him to pick me up, all that time he was already dead.

I should have known, shouldn't I? Shouldn't I have felt it? I was so happy. And he was already dead.

Wednesday, August 17, 1994, 4:30 a.m.

I don't understand why Tom was drinking. That doesn't make any sense. Unless . . . unless he and Mike got into a conversation, got over their fight, and had a few drinks together. That's the only explanation I can think of. They must have been drinking together. But then, what . . . Tom went for a drunken solo walk down on the jetty?

Friday, August 19, 1994, 6:00 p.m.

I'm such a mess. I can't pull it together. I've been working, kind of, going through the motions, but I can't seem to remember much of the last few days so I don't know what I actually did in those hotel rooms. I think maybe Rosa followed me from room to room, cleaning up after me, doing what needed to be done. I feel broken. I knew him for exactly five weeks. That's nothing. People will say that I have no right to mourn him. Not like his real friends. Not even like his shitty family. I am the only person in the world who knows what we had. I . . . oh God, I can't write anymore.

Hannah

SEVEN

Camila and Hannah said nothing as they walked away down the path of the inn toward the car. Hannah had that crawling sensation of being watched, was conscious of Angie's eyes on their backs until she heard the latch of the door close behind them. They climbed into the car, closed the doors.

"Jesus," Camila said, with a burst of energy. "That was so risky. I nearly had a heart attack when you asked her if she had any reason to think that Dandridge went to the Fitzhugh house that night. I thought . . . you know, suggesting it even might lead her down a path we don't want her to go down."

"Better to know than wonder what she might say when there's someone other than us in the room."

"Maybe," Camila said, frowning. "But you need to be careful. Like I said, witnesses can be suggestible. We're here to help our client, not find more people who are willing to say he could have done it."

"Right," Hannah said. "Sorry. I wasn't thinking." Camila's sharp eyes were still on her but after a moment she moved on.

"We got so much, though. Sean is going to lose his mind that he missed this. Parekh will be thrilled. I mean, this is major corroboration for Dandridge's alibi. And did you see her? She's like the perfect PTA mom. Put her on the stand and the jury is going to love her."

"I don't know," Hannah said. "I mean, she says she went home at ten. And that she went home angry, that she had argued with Neil Prosper. A prosecutor could do a lot with that. All we can show is that Prosper and Dandridge were drinking and smoking weed together at ten P.M. There is nothing to stop either or both of them from leaving the house an hour or so later, going to the Fitzhugh home, and committing the murder."

"Except that we know they didn't," Camila said.

"Sure," Hannah said. "But you know, Camila, even if this stuff helped at trial it's not going to help at the preliminary hearing. We're the defense. The judge wouldn't even let us call her as a witness. I think Parekh's looking for slam-dunk stuff."

"We need to get to Neil Prosper," Camila said. "Have you got the number? Let's call Sophia from here."

"Right now?" Hannah asked.

"No point in hanging around."

They dialed the number on Camila's phone, put it on speaker. It went to voice mail and Camila tried again. This time the call was answered by a harried-sounding woman.

"Hello?"

"Am I speaking with Sophia? Sophia Prosper?" Camila said.

There was a pause. "My married name is Prosper-Reynolds."

"My name is Camila Martinez. I'm a law student at the University of Virginia and I volunteer at the Innocence Project there." There was silence at the other end of the phone. Camila locked eyes with Hannah, made a face, then continued. "I'm working on the Michael Dandridge case, and it would really help if I could talk to your brother, Neil. I'm wondering if there's any way you could put me in contact with him."

"Why are you calling me now?" Sophia said.

Camila threw Hannah a pained look. It took her a second before she found the words. "Um . . . According to Michael's file, his original defense attorney did try to track Neil down, but he couldn't find him. No one has ever managed to speak to Neil about that night, and you know, Michael says he was with Neil in his apartment when the murder happened. So for us to be able to talk to Neil, that's absolutely key to his defense."

"Dandridge has already been convicted, hasn't he? What do you mean, his defense?"

Camila's eyes locked with Hannah's and she held up crossed fingers. "Michael's conviction has been vacated, Sophia. That means that the federal court thought that there was so much wrong with the original trial, that the prosecution broke so many rules, that the court decided that the conviction couldn't stand. But the original prosecutor and sheriff are still in their positions, and they've decided to try to prosecute him again. Right now, we're getting ready to defend him for a second time."

"Look, I don't want to speak to you about Neil, or Dandridge, or anything else. This has nothing to do with my family and I don't want to get dragged into it, okay?"

"I understand," Camila said hurriedly. "We don't want to involve you in anything. We just want to talk to Neil. Even ten minutes of his time would make such a difference."

"And then what?" Sophia said. "You take whatever he tells you and you use it and you draw trouble on all of us. Sorry, I can't help you." And she hung up.

"Shit," Camila said. She punched the seat. "Shit. I screwed that up."

"It's not your fault," said Hannah. "She was pretty clear. I'm not sure there's anything you could have said that would have made her agree to help us."

"Well, we're not giving up," Camila said. She opened the car door and jogged back up the path to the inn.

"Camila?" Hannah called, but Camila didn't slow or stop. Hannah watched as she knocked on the door, as Angie opened it, and the two women talked. Angie disappeared back into the house for a few minutes, while Camila stood at the door, her arms folded across her chest. A few minutes passed before Angie came back, exchanged a few more words with Camila, and then Camila was jogging back to the car.

"I got it," she said, as she climbed back into the driver's seat.

"Got what?" Hannah asked.

"An address for Sophia Prosper, Prosper-Reynolds, whatever she's calling herself," Camila said. "She lives in Williamsburg. It's basically on our way home." She grinned at Hannah, held up her hand for a high five. "Don't leave me hanging," she said.

"Angie just handed that over?" Hannah asked. She forced a smile and returned a weak high five.

"She wasn't sure about it, but I gave her the hard sell . . . just repeated her own words back to her really, about Michael's whole life being taken away from him and just wanting to get to the truth." She made a *let's go* gesture.

"You want to go right now?"

"No time like the present," Camila said. "Come on, Hannah, we're on the trail here. We're killing this thing. Beyoncé had it right, girl. We *run* this mutha."

Despite everything Hannah laughed.

"What we need now is music," Camila said.

"And food."

"That too. Angie said she's a marketing manager. Sophia is, I mean. So let's go eat, and then let's drive to her place and wait for her to get home. I really think we'll have more luck in person."

They went to the York Pub, where they ate crab cakes and side salads. The food was good and the atmosphere was better—the place was half full, despite the fact that it was only three o'clock in the afternoon and lunch hour had long passed. A handful of groups were already drinking—beer or happy-hour margarita pitchers. Camila cast them an envious eye.

"I almost wish we were staying," she said. "We could get lit and talk about our first boyfriends."

The pub was the kind of place that drew you in. There was a happy buzz of conversation. Hannah felt another little knot of tension unravel.

"So tell me about U Maine," Camila said. "Are things very different from UVA?"

Hannah finished her last mouthful of crab cake. "Not as much as you'd think," she said. "But I've only got a couple of classes. I'm just doing enough to stay on top of things for next year."

Camila nodded, eyes hooded. "So being here, for you, really is about your mom, huh?"

Hannah nodded, and just like that the tension was back. She pushed her plate away. "Did you see the carrot cake up there? I'm going to get some, and maybe some coffee. Can I get you anything?" Camila didn't take much convincing. By the time Hannah had been to the counter, ordered, and returned, Camila had finished her crab cakes, but the conversation hadn't moved on.

"It must be difficult for you," she said. "Do you have other family?"

Hannah hesitated. "Nope. No other family, really. Or I suppose there is, but we're not in touch."

"Not with anyone?" Camila asked.

"Well, my mom's mom is dead, and she hasn't been in touch with her dad in years. My father's family didn't want anything to do with us. He was . . . I guess he was wealthy, and my mother came from nothing, so . . ." Shit. It was hard to keep Camila at bay. She was good at asking questions, probing away gently until your back was up against the wall.

"Man, that's really tragic," Camila said, brow furrowed.

"What about you?" Hannah asked.

Their conversation was interrupted briefly by the waitress, who delivered two slices of cake and two cups of coffee. Both women were quiet for a moment as they ate. The cake was incredible, the coffee even better.

"Well, my dad bailed when I was twelve," Camila said. "He lives in LA now, I think, although the last time he was in touch was a phone call maybe two years ago? But my mom remarried and I'm really close to my stepfather. I think of him as my dad, really. My mom's a nurse and she works two jobs. I've got two sisters and she is like, *determined,* that we are all going to set the world on fire. She never let us get weekend or evening jobs, you know? It was always about study, study, study." Camila's tone was chatty, very friendly, intimate. Hannah told herself to be careful not to be fooled. They weren't going to be friends. "I had to maintain a perfect GPA or man did I get it. I got financial aid for undergrad and grad school, obviously, otherwise there's no way. But the deal is when I start earning, I start contributing to the family finances. I guess it's a form of financial indenture. I don't know how many years I'll have to serve. That depends on my sisters."

"What are they like?" Hannah asked, drawn in despite herself.

Camila put her head to one side. "Pretty good. I mean, we fight, sometimes, you know, sibling stuff, but we're close. They know if they need me I'm there, every time, and I guess I know they're there for me too."

"Right," Hannah said, nodding as if she got it. She thought of the home she grew up in, one that had alternated between chaos and silence, and imagined a mother who worked two jobs and pushed you to achieve. It was a stray thought, but guilt followed hot on its heels. Laura struggled sometimes, but she had good reason, and she had always done her best. And sisters might be nice, but there was no way Camila's relationship with her mother came near the bond Hannah shared with Laura.

"Has your mom been sick for long?" Camila asked.

Hannah looked down at what was left of her cake. "Her health has never been great. She's had a tough road."

"Is she expected to stay in remission?" Camila asked.

Hannah swallowed. "Do you mind if we talk about something else?"

"Of course," Camila said. "Of course, sorry."

Fifteen minutes later they made their way to the car. It was a thirty-minute drive from Yorktown to Sophia Prosper's address. They talked on the drive about how to approach the conversation, but really, it was difficult to know what to do or where to start until they got there and got the lay of the land. They pulled up outside the home, and sat in silence for a long moment.

"Jesus," Hannah said.

"She must be a very successful marketing manager," Camila said. The house was large and built in the style of a French country home, all redbrick and shuttered windows. The landscaping was beautiful and the whole thing said money.

"I guess. Or maybe her husband makes a lot of money?" Hannah asked.

"That or it's family money," Camila said. "Her parents—hers and Neil's—were very wealthy."

There were no cars parked in the driveway, but there was a double garage off to the side, so maybe Sophia was already home. They would need to ring the doorbell and find out. Camila put her hand on the car door handle and took a deep breath. "Okay," she said. "Here goes."

They stood in the doorway and rang the doorbell, but the house was quiet and there was no reply.

"What now?" said Hannah. Before Camila could respond they heard the sound of an approaching car and turned to see a silver-gray Range Rover pull into the driveway. The driver was a blond woman, slim and pretty. There was a young girl—maybe fourteen—in the passenger seat, and another a few years younger in the backseat. The girls looked at them with frank curiosity. Their mother looked with suspicion.

"Here we go," said Camila. The girls climbed out of the car. They were wearing jodhpurs and riding boots. Their mother—presumably Sophia—went to the backseat and lifted out an infant car seat. She held it with one hand and turned to Camila and Hannah.

"You called me earlier," Sophia said, and there was nothing friendly about her tone. She was quite astonishingly pretty up close, with perfect skin and delicate features. Her clothes were casual but expensive.

"We're sorry to just show up like this, Mrs. Prosper-Reynolds," Hannah said. "We understand that this might be difficult for you."

"But it's so important," Camila put in, oozing sincerity. "We're talking about a man's life here, and a terrible injustice."

"Mom . . . ?" said the older girl.

"Not now, Beth," said Sophia. "Take your sister to the kitchen and make her a sandwich. Then get your homework started." The girls didn't move until Sophia followed her instructions up with a sharp, "Now, Elizabeth." The sisters made their way toward the house, the older girl dragging her feet. The baby was fussing, and Sophia shifted the weight of the car seat from one hand to the other.

"If we could just have a minute—" Camila said.

"I haven't heard from Neil in years. He was a drug addict and my parents cut him off. For all I know he died years ago. That's all I have to say to you. If you come here again, I'm calling the police," Sophia said. "I made it very clear to you on the phone that I had nothing to say. Now you show up at my home. This is harassment. You're just lucky my husband isn't here. Now get off my property." She turned her back on them, and still holding the baby seat in one hand, stalked away into the house.

"Bitch," said Camila, none too quietly.

Hannah took her by the arm, pulling her back toward the car. "Come on, before she calls the cops." They got in the car.

"Damn," Camila said. "Damn. I don't believe a word she says. She's definitely hiding something. Protecting her brother. Did she seem kind of freaked out to you? I mean, underneath all that attitude?"

"Maybe," said Hannah. "Or maybe she really has lost touch with him and she never liked him much and she thinks Dandridge is guilty as hell and wants nothing to do with any of it. You know, Camila, it is possible to feel that way."

"If you close your eyes and your ears and you're absolutely determined not to learn the truth, sure."

Hannah opened her mouth to say something, then shut it again determinedly, but Camila was too sharp.

"What?" she said. "You don't agree?"

Shit. She couldn't backtrack now. It would be too obvious and only serve to make Camila suspicious. "I don't think it's as clear-cut as you want it to be," said Hannah, carefully. "Okay, so he claims the sheriff beat him up, but there's no proof of that. And the prosecutor hid the DNA evidence that might have helped the defense. We all know that prosecutors used to do that kind of thing all the time. But that's one hair that Sarah could have picked up somewhere, some kind of contact transfer. It doesn't prove that someone else was the killer. It doesn't prove that Dandridge wasn't."

"What are you saying? You think he's guilty?"

"No, I'm not saying that. I'm saying there's no point in putting blinders on. You said it yourself. We have to see the bad facts as well as the good facts, right? If we ever want to convince a jury. And right now I think we have more bad facts than good. Which means, I guess, that we have to raise our game. We have more work to do."

Camila was distracted. She was watching the house. Hannah turned to see what she was looking at. One of the girls, the older daughter—Sophia had called her Beth, hadn't she?—had come out. She had a basketball—there was a hoop attached to the wall of the garage—and as they watched she started to dribble the ball and take shots at the hoop. Her attention was on the car though. She kept shooting small glances their way.

"What's that about?" Camila said.

"I don't know."

"Do you think she wants to talk to us?"

The girl stopped dribbling, stopped shooting, and turned, ball in hand, to stare at them.

"What do we do?" Camila said.

"If Sophia sees us, she'll call the cops. Round here that means the sheriff's office. As in, Sheriff Pierce."

"Let's walk," Camila said. She didn't wait for Hannah's reply, just got out of the car and started walking down the sidewalk away from the house. Hannah hesitated, then hurried after her.

"What about the car? If Sophia looks out of the window and sees it . . ."

"Well, we're just walking. We're walking *away* from her house. The car is parked on the street. Nothing illegal about any of that."

Camila was nervous, Hannah could hear it in her voice, but she still turned her head and smiled at Beth with the basketball, before they walked on.

"Is she following?" Camila asked after a moment.

"I don't know," Hannah said. "Not yet, I think."

"Let's give her a minute."

They kept going, down the street.

"How much farther are we going to go?" said Hannah.

There was a small park with swings and a climbing gym at the end of the street. "There," Camila said, nodding in the direction of the park. "Let's go there."

They sat on the swings and waited.

"You're right, by the way," said Camila.

"About?"

"I shouldn't have blinders on about the case. It won't help our client. I'll do a better job, keep an open mind."

"Right," said Hannah. She looked at her shoes.

"There she is," said Camila.

Hannah looked up to see Elizabeth Prosper-Reynolds making her way down the street toward them, basketball still under one arm. It seemed to take a long time for her to reach the park and when she did there was no hesitation. She walked right up to them.

"It's Beth, right?" said Hannah.

The girl nodded. She was pretty, like her mother, though her eyes were brown instead of blue. She had changed out of her riding pants and boots into a pair of sweats, sneakers, and a T-shirt.

"I'm Hannah. Were you wondering why we were talking to your mother?"

Beth shook her head. "No."

"Because you overheard?" Hannah said.

"Yes. You were asking about my uncle."

"That's right," said Hannah. She had no idea what to say next. Turned out she didn't have to say anything.

"I know where he lives," Beth said. "And so does my mother. She lied to you. And I heard what you said. This is about that guy, Dandridge, right? I read about him online. Do you really think he's innocent?"

Hannah hesitated, but Beth rushed on. She was flushed, worked up.

"I mean, if he's innocent, then we have to do the right thing, right? We have to tell the truth." She scowled. "It's just so typical of my mother. Say one thing and do another. Like, there's always a double standard. She goes on and on at *me* about always telling the truth, but she lies all the time."

"Do you know where we can find your uncle Neil, Beth?"

"If I tell you, are you going to tell him you found out from me? Will you tell my mother?"

"Absolutely not," Camila said. "Whatever you tell us we'll keep strictly between us."

The girl reached a hand into the pocket of her jacket. She drew out a folded piece of paper and thrust it toward Hannah. "We visited him last year." Then she stared at the piece of paper in Hannah's hands, as if she wished she could take it back. "Don't tell them I told you," she said again. And she wheeled away back the way she had come, bouncing the ball every few steps. Hannah waited a moment before unfolding the piece of paper.

"What is it?" Camila asked.

Hannah held it up to show her. There was an address, in Charlotte, North Carolina. "I think, maybe, we've found him," she said.

IT WAS AFTER EIGHT P.M. BY THE TIME THEY GOT BACK TO CHARlottesville. The phone call with Laura had been arranged for seven.

Hannah dropped Camila at home and called Laura right away. There was no answer. She tried again, and sat in the car and listened to the phone ring. She imagined Laura's cell phone, sitting on the coffee table in their living room, abandoned, while Laura went . . . where? Maybe it was nothing. Maybe she'd just muted her cell so she could have an early night. Maybe.

Damn. Damn damn damn.

LAURA

DIARY ENTRY #6

Monday, August 22, 1994, 8:00 p.m.

This morning I went to the cops. I asked Rosa to drive me. She said yes and didn't ask any questions. At least, not then. At the police station they were very kind. I told them I was a friend of Tom's and that I had questions about his death. I asked to speak to the investigating officer. His name is Daniel Fawkes. Lieutenant Daniel Fawkes. He came down to meet me, told me how sorry he was about Tom. He took me into a little room, insisted on getting me coffee. He's a big guy, Fawkes. He has a couple of tattoos and a buzz cut and sharp, no-bullshit eyes. Which I figured was a good thing. I was relieved they had someone smart working the case. A young guy. Not some old fart just clocking in the hours. He checked me out—a quick glance up and down—and I wished he hadn't, but I didn't think too much about it.

I told him about Tom and Mike. I told him about the fight. I told him that it didn't make sense to me that Tom had suddenly decided to get drunk alone then wander down by the jetty. Why would he even do that? I asked him where Mike had been when Tom went into the water. Had Mike found him? Had Mike been drinking with him? He looked at me with these dark eyes and I couldn't tell what he was thinking. He asked me questions. He wanted my full name, my date and place of birth. I thought I saw a flicker in his eyes when I told him my name, I thought I saw his expression grow colder, but I told myself I was paranoid, and kept talking. I answered all his questions. How and where had I met Tom? What was the nature of our relationship? When had I last seen him? What had we talked about?

After a few minutes I stopped talking. He sat there looking at me and I looked right back. I said, "Why don't you care about this?"

"Who says I don't?"

I didn't know what to say, but I could feel it rolling off him by then. His contempt for me. His complete disdain.

"I . . .

"I'm just waiting for you to work this around to asking about Tom's parents, that's all."

I didn't understand what he was saying.

"That's why you're here, right? You think that playing the grieving girlfriend will get you some kind of payout, or something?"

I sat there and I couldn't say a goddamn thing. I sat there and let him talk.

"I know all about you, Laura. The worst of it is, the way the world is now, I wasn't even surprised. Except that after everything you did, you came back looking for more."

Daniel Fawkes didn't hold back. He was more than happy to explain that Michael had told them everything. That Tom had been seeing a local girl (me). That Tom was a good guy, a very good guy, but a bit naive when it came to women. Michael said that I already had a boyfriend, that I was playing a game with Tom . . . interested in him because of his money. He said Tom found out I had been using him on the day he died. So he sat up late with his best friend Michael, drinking and talking. Around eleven o'clock Mike decided to go to bed. He was exhausted. He said good night and he left Tom in the library.

Fawkes said, "Mike assumed—not unreasonably—that Tom would go to bed too. But it seems he went down to the water. Maybe he went there to *think. It's the kind of thing people do, when they're sad and they've been drinking. We're calling it an accident. It's better for his family that way."*

First I thought I was going to be sick. Then I pulled myself together and I tried. I sat in that room and tried so hard to convince him that the story Mike had told him was complete bullshit. Even though he looked at me like I was dog shit. Even though I could see I wasn't getting anywhere.

I promise. I really, really tried.

Afterward I got back into the car with Rosa and I stared out of the window. I still haven't cried.

Monday, August 22, 1994, 10:00 p.m.

Rosa came to my room with a bottle of wine, poured me a glass, and basically forced me to drink it. She held my hand and told me that she was sorry. I told her that the police didn't care. That they were pretending it was an accident. She shrugged, like that made sense. I said I couldn't understand why they believed everything Mike said. Why they weren't even investigating, and she said that that was probably because of the Spencer family.

"You can't be surprised, Laura. People like the Spencers, if they don't want an investigation, that is how it will be."

I started to get worked up. "You're saying they bribed the police?"

"I'm not saying that. It doesn't have to be so blatant. There would just be . . . pressure. This is America. Money talks."

"But his parents . . . why wouldn't they want the truth?"

"If they believe Tom killed himself, they will not want it confirmed. They will not want people speculating about his reasons. It's better for it to be an accident."

"It wasn't an accident. *That's what I've been saying. Why would Tom go home and start drinking, so late at night? Why would he go to the boat by himself?"*

"You might never know the answers to your questions. You knew him, but . . . forgive me . . . you did not know him."

I pulled my hand away. She didn't get it. She looked at me with that flat expression that gave nothing away. For a moment, I hated her.

"You think his friend killed him?" That was what she said. Just blandly, as if she were asking if Mike had taken out the trash. My mind flashed through everything that had happened, right from the beginning. The phone call I'd overheard—an argument about money. Mike's obsession with Tom's father's boat. His mysterious sailing trip north. Why would a rich Virginia college kid have friends in a fishing port in Canada? His bullshit story about his "friend" Dom. And his obsession, his complete insistence that they sail the boat back to Virginia. His fury when he realized that Tom was serious about flying home instead. Last of all I thought about Daniel Fawkes's face as he looked at me and spewed out Mike's story. Why would Mike go to the police and tell them a bunch of lies about me? There could only be one reason. I told Rosa I thought he killed Tom. She told me it didn't matter. So I explained again.

"Rosa, what I'm saying is that I think maybe Mike was running drugs. I know it seems crazy, but . . ."

"I'm not telling you you're wrong. I'm telling you it doesn't matter."

I stood up and knocked back the rest of the glass of wine she'd given me while she kept talking.

"Listen to me, Laura. You are a young girl, with no money, and very few friends. You have no proof of anything. These are rich people. You went to the police. You tried to talk to them, and you saw what happened. Perhaps this Michael killed your friend, but if you pursue this you will be the one who is hurt."

It went on like that for a while. Me, shaking my head again and again and Rosa, trying patiently to explain to me her theory of rich people. Which was basically that they're dangerous. That getting mixed up with them always ends up in disaster for people like us. (The like us al-

most ... almost ... made me laugh. I'd bet what little I have that Rosa has a fortune salted away. But if I pointed that out to her, I'm fairly sure she'd say back that there's rich and then there's rich, and I guess she'd be right about that.)

I listened to her, or at least I made sure I looked like I was listening to her, but all the time I was planning. I need proof. If I had proof I could go to the cops, or maybe to Tom's parents and tell them everything. So I listened to Rosa and I drank with her and I agreed with everything she said. I'm not sure that she believed me. Rosa is shrewd. But she left after an hour or so, which is good. I need to be alone now. I have things to do.

Hannah

EIGHT

THURSDAY, AUGUST 29, 2019

"We'll have to be careful," Rob Parekh said. "It seems clear that Prosper doesn't want to be found."

They were sitting in the Project offices—Parekh, Camila, Hannah, and Sean. The day hadn't started that well. Hannah still hadn't succeeded in getting Laura on the phone. She'd reached Jan an hour before, and Jan had said she'd call as soon as she'd been to the house. Waiting on that update was incredibly distracting and Hannah had to force her attention back to what was happening in the room. Which wasn't much. Camila had been intent on delivering their update to Robert Parekh first thing Thursday morning, in person, but Parekh was less excited than they'd expected. He seemed distracted too, under pressure.

"I think we should follow up quickly," Camila said. "I think there's a risk that Beth, the girl who gave us the address, will have second thoughts. If she comes clean to her mother that she told us, Sophia might call her brother and he might go into hiding."

"I've looked up the house," Hannah said quietly. "Online. It's in the suburbs in a very exclusive area. Expensive."

"It's been eleven years," Parekh said. "That's a lot of time. Enough time for Prosper to build a new life. If he's done well for himself, that could work for us or against us." Parekh was sitting on the edge of his desk, hands lightly clasped in front of him. "If he's married, with kids, then he's less likely to leave town as soon as he sees us coming. On the other hand he's really not going to want a nice quiet life to be pulled apart by a murder trial, which makes him less likely to be cooperative. It's odd that the sister lied. But maybe they're afraid of publicity. They don't want the Prosper name associated with Dandridge."

"I think he's probably changed his name," Hannah said.

"Oh?" Parekh's eyes were on her, measuring and assessing. Hannah shifted in her seat.

"Well. You've been looking for Neil Prosper for a while," she said. "And Dandridge's previous attorney searched for him at length."

"I'm not sure we can take him at his word about that," Parekh said. "There are a hell of a lot of gaps in his work."

"Okay," Hannah said. "But we know that Prosper essentially disappeared after the murders. There's no record of him online, on social media. That might have made sense if he was still a drug user or an addict, living at the edges of the system. But if he is living in an expensive house, with a family, going to work every day— Well, I think it's very hard for people to have absolutely no internet presence at all in those circumstances."

"Did you check the property records for the address? Find out whose name it's registered under?" Parekh asked.

"I tried," Hannah said. "The property is registered to a corporation and I didn't have any luck in tracing the ultimate owners."

"You don't think, if he changed his name, that Beth would have said something about that?" Camila said.

Hannah shrugged. "Maybe, maybe not. She might not know. He could still be Uncle Neil to her. Or I could have it all wrong. It's only a theory."

"Okay," Parekh said. "Well, I guess we're going to find out one way or the other shortly." He clapped his hands together. "Great work, girls." He looked at his watch. "I have a lot to get through today, so I need to wrap this up. Are you up for another road trip? To check out this address?"

"I can't," said Camila, shaking her head. "I have a test this afternoon, and my mom has some stuff going on at work. She needs me to check in at home."

"I can go," Sean said.

"Hannah?" Parekh asked.

Hannah nodded. Her reaction to the request confused her. She was worried about the outcome of the trip—it was always possible that they would uncover something that could help Dandridge in court—but she also felt an unexpected little boost of happiness. She could go to North Carolina without worrying about Laura's routine or thinking about anyone but herself. That felt good.

"Okay, well, that might be better anyway. I think I'd like Sean along in case Prosper reacts badly."

Hannah looked at Sean, and wondered exactly what Parekh expected him to do in the event that Prosper got aggressive.

"Sean, I'd like you to squeeze in a visit to Michael too, if you can. Maybe on the way back from North Carolina. He's getting antsy with the hearing coming up next week, and I'm needed here. Introduce yourself. Spend some time with him, all right? Boost his confidence a little. Bring Hannah with you if you like. It would be good for you to meet him too, Hannah."

Before Hannah or Sean could respond, the door to Parekh's office burst open and Jim Lehane and Marianne Stephenson came in in a flurry of anxiety and paperwork.

"Rob, the goddamn filings are messed up," Lehane said. He tried to thrust some papers into Parekh's hands. Parekh was slow to take them.

"What?" he said.

"The filings. The motions," Lehane said. "In the Dandridge case, I mean. We filed the wrong motions and now the deadline has passed."

"I can't understand it," Marianne Stephenson said. "It doesn't make any sense."

"The document numbers were all mixed up," Lehane said. "We filed electronically and we just picked up the motions through the document management system. I filed most of them myself and I made damn sure I had the right document name and number. But I just happened to open a document today—I was going to cross-reference a section in a motion I'm writing today—and I realized it was all wrong. We've filed a bunch of old motions from the federal case."

Parekh stood up. His fury was unmistakable but he kept it in check. Barely. "How. The fuck. Did this happen," he said. "Marianne?"

"I've called in IT," Marianne said, her face and voice tight with anxiety. "But it's the college system. It will take them days to look at it. I've tried to figure it out myself. We run backups on the system every night. I was going to go back over them to see when the document naming system went wrong, but the backups seem to be corrupted. I can't load them."

"Christ," Parekh said. "This is . . . unforgivable. We have to be better than this."

"We *are* better than this," Lehane said.

Marianne was wringing her hands. "Nothing like this has ever happened before. You know that. I am so careful. I don't understand . . ."

"We have no backups?" Parekh asked. "We'll have to rewrite the damn things from scratch." His face lost color, and he sat back on the desk. "That's days of work. We'll never get the judge to accept them."

But Lehane was shaking his head. "It's not quite that bad," he said. "I've got versions on my laptop. Most of them, at least. They're not final versions, but I think they're pretty close. We'll have to go through them all, check them, make final edits again, I guess. Then see if the court will accept late filings."

Parekh stood up. "Bring in your laptop, Jim. Let's get to work. I'll call the clerk. See if I can sweet-talk her into allowing a late filing. But I'm not holding my breath."

Lehane left the room. Marianne Stephenson stayed.

"I'm so sorry, Rob. I don't understand . . ."

He held up a hand. "We don't have time for this, Marianne. Just see what you can do about getting to the bottom of what went wrong, okay? And from now on the Dandridge files stay off the main system."

Marianne swallowed. She looked like she was close to tears, but she left the room with purpose in her step and her head held high. Parekh seemed to realize in the same moment that Hannah, Sean, and Camila were still sitting there, frozen.

"Let's go, people," Parekh said, irritated, and they hurried out of his office.

"MAN, I CAN'T BELIEVE IT. IT'S NOT LIKE MARIANNE TO SCREW UP like that," Sean said, once they were out of the office and walking down the corridor.

Camila was frowning. "You're assuming it was Marianne. It might have been Jim. Just because he went in there shouting the loudest doesn't mean it wasn't him."

"Right," said Sean.

"Or maybe it wasn't anyone. Maybe it was just a glitch." Camila's frown deepened. "If it was a glitch, it's not going to be isolated to one case. I'd better go and check my stuff. As if I didn't have enough to do today." She sighed. "Do you have anything you want me to look at for you, Sean? If you're going to be on the road today?"

He shook his head. "I'll bring my laptop, check it tonight. But thank you. That's a nice offer."

"Do you think they'll get permission to file late? In the Dandridge case, I mean," Hannah asked.

Camila shrugged. "Who knows? I guess we don't have any friends in Yorktown right now. There's a lot of politics with this case. But Rob Parekh is pretty smart. Maybe he can find a way to put pressure on the judge."

They were quiet for a moment before Sean spoke again.

"Do you mind, Camila? Not going to North Carolina, I mean. It was your lead. Yours and Hannah's."

She shook her head. "Not really. Taking another day or couple of days would be hard right now. I just wish Parekh wouldn't call us *girls*. It's patronizing."

"I'm not sure he means it the way it sounds," Sean said. Camila cast him a look, and he held his hands up. "Okay, okay."

"I think you might be right," Camila said to Hannah. "About Prosper changing his name, I mean. It makes sense."

"Do we have any pictures of him?" Hannah asked. "In the files? If we track him down, but he's going by a different name, how are we going to know it's him?"

"There's the yearbook Camila found. But he was eighteen in that. Maybe there's something more recent in the case file," Sean said. "I'm not sure." He looked back over his shoulder toward the office. "I'll go back in and have a look now, and then—do you need to go to your place to pick up some stuff, Hannah? I can follow you there if you like? That is . . . I thought I'd drive, if you're okay with that. I figured you might like a break . . ."

Hannah shrugged. "Sure. My car's here, in the parking lot. I have an overnight bag in the trunk that I packed when Camila and I thought we were going to stay in Yorktown. I can bring that, just in case. Otherwise, I'm good to go. But I'll wait here for you, if that's all right. I'll take a minute and just check in on my mom."

Camila left. Sean went back into the law school building in search of the photograph. Hannah retrieved her bag from the trunk of her car and telephoned her mother. Laura answered the call on the first ring.

"Hannah."

Shit. Laura's voice was a rasp. She'd obviously been crying, which meant she'd been drinking. It took only Hannah's name, said in precisely that way, for Hannah to understand what kind of state her mother was in.

"Oh, Mom."

"I'm sorry. I'm so sorry. But you didn't call me. You said you would and then you didn't."

It would be useless to protest that she had called, just later than planned. "It's okay. Please, it's okay. Where are you? Are you home?"

"Yes."

"That's good. Did you see Jan today? Did you go to your meeting?"

"I saw Jan. I can't stop thinking about you out there. About the risks you're taking. So then I . . . I'm sorry, Hannah."

Laura didn't drive. She'd lost her license a few years back and since then Hannah was the only one who drove the car. So how had she gotten her hands on alcohol? Jan wouldn't have bought it for her. Laura must have had a stash somewhere. Damnit. Damn. That felt like such a betrayal. Or no. More likely she'd just called a cab and had it drive her to the liquor store. Laura couldn't help the drinking. She'd been through so much that had stripped her raw, torn away all of her defenses, and now sometimes the world was just too much for her. Alcohol was the anesthetic she chose to numb the pain. Hannah understood all that but sometimes it was hard. Sometimes she felt let down or hurt or just overwhelmed. That wasn't okay. That was taking Laura's trauma and making it all about herself. She needed to be stronger than that.

"You know you can't drink anymore, right? You have to stop now or you will hurt yourself."

"I'm sorry." Laura was crying harder now.

Hannah drew a breath. "Do you need me to come home?"

"I ... I don't know ..."

Hannah closed her eyes for a second. "The most important thing is that you're okay. All of this . . . none of it is worth doing if you're going to be hurt by it." The whole point of everything was to help Laura. To heal her.

"I'm all right." Laura's tone was stronger.

"Are you sure?"

There was a moment's silence and then Laura spoke again and she sounded stronger, more together. "Do you feel like what you're doing is making a difference?"

"Yes. Yes, I definitely do." She lowered her voice. "Dandridge's defense is weaker than I expected. I think what I'm doing is keeping everyone off balance. And there'll be other opportunities. I'm just getting started."

"I wish you didn't feel like you have to do this. I'm worried about the risks you're taking. If you get caught, if they find out that you've been lying . . . they won't allow you to graduate. You could lose everything you've worked for. But I understand why you're doing it.

And . . . I . . . ." Laura let her voice trail off and she was silent for a long moment before she spoke again. "Maybe it *would* make a difference if I could believe he'd finally paid the price for what he did."

Hannah felt a flood of emotion that left her almost giddy—surprise and hope, combined with a fierce need not to let her mother down. "I'm going to call Jan. She'll come over again and help, if you'll let her. I'll ask her to stay with you for the rest of the day, okay?"

"Yes, all right."

"And I'll call you tonight, fill you in on everything, and you can let me know how you're doing."

They talked a little bit longer until Hannah saw Sean coming back out of the building. He waved at her. Hannah waved back, held up one finger in a *wait* gesture. She ended the call with her mother, then quickly called Jan and explained the situation. The other woman agreed to go to the house and cook dinner and to visit three times a day for the next couple of days. Hannah said she would check in as soon as she could, then hung up and joined Sean.

"You okay?" he asked, giving her a sideways look.

"Yes, yes. Fine."

"Everything okay with your mom?"

For a split second she blanked about the cancer story and was struck dumb, thinking irrationally that he had somehow overheard her conversation. Then memory came back.

"Uh . . . she had a bad night, but she's okay. She's reading."

"That's good. Good that she's feeling okay today, I mean, and up to reading." Sean took her bag from her and put it in the trunk of his car. They climbed in and he started the engine. "It can't be easy for you," he said. "You know, Rob's a workaholic, but don't let him push you around. If you need to be with your mom you need to tell him that. He'll have to deal with it."

"No. It's okay. My mom . . . she wants me to live my life. I want to be with her, of course, but she gets upset if she thinks I'm giving up opportunities to be with her."

"I hear you. My mom is exactly like that. Independent as all get out. Hates it when I try to take care of her. Makes it hard to celebrate her birthday, or Mother's Day."

For a moment Hannah thought he was being sarcastic, but his expression was entirely sincere. "Really?"

"Sure. I mean, obviously, it's different for me. My mom's not sick. And I get back to see her a couple of times a semester. It must be really hard for you." He turned on the radio. Adele came on, singing her heart out about love and loss. He flipped the channel. "Nope."

"Not a fan?"

"Definitely a fan. Just too sad for today. We need something with some energy." Lizzo came on with "Truth Hurts." "Oh, yeah." He turned it up, grinned at her. "Now we're talking."

It was a four-hour drive to Charlotte. After a while they moved from the radio to music apps and playlists and mostly they just listened and talked music. When they were about two hours into the drive Sean changed the subject.

"Rob told me about your murder rule case."

"Did he?"

"It sounds like it has a lot of potential."

"Yes. I think so." Guilt ate at Hannah. Had she thought about Nia Jones once in the last couple of days? Nia Jones, who'd spent twenty-four years in prison and was facing eleven more? That wasn't good enough. She would have to do something to move the case forward while she was still in a position to do so.

"I've never liked the murder rule," Sean said. "This idea that people should be fully legally responsible for acts they didn't commit, or didn't intend to commit. It undermines our whole concept of justice."

"Hmmm."

He glanced at her. "You don't agree?"

She shrugged. "I don't know. I think it's a good idea to make people take responsibility for the consequences of their actions, even if those consequences are unintended, within reason. It's all a question of foreseeability. If you could reasonably foresee that a death might result from your actions, or in, you know, the overall action you're taking part in, like an armed robbery, for example, then you should pay the price."

Sean grimaced. "When you put it like that it sounds okay. But the reality of the case law is that a lot of the time, felony murder is just another stick used to beat poor people. The kind of people who commit stupid crimes or get caught up in something bigger than themselves because they're out of options."

Hannah made a sound that could be taken for agreement. She didn't agree with him and the part of her that wasn't on a mission wanted to keep the conversation going. She had questions she wanted to ask him too—about why he had volunteered for the Project, what he really thought about Robert Parekh, and why he was so convinced of Dandridge's innocence—but questions from her would likely prompt questions in return and it would be much safer if she kept things light and simple. She allowed the conversation to peter out and used the quiet moments to think about the upcoming interview. It was incredible how convinced Camila had been that Neil Prosper would be useful, rather than detrimental to their cause. Really, there was no reason at all to think that he would be a good alibi witness for Dandridge. Even if Prosper claimed to have been with Dandridge all night the night of the murder, how useful would that evidence be now, eleven years after the original trial? It would be easy for the prosecution to paint Prosper's abrupt departure from Yorktown in the worst possible light. Surely any objective person looking at the facts would recognize that Prosper had to have been running from something. And yet Camila was clearly excited, Sean almost as positive, and even Parekh, who at least seemed to have some degree of skepticism about the situation, seemed to be hopeful overall. Why? Because they were all so genuinely convinced by Dandridge's innocence that they couldn't see any other possibility? Or was it an intentional suspension of disbelief? Something like the mechanism defense attorneys adopted to allow them to defend guilty or possibly guilty clients and still go home and sleep at night. Either way, it was a weakness. Hannah sat and looked out of the window, and thought about ways that weakness could be exploited.

IT WAS THREE-THIRTY P.M. WHEN THEY PULLED UP OUTSIDE 6826 Alexander Road, Charlotte, North Carolina. Hannah looked down at the piece of paper in her hand, the one Beth Prosper had handed her a couple of days before, then looked back at the house.

"Jesus," she said. She'd told Parekh that she'd looked the house up online, and she had, but as the house was on a private road she hadn't been able to access any street-view photographs of the actual property, and she hadn't been able to find any real estate photographs. She'd expected, based on the neighborhood, that the house would be expensive, but nothing had prepared her for the real deal. The house was set back among the trees, with a winding gravel drive. The facade of the house was all beautifully painted plaster and high arched windows. She looked around. The neighboring houses were similarly set back and private.

"His sister, Sophia, said that he was cut off by the family?" Sean asked.

"Yes."

"Doesn't look like it."

They got out of the car and walked down the drive. It was very quiet. They could hear only birdsong, and the sound of the gravel crunching under their feet. As the driveway curved around, they caught a glimpse of a gleaming swimming pool and a pool house to the rear of the house. They kept walking, reached the porch, and Sean rang the doorbell. They heard it ring inside the house and waited. But it was too quiet. The house felt like it was empty. They waited for a minute, then Sean tried the doorbell again. Still no answer.

"What do we do now?" Hannah said.

"I guess we wait."

They walked back down the drive. The air was cool and sweet with the smell of late-blooming flowers. Hannah thought about money as they walked. Thought about how it insulated you, wrapped you up in a bubble of beauty. Thought about what a person might do to stay inside that bubble. They reached the car and Hannah stopped with her hand on the door handle.

"I think I'm going to try the neighbors," she said. "See if I can find out who owns this house. If it's Neil Prosper, or someone else."

Sean nodded. "That's a good idea." He looked around.

The first house was just as beautiful, as manicured and deserted as the Prosper house. The neighboring house to the left, however, was a little tired looking, a little more lived in. Hannah pressed the doorbell, but didn't hear it ring, so she knocked loudly instead. The house was so big, the front door so solid, that it was hard to believe that the knock would be heard in any room but the entrance hall. Hannah waited, tried again. Then stood back from the house and looked around. A moment later she heard footsteps echoing from deep within the house. A moment after that and the door was opened by a very thin, very old woman. She was dressed in an emerald-green cardigan over a silk blouse, and her gray hair was pinned back just so. Her pants were tailored gray wool, and her shoes the softest leather.

"Can I help you?" she asked.

Hannah summoned her friendliest smile. "I'm so sorry to bother you," she said. "My name is Hannah. I'm a student at the University of Virginia, and I'm just in Charlotte for the weekend. My dad asked me to look up an old friend of the family's, and I was supposed to meet them at their home, but now I'm wondering if I got the address wrong." She fished Beth's piece of paper out of her pocket.

The old woman raised an eyebrow and the expression spoke volumes. She was a little suspicious, certainly, but mostly unimpressed at this, the latest evidence of a younger generation who could not be relied upon to keep their social engagements and maintain basic manners.

"Um . . . it's 6826 Washington Drive," Hannah said. "The Prosper family? Neil Prosper?"

"Oh no. We're 6824, and next door belongs to the Swifts. Johnathon and Amanda Swift."

"Oh," said Hannah, creasing her brow. "I think we might know them. Maybe that's why I got the address wrong. Is that the Virginia Swifts? From Yorktown?"

Suspicion faded from the older woman's face, even as her condescension grew. "Yorktown? Now why would you think that? Amanda Swift is North Carolina born and bred. And Johnathon owns a string of coffee shops all across the state. He didn't start that business in Yorktown, let me tell you. No, you'd better telephone your father, young lady. You've certainly mixed things up as much as a person could."

With the sincerest apology she could muster, Hannah withdrew. The older woman watched her until she'd reached the gate.

"Well?" Sean said, as Hannah climbed into the car.

"The house is owned by a family called Swift. Johnathon and Amanda Swift."

"Johnathon Swift," Sean said.

"Yes," Hannah said. She was already busy with her phone. A couple of moments later she was looking at a profile picture on a business social networking site—that of Johnathon Swift, CEO and Founder of Swift Coffee. He was as blond as Sophia Prosper, with the same narrow, straight nose, blue eyes, and delicate mouth. On Sophia those features had made her beautiful. On Swift they made him look weak. But appearances, Hannah knew, could be deceiving.

"It's him," she said, clutching her phone. "It's definitely him."

"Show me," Sean said. He grabbed her hand to pull the phone closer. "Yeah. He's changed, since the yearbook picture, but not that much. Man, I can't believe we've found him," he said. "As easily as that. After so many years."

Hannah wanted to point out what Parekh had said—that they didn't even know for sure that the original attorney had looked for Prosper. Maybe he hadn't been difficult to find at all. Maybe no one had tried.

"I think we should leave for a few hours," she said. "The woman I spoke to is the kind who would call the cops if she left her house for some reason and saw us still sitting here. I gave her a story about looking for a family friend. She thinks I came to the wrong address."

Sean looked at his watch. "All right. Let's get some food, come back here after five, when he's likely to be home from work."

"Let's do it," Hannah said. She was looking forward to the interview, and couldn't help but feel a little sorry for Sean, for the disappointment she was sure was about to come his way.

LAURA

DIARY ENTRY #7

Wednesday, August 24, 1994, 10:00 a.m.

I felt confident. Sure that I was doing the right thing. I'd had a glass of wine (maybe two) for courage at the hotel and I was all fired up, sure that I was about to expose Michael and make him pay for what he'd done. I wasn't afraid. After all, I was the one creeping around outside, about to expose all their dirty secrets, while they sat inside, oblivious. And I was very careful, very quiet. I rode down the street until I was within sight of the house, then I ditched my bike in the trees. There were cars parked outside the house, four of them, and even though it was past midnight there were lights on inside. Obviously the family was still in the house. I had a flashlight with me, but I didn't turn it on. The moon was bright enough that I didn't need it.

I skirted around by the pool, pushing away memories, and made my way down the path that led to the beach. The yacht was still there, tied to the jetty. I hurried, wincing a little at the slap of my sneaker on the wood. It was so quiet. Other than my noisy arrival the only sound was the gentle lap of tiny waves on the shore. I was absolutely sure I was alone. I stepped onto the boat and went below deck and there he was, just sitting there in the shadows.

Shit. Shit. He was so calm. He asked me what I was doing on his boat.

I said, "It's not your boat." I was angry, and I was too stupid to be afraid.

"It is, actually. Thomas Spencer Senior gave it to me. Something to remember his son by."

There was so much mocking sarcasm in his voice; he barely held back from outright laughter, and something in me just snapped. I walked the few steps across the little room to him and I slapped him, hard, across the face. He let me do it. Then he stood up and he punched me. His fist connected with the side of my temple. I fell sideways and I was unconscious before I hit the floor. I don't think I was out for long. When I came to I was lying on my side, and my arm was bent underneath me. I had landed on it when I'd fallen. Michael was sitting on the small couch looking down at me with this expression on his face . . . like a benign kind of interest.

I scooted backward away from him. My head was throbbing, the entire left side of my face was on fire.

I said, "You killed Tom."

"Yes."

"Because you were running drugs. Or trying to. And he found out."

He put his head to one side. "You are nearly right. He didn't find out. But I think he probably would have. Mostly I killed him because he pissed me off."

I think that was when I finally realized just how stupid I had been. To accuse him. What had I thought? That he'd applaud my amazing insight and then let me go?

"The drugs are gone now, of course. That's why you're here, isn't it? To search for proof. I thought you might come, but you're too late. We moved them a couple of days ago. The people I've been working with weren't thrilled with me, but they understood the need for a change of plan, after Tom's death and the possibility of a police investigation. Although, you know, Laura, I don't think it was necessary? I think I could have kept the drugs onboard and brought them back to Virginia whenever it suited me. It would have been easy. Everyone's accepted my story." He leaned forward. His tone was comfortable, conversational. I should have run. Maybe I could have gotten away if I'd run right then. I didn't move. I couldn't. It was like I was hypnotized by him as he talked and talked.

"If I were you, I would be really offended. People who haven't even met you are very willing to accept that you are a dirty little slut, and they are eager to believe that Tom was a naive, heartbroken idiot. Tom's parents are so desperate to avoid the so-called truth about his suicide leaking out that they just want to get him home and bury him and sweep the whole sad story about his summer romance under the rug."

Mike stood up and crossed to me. He knelt beside me, quite casually, and then he reached out his hands, put them around my neck, and started to choke me. I lashed out, tried to scratch him, gouge his eyes. He let go of my neck and I gasped for breath, but then he pulled me down until I was lying flat, straddled my body and knelt on my arms so that I couldn't move them, couldn't fight him. He started to strangle me again. He was so much stronger than me. There was absolutely nothing I could do to stop him.

He strangled me until I lost consciousness. When I woke up he was sitting beside me, looking down at me. "I could kill you," he said. "Quite easily. I could take your body out to sea and dump you and no one would ever find you. But then, there might be questions, I suppose. Two deaths in such a short period of time, even if one of them is just little old you, might be problematic, even for the cops. So maybe I won't. I haven't decided."

I cried. For the first time since Tom died I just lay there and cried, and it wasn't because he was dead but because I was afraid for myself. I didn't try to fight back or run away or even say anything. I'm so pathetic. I fucking hate myself right now. Mike looked at me with disgust. I was so sure he was going to kill me and just as sure that I couldn't do anything to stop what was about to happen. I was so afraid, I . . . oh God, I peed

my pants. He didn't like that at all. He hit me again, told me to clean myself up and kicked me until I started moving. He talked as I scrubbed and
cried. He blamed everything on his father, said his father had made a bad
investment and nearly lost all their money and wanted Mike to give them
his apartment and his car. For a moment Mike sounded genuinely upset.

When I had cleaned up he made me take a shower, and then he held
me down and he . . . I don't want to write the words. I don't want to. If I do,
it makes it real.

But I can still feel the pain of it. Everything hurts, so much. The worst is
this feeling inside my head. I don't know how I'm ever going to get it out.
You can't clean inside your brain. How can I stop this feeling? Maybe if I
get drunk. Oblivion. I would do it if I could feel safe, but I'm not safe now.
He might come back.

He raped me. He used a condom. He made me shower a second time.
Then he told me I could go. He promised he'll kill me if I ever talk to the
police again, or one of his drug-running friends will kill me. He told me
exactly how. I believe him. I think he wants to do it. I think he's just biding
his time.

Hannah

NINE

They found a café that served an all-day breakfast. Sean ordered a breakfast burrito, Hannah a Cajun chicken sandwich, and then they waited, while Hannah thought about how hungry she was. She couldn't remember if she'd eaten breakfast. The food came quickly, and it was really good.

"So let's work it out," Sean said. "What's the time line here?"

Hannah had just taken a bite of her sandwich. She thought about it as she chewed and swallowed. "I think we don't have a lot of facts to go on. We do know that Sophia lied. She said she wasn't in touch with her brother, that she didn't know where he was when clearly she did. Beth was able to give us his address. And Neil Prosper has that coffee chain. He's obviously very wealthy. What are the chances he built that up without seed money from his parents? So I think she lied about Prosper being cut off by their parents too."

"Okay, so we know that Prosper spent the evening of the murder with Dandridge. And that within a few days of Dandridge being arrested, Prosper had left town and essentially, as far as we know, never came back. And his family has very deliberately covered his tracks. Making him difficult to track down. So why would the Prosper family do that? Is it a reputation thing? They're a wealthy old

Virginia family. You think they didn't want to be associated with a murder trial?"

This again. Hannah made a face. She couldn't help it. She liked Sean, but this was just stupid.

"What?"

"I just don't think we can jump to that conclusion."

Sean looked interested. He sat back in his chair. "Tell me."

"I just think there might be other reasons for him to run."

"Like?"

"Well, I hate to say this, Sean, but I think Prosper running is a bad fact. Don't you think Parekh looked worried when we told him about it? I mean, our client claims to have spent the night with this guy when the murder takes place, and then the guy runs. I don't think that looks good at all. Innocent people don't run. What if they did it together?"

"You think Dandridge and Prosper might have killed Sarah together?"

"I think, if I were the prosecution, it's exactly what I would suggest the moment I see Prosper on the stand. He ran. If I'm the prosecutor, I'm going to *want* to tie Prosper and Dandridge closer together. It makes Dandridge look worse, that his alibi ran away, not better."

Sean thought for a moment then shook his head. "Oof."

"What?"

"Nothing." He stood up, fishing in his pocket for money for a tip.

"Tell me," Hannah said, her anxiety spiking. She should have kept her mouth shut.

"It's just, I can absolutely see why Rob wanted you on the case. You have a different way of looking at things."

WHEN THEY PULLED UP OUTSIDE THE PROSPER HOUSE IT WAS SIX P.M., and there was a large Mercedes sedan and a Tesla Model X parked in the driveway. They parked outside, walked down the driveway, and again Sean rang the doorbell. This time little feet came running. A boy, about five years old, opened the door. He hung off the door frame, looked up at them in a friendly sort of way.

"Hi," he said.

"Hi," Sean said. "Is your dad home?"

"Uh-huh." The boy didn't move, just stared up at them curiously.

"Do you think you could run and get him for me?" Sean asked. But there were heavier footsteps already approaching. Johnathon Swift appeared, wearing slacks and an open-necked blue shirt, but otherwise looking just like his profile picture. He put a hand on the little boy's shoulder, looked at Sean and Hannah with an expression much like his son's.

"Can I help you?" he asked.

"Mr. Swift," began Sean. "My name is Sean Warner." He pulled out a business card and handed it over. Hannah caught a flash of the Innocence Project logo on the card. "I'm a law student at the University of Virginia, and a volunteer at the Innocence Project. This is my colleague Hannah Rokeby. We'd like to talk to you for a few minutes about Michael Dandridge."

Swift, or Prosper, flinched. His hand tightened around his little boy's shoulder as he looked down at Sean's card. Then he looked back at Sean. "I don't . . . ," he began. But he stopped, changed direction. "Peter, can you go in and find Mommy, please?"

The little boy ran off into the house.

"I don't have anything to say about Mike," Prosper said. "I can't help you. I'm sorry." He started to close the door and Sean put a hand out to stop him.

"Mr. Prosper, I'm sorry, but the next step after this is a subpoena. I know you don't want that. But if you talk to us now, and tell us everything you know . . . if it isn't useful then maybe there'll be no need for a subpoena. Please, we just have a few questions. I'm sure it won't take long and then we can leave you to your evening with your family."

He wanted to say no. Hannah could see it written all over his face. But he hesitated and then, maybe because the subpoena line had worked, or maybe just because he had questions of his own, he changed his mind.

"You'd better come in," Prosper said. He led the way into a beautiful library. It was modern and bright, and large enough to comfortably house an oversize custom-made desk as well as two small couches, which faced each other to facilitate conversation. Prosper took a seat at one and gestured for Hannah and Sean to sit in the other. "How did you find me?" he asked.

Hannah was determined not to throw Sophia's daughter under the bus. "Someone saw you," she said. "Or rather, saw your photograph online. Someone from Yorktown. This person knew you in the old days, and still knows your sister today. She recognized you."

Prosper scowled. "I'm not in touch with Sophia. She has nothing to do with any of this."

"Okay . . . ," Hannah said, a little thrown by his vehemence.

Sean leaned forward. "Mr. Prosper. As you know Michael has been in prison for eleven years for the murder of Sarah Fitzhugh. We believe that he is innocent of that crime. In fact, his conviction has already been vacated by the federal courts. Notwithstanding this, the state prosecutor is planning on trying the case again. Michael is still in prison, and he will have to go to court again to fight for his freedom in just a few days. I don't know . . . are you already aware of all this, Mr. Prosper? It's been widely reported in the newspapers."

"My name is Johnathon Swift," Prosper said. "I haven't been Neil Prosper for years." His voice was tight and his face flushed. Was that anger? Or something else?

"Mr. Swift, then." Hannah broke in, her tone conciliatory. "I don't . . . maybe you're not aware that Michael Dandridge gave your name when he was asked for an alibi for the night of the murder? He said that he spent the night with you, drinking and listening to music. Is that right?" She waited for him to deny it.

Prosper visibly squirmed. Seconds passed when he didn't speak. Finally, he said, "I'm not obliged to speak to you, right? I mean, not legally."

Hannah opened her mouth to speak, but Sean got there before her. "Not right at this moment," he said, evenly, "but if you don't speak to us voluntarily you will be subpoenaed to the trial where you will be obliged to respond to questioning. If you object, Michael's defense lawyers—our colleagues—will be entitled to treat you as a hostile witness, and you will be cross-examined. If you lie to the court, that would be perjury, and you may be sent to prison."

The word hung in the air. Prosper was staring at Sean with a combination of dislike and fear. "What makes you think I'd lie?" he said.

Sean hesitated. "I think you've worked very hard to avoid telling the truth for eleven years. Presumably, there's a reason for that."

Tension sparked between them and there was silence for a long moment. Shifting in her chair, Hannah said, "Mr. Swift, if you didn't spend the evening with Mr. Dandridge, or if you spent only part of the evening with him, you are free to say so, you know. We do want to hear the truth, whatever that might be." Was that too obvious? She risked pissing Sean off, even making him suspicious, but it would be worth it if it put the alibi witness idea to bed once and for all.

But Prosper turned his gaze to her and said, "I'm not going to answer your questions."

Sean and Hannah exchanged glances.

"Are you saying . . . are you saying that you are concerned about self-incrimination?" Hannah felt herself flush. God. This was too good. She half-expected Prosper to stand up, to say he was going to call his attorney, to ask them to leave. But he didn't do any of those things. He just sat there and looked at them, and the tension grew.

"You're not going to answer our questions," Sean said, eventually, carefully.

"No."

"You can't help us."

Prosper nodded. He and Sean had locked eyes. It was like they were having a different, unspoken conversation now. One that Hannah wasn't hearing.

"You can't be *seen* to be helping us," Sean said.

Prosper nodded again.

"Because of Sophia. Because of Sophia and her family."

"Yes." There was relief on Prosper's face as he nodded for a third time, the relief of someone who is finally understood. But there was fear in his eyes too. Unmistakably. Hannah started to feel uneasy.

"Okay," Sean said. He was very serious now and he looked older, somehow. Warm, easy, jokey Sean had disappeared and this was another version of him. Clever, focused, compassionate.

"What can we do to help you?" Sean asked.

Prosper shook his head. "I don't know."

"Let me talk to my boss. His name is Robert Parekh. If you've been following the case, you might have read about him. He wants to meet you. He has experience with situations like this. I'm sure he could help you. Help Sophia."

Prosper hesitated. Hannah could almost feel him teetering on the point of making a decision, falling one way or the other. Eventually, he shook his head again. "I'm sorry. I really am sorry. But there's nothing I can do to help Michael." He stood up. "I'll show you out."

They followed him to the front door. They thanked him for his time. When they were outside but before Prosper had shut the door, Sean turned around and asked one more question.

"Can you tell me one thing, Neil? Is it Jerome Pierce? Is that who you're afraid of?"

Prosper didn't answer. He turned away, went inside, and closed the door.

LAURA

Monday, August 29, 1994, 10:45 a.m.

I'm writing this on the bus on my way back to Boston. Rosa fired me this morning. Tom's father phoned the hotel owner and told him he wanted me gone and just like that I lost my job. I feel like shit. Like complete shit. Like I'm disgusting. Like everything they all believe about me is really true.

Rosa said I had to pack up and go right away, but she gave me an envelope full of cash—one week's wages and what she said was my end-of-season bonus. I think it might have been her own money. I could see she felt bad about everything. I wanted to tell her that I understood. She didn't have a choice. She can't afford to lose her job either. I wanted to hug her, but I couldn't. I just left without saying anything. I can't even cry anymore. I think maybe something inside me is broken.

Tuesday, August 30, 1994, 11:00 a.m.

I'm back in Boston now. Jenna is too. I stayed with her last night. We talked and talked and I told her nothing. Nothing about Michael Dandridge. I told her about Tom, that I'd fallen for a guy and that he died in an accident. An accidental drowning. But it came out all wrong. I sounded like a robot. I couldn't explain anything properly. She hugged me and I al-

most shrugged her off. I can see that she wants to comfort me. She's trying, really hard. I can't seem to let her in.

I'm a different person than the person I used to be. I feel like Michael's watching me all the time. Everywhere I go. I know he's in Virginia and very far from here but I can't let go of the fear. I'm not sleeping much. I feel sick all the time and I'm full of guilt. Michael Dandridge murdered Tom Spencer and I let him get away with it. I've thought about going to the police here in Boston, but I'm too afraid. They won't believe me, but they might make a phone call, or something. Michael will hear of it, and he'll find me, and then he'll kill me for sure.

Thursday, September 15, 1994, 2:30 p.m.

The night before last I had a dream that I got my period. Then I woke up and I knew, without even really thinking about it, that I'm pregnant. I can't believe it took me this long to realize, but I'm almost exactly eight and a half weeks pregnant. As soon as I woke up, I went and got a test and of course it was positive. I called Jenna and we went for a long walk around Griggs Park. Jenna is one hundred percent sure that I should have an abortion. She says I have to stay focused. I'll never get back on track if I have a baby now, and worse than that, what kind of life can I give a kid with absolutely no money, no home, no support? I know she's right. I found another apartment to rent and it's even shittier than the last one. Small, damp, and ugly. I'm pretty sure the guy in the place next door is dealing. How could I bring a baby up there? How do I work, even, with a little baby? It's hard to believe that things could get much worse than they are right now, but I know I'm kidding myself. Things can always get worse.

I loved Tom but I have nothing of him, not even a picture. I think about him so much that sometimes his face starts to go out of focus, and I wonder if I even remember what he looks like properly. Last night I closed *my eyes when I was in bed and I put my hand on my belly and I thought about the little bean inside and I pretended that I could feel Tom's hand covering mine. For a moment he was alive again. It was the first time I'd felt safe since the night on the boat.*

I don't know. I don't know what to do.

Hannah

TEN

They drove a little way from the Prosper house before pulling in again so that Sean could call Robert Parekh and fill him in on the interview with Neil Prosper. Hannah tried to sort out her own thoughts while she listened to Sean's side of the phone call. On the positive side Prosper was clearly useless as an alibi witness. He wasn't willing to talk. On the other hand everything had gone sideways there, just at the very end. What was that all about?

Sean finished his phone call.

"Well?"

"Rob's not happy. He thinks your point is a good one. If we try to put Prosper on the stand as an alibi for Dandridge, the prosecution will use the fact that he left town and changed his name to make both of them look guilty."

"What did you mean, when you asked Prosper if he was afraid of Pierce?"

"Rob's heard a few rumors. Like maybe Pierce's squeaky-clean disciplinary record is more to do with the fact that he's skilled at intimidation—people are afraid to go up against him. And look, if he was willing to beat Dandridge up to get a confession, he's not going to stop there, is he? I could see Pierce going after Prosper, running him out of town. Maybe threatening Prosper's sister to keep him in line."

Hannah thought about it. It was within the realm of possibility. If it was true, Pierce wouldn't be the first police officer to cross a line in pursuit of a conviction. "Maybe."

"Maybe?" Sean gave her a teasing look. "I only get a maybe?"

She smiled at him. "Maybe. I'm just saying, we have to wait for the facts, that's all."

"Hannah-of-the-facts, that's what we're going to call you from now on."

She turned her face away from him as her smile widened. He was too easy to like.

"Okay, we have two options," Sean said. "It's too late to visit Dandridge today. We can go straight back to Charlottesville now, but we won't get in until after eleven, and tomorrow we'll have to drive out again to Greensville and we'll lose a lot of the day. Or . . ."

"Or what?"

"Or we can drive to Greensville now, stay overnight, see Dandridge first thing, and then head back to Charlottesville. We should still get back to the Project's office by midmorning and have most of Friday to work. What do you think?"

"I don't mind." Hannah took out her phone to look up hotels. "It makes sense to stay near Greensville overnight. Is there a place you usually stay?"

"Well." He gave her a sidelong look. "Zero pressure. We can stay in a hotel, or whatever, but my mom lives about half an hour outside Greensville. She loves visitors. If I message her now there's a solid chance she'll even make dinner . . . But not if you don't want to, of course."

Hannah didn't want to. She needed to call Laura and the last thing she wanted to do was spend the evening making small talk with a stranger. But there was no polite way to say no to the invitation. "Of course," she said. "That sounds really good."

They pulled up outside Sean's mother's house just before ten o'clock. By then Hannah was tired and hungry and all she wanted was an empty hotel room, a shower, and a room service menu. The house was pretty, a renovated 1940s redbrick with a small but very pretty yard. Everything was beautifully lit, so even in the dark Hannah couldn't miss the mature trees, the manicured lawn, the flowering shrubs.

"So your mom is a gardener."

Sean was getting the bags out of the trunk. "That's all my uncle," he said. "He loves to garden and his place is tiny, so when he gets tired of working over there he comes here and goes nuts. My mom loves the yard but they bicker all the time when he wakes her with the mower or whatever. I think they just like to argue. It reminds them of their childhood, or something." He led the way to the front door and opened it with his own key. The smell of something cooking met them as soon as he opened the door. The hallway was brightly lit. Sean dropped their bags at the bottom of the stairs, then turned and ushered her inside.

"Mom?" he called.

"Kitchen."

They found Abigail Warner sitting at the table in a comfortable, if slightly messy kitchen. She had a glass of red wine in front of her, and an iPad. She was watching an episode of *Queer Eye* and there was a dog, an older-looking golden retriever, asleep at her feet.

"Oh my God. Mom," Sean said, with a glance at the iPad. He leaned in and gave his mother a hug. She pulled him closer and kissed him on his cheek and then his forehead before letting him go.

"What?" she said. "You know I love it." Abigail turned the screen off and smiled up at Hannah. She had curly dark hair to her shoulders and eyes that were the exact same color as her son's. "It's Hannah, right?" Abigail reached behind her and pulled out a walking stick. She maneuvered herself out of her chair and with the help of the stick made her way to Hannah and gave her a one-armed hug. "Welcome. You must be so tired. Grab a seat, and let's get you fed. Please tell me you're not a vegetarian?"

"Nope," said Sean. "She's an omnivore like the rest of us." He'd cuddled the dog—introducing him as Howard the Wonder Dog—and was already grabbing plates from a cupboard and bringing them to the table. On his way past he took Hannah by the shoulder and pushed her gently into a chair. "Sit. You can't help. You don't know where anything is."

"Sean, I just defrosted some stroganoff. You get that out of the oven and bring it to the table. I made fresh rice, and there's bread, and wine, and with that we shall have to do. Next time, give me some notice and I'll get some fish, all right?"

Hannah watched, uncomfortable that she was doing nothing while others did all the work, particularly Sean's mom who clearly had a disability. Sean had never mentioned it. In fact he'd specifically said his mom was well. Was it something that she'd been born with? Abigail was drinking too. Was that a good idea? She walked with a heavy limp and obviously needed the walking stick. Why was Sean letting her do so much in the kitchen? She should be sitting down. And he'd said he only saw her a couple of times a semester. So, what, he left her to fend for herself in the meantime? Unless . . . maybe his dad? There'd been a family photograph on the table in the hall—a photo of a much younger Abigail, a handsome man, and what was presumably baby Sean. Where was this handsome man now?

Sean poured wine for everyone and Abigail served dinner and there was absolute silence for the first minute while everyone got started. The food was rich and filling and welcome after a long and difficult day. Abigail finished her glass of wine and poured another. Sean was drinking too. Hannah took a sip from her own glass and told herself to stop worrying. Abigail was not her responsibility.

"So tell me about your day? What were you two up to that brought you over to Greensville? Visiting the prison?"

Sean shook his head but he had a mouth full of food and couldn't speak.

"Uh . . . we were in Charlotte," Hannah said. "Interviewing a witness. We're visiting a prisoner in the morning." She still felt uncomfortable.

Sean swallowed, gestured with his fork. "The interview was interesting. The witness is a possible alibi for our client, but he ran after the arrest eleven years ago. Got out of town and basically hasn't been seen since. We think that's due to police intimidation, but we're worried the prosecution will use it to make our client look bad."

Abigail made a face. "Well, I can see that. Sounds like it will be a difficult call." She reached out with the wine bottle and topped up everyone's glasses. "Would he make a good witness? How do you think he would do on the stand?"

"I don't know. It's too early to say. And we don't really have time to find out."

"Are you a lawyer, Abigail?" Hannah asked.

"It's Abbie, please. And no, not a lawyer, thank goodness. One in the family is enough." She smiled at Sean.

"She's an office manager for a law firm. That's what she does. She herds lawyers all day. Badgers them. Snipes at them. Until they do her bidding."

"I do not."

"Do too."

That sort of thing went on for a while. Gentle teasing. Inside jokes. They were very easy with each other. Unusually relaxed and comfortable. It wasn't anything like a normal family relationship. More like a friendship. When they finished eating, Hannah stood quickly and insisted on cleaning up. She gathered the plates and started to scrape scraps into the garbage bin, tried to find the dishwasher, and shot a dagger look at Sean when Abigail stood up and started to help. He was looking at his phone and didn't notice. It got awkward quickly. Abigail kept chatting, kept things friendly and light, but she took over the cleaning and made it clear, without saying anything directly, that she didn't want help. Soon Hannah found herself standing uselessly off to the side, holding again her glass of wine, pressed into her hand by Abigail.

"Are you sure I can't help?" Hannah said.

"Everything's done. Not to worry."

"Is there ice cream?" Sean asked. His head was now buried in the freezer.

"There is not," Abbie said. "You ate it all the last time you were here, remember?"

"And you didn't get more? Shame on you."

"Let's go into the living room, catch up before bed."

They went through into the living room, sat, drank wine, and talked. The conversation meandered, from the Innocence Project to the headlines of the day to Abbie's work and back. They talked a little about Sean's father. There'd been a car accident when Sean was ten. Sean's father, David, had been killed. Abigail had suffered severe injuries to her back and right leg.

Hannah found herself staring at Abigail's legs. You couldn't tell that she was injured in any way when she was sitting like this, wearing long pants.

Sometime later Sean disappeared upstairs to look for a textbook he thought he might have left behind. Hannah looked around for her cell phone to check the time—she didn't wear a watch—she'd lost track of the evening but it must be getting very late. Tiredness was pulling at her and she was feeling the effects of the three—four?—glasses of wine she'd had. She should be in bed. But there was something about Abbie Warner. Something about her company. Abbie was like her son. Warm, and easy to like. And Hannah was so tired. Too tired to move.

"Tell me about you, Hannah," Abigail was saying now. "What drew you to the Innocence Project?"

"It's a great opportunity to learn. I want to get practical, hands-on experience. It's harder to get experience like this in Maine, you know? Working on the Project is the kind of thing that might get me noticed when I graduate."

"Interesting." Abbie smiled. "Most students tell you that they're drawn to the Project because of the moral or ethical dimension. They say they want to help people." There was no condemnation in her tone. Just curiosity.

Hannah made a face. "I think that's just naive, really. I mean it's all a bit of a game, at the end of the day. Isn't it?"

"In what way, a game?"

Hannah made an expansive gesture. "The whole thing. Life. Society. Whatever. The Project too. Like, take Robert Parekh. Did you know he was on the cover of *Vanity Fair*?"

"You weren't impressed?"

"I don't know what the point of that is. I mean, was that article about advancing the work of the Project or was it about raising his profile personally? And then there's a whole other issue. Like, the whole article lacked any kind of nuance, any consideration that there might be any other take but Robert Parekh's. Is he really this great hero? Maybe he just likes to look that way. That magazine cover, that article, it's just a puff piece. They're selling a fantasy, right?"

Abbie shook her head. "I can't say that I'm following you on this one. Why would a journalist or the magazine want to sell that fantasy? I could see it happening with a movie star maybe. You know, some A-lister with a powerful publicist. You get them for your cover and you sell copies. But for a lawyer? What's the motivation?"

"I'm not saying complicit, exactly, or at least not consciously so." Hannah put a hand to her forehead, trying to think. She felt like she was losing the thread of her argument. "Like I'm not saying the journalist is lacking integrity, necessarily. I'm just saying that it's about narrative, isn't it? We, I mean people, all of us, we love a story. We want a hero. We want a bad guy. We want a beginning, a middle, and an end. And life is more complicated than that but we love it when we're served up a story and sometimes if we don't get it, we make it for ourselves. We believe only the facts that suit the story we like and we ignore everything else."

"So which is it? Journalists are writing puff pieces or the audience is believing what they want?"

Hannah flushed. "Both. I think that journalists, or really, I suppose I mean opinion writers, they're just giving us what we expect, aren't they? The Robert Parekh story fits the accepted narrative. He's out to save the poor, wrongly convicted prisoner. Parekh therefore must be a good man motivated by a need to do the right thing. There's no room in the narrative for the truth, which might just be that he's an egoist who loves the attention, right?"

Abbie Warner looked at her steadily, and her expression was sad. "It seems like a very hard way to live your life, Hannah. To go through this world so alone, believing in no one. Tied to no one."

"I didn't say that," Hannah said, stung. "I didn't say I didn't believe, or that I wasn't tied."

"Oh?"

"I believe in . . ." She let her voice trail away, suddenly lost for words.

"What? What do you believe in?"

It took her a moment. "I believe we choose our people. That we choose them and we love them and we do everything we can to protect them and keep them safe. And that's it."

"You're talking about family," Abbie said. She considered Hannah, head tilted to one side.

"I guess."

"So why the Project, then?" Abbie asked.

"Sorry?"

"I understand what you've said to me," she said. "What you've explained. I'll tell you that I don't agree with it. As a philosophy, I think it stinks. I think it's a dangerous, self-defeating way to think. If everyone in the world thought the way you did, we'd descend into some sort of anarchic tribalism, wouldn't we? But let's say you really believe everything you've said to me tonight. Why the Project? Why are you there? I'm not sure I buy your work experience thing."

From anyone else the words would have seemed hostile, confrontational, but Abbie gave off a different vibe. Like she wanted a tough, but mutually respectful debate and assumed Hannah would want to give it to her. Still, Hannah was thoroughly thrown. She stared back at the other woman, aware of the flush in her cheeks, feeling that her wineglass was suddenly too heavy. She put it down on the coffee table. "It's complicated," she said.

"I think I'm a pretty smart person," Abbie said. "Why don't you try me?"

"Well, why does Sean work there?"

"Oh, Sean's easy. He's a romantic. He believes that he can save the world. Righting one wrong at a time."

Hannah raised an eyebrow.

"You don't believe me?" Abbie said.

"No, I do. I mean, I could see that about him. I just think . . . I mean, Sean's so smart . . ."

"You think smart people can't be romantic, or idealistic? Sean's the best kind of romantic. He has a romantic's soul and the mind of a pragmatist. He wastes no one's time with fantasies, least of all his own. He sees the world as it really is and then he sets out to make it better."

Hannah studied Abbie. "You make him sound like a saint."

Abbie laughed. "God no, far from that. Just a boy. Just a good and decent boy."

Sean arrived back in the living room just in time to hear the end of Abbie's comment. "Who's a good and decent boy, Mom?" he asked, smiling.

"I was talking about the dog," Abbie said. She leaned forward and rubbed the sleeping retriever behind the ears. "He's the only one who gives me any love in this house."

Sean rolled his eyes and Hannah smiled politely. She was feeling the effects of the wine, but more than that she was feeling as if she had just been very thoroughly smacked down.

"More, Hannah?" Sean asked, gesturing to her glass, which was still a quarter full.

"No, thank you," Hannah said. "I think the day has just caught up with me. Do you mind if I go to bed? I'm exhausted."

Hannah sat on the bed and pulled out her phone. She called Laura's number. It rang for a while before Laura answered.

"Hannah? It's so late."

Hannah glanced at her watch and started guiltily. It was after eleven P.M. "I'm sorry, I lost track of time. I'll let you go, call you tomorrow."

"No, no." Laura yawned. "It's fine. It's just . . . I'm exhausted."

"Of course you are. You've had a hard day."

"Yes. It's always hard without you."

"I know, Mom. I'm sorry. Why don't you tell me what you did to-day, and then you can go to sleep while I stay on the line for a while. That will make it a bit better, right?"

Hannah lay back on the pillow and closed her eyes and listened to her mother tell her about her day spent at home, reading, taking a walk in the garden and a long bath, while Jan cleaned and cooked. She told herself she was glad that Laura was safe and cared for. She told herself that she and her mother had a strong, healthy, loving re-lationship. She told herself a lot of things. And then she slept.

LAURA

DIARY ENTRY #9

Wednesday, November 16, 1994, 1:40 p.m.

I've decided to have the baby. Jenna doesn't understand. I can't really blame her for that. She doesn't know everything that happened and that's made things hard between us. We don't see each other as much anymore. I'm five months pregnant now and I've been tired and sick, but I've been working as much as I can, saving. I know it's not going to be enough money and I'm not raising our baby in a dump. That's why I'm on a bus to Virginia. I should have fought harder for Tom back on the island, but I've realized that it's not too late.

At least I know exactly where I'm going. I still have a book of Tom's that has his name and address printed on the inside cover. The bus I'm on now goes direct to Washington, D.C. When I get to D.C., I have to walk to Farragut West Station (that's only going to take a few minutes) and then I can get another bus on to McLean. From there I'll have to get a cab to the house. I left just before eight this morning, and I should be at the house by seven tonight. Right now, I'm really scared.

I miss my mom. I always felt safe when she was alive. I never realized how much that was worth until it was taken away. I keep thinking about what life was like before she died. I was going through that bratty teenage stage where you realize your perfect parent is actually a human being with flaws just like everyone else and you decide to punish them for it. We were fighting a lot. I was such a bitch, because there was so much she had to deal with and I didn't help with any of it. I just watched her try, and criticized her. But even with the stupid fighting, life was so good when I had my mom. Despite everything, until she died I could still be a kid. I would give anything to be able to go back, to do it all again but do it right this time. I'd show her every day how much I love her, how much I appreciate her.

My mom died on a Monday morning, at ten-fifteen. She'd been sick for a year by then. I was at school. I found out later that the hospice called my dad at seven and told him that she would likely pass soon, that we should come in. He couldn't deal with it, apparently, so he just hung up the phone, didn't go in to see her, didn't tell me about the call. I went to the hospice for a visit after school that day, same as I had every day for the three weeks Mom had been there. The hospice director had to take me into her office to tell me that Mom was dead.

My father refused to get out of bed. I was sixteen years old, and I had to arrange my mother's funeral.

After she was buried we went back to a weird kind of normalcy. I kept going to school. Dad mostly stayed at home. He'd been in and out of work for most of my life. Every time he got fired it was not his fault. His manager had it in for him. The CFO was corrupt. My mom had earned all the money in our house. She stayed sunny and positive and worked really long hours as a supervisor at a pharmaceutical company. But no matter how hard Mom worked, we always seemed to be broke, which pissed me off, and I hated that she was never around when I needed her. I was so clueless. Things happened at our house that never happened at my friends' homes. Debt collectors, repo men showed up so many times that I knew them by name, but I just went to my room and closed the door and pretended it wasn't happening.

Before she died Mom told me that there was an insurance policy. Two hundred and fifty thousand dollars that went straight to my dad after she passed. I had to beg him for pennies. He gave me cash on Mondays and Fridays, just enough to cover basic costs. I did the cooking and the cleaning and I kept on going to school, so it probably seemed to other people that my life hadn't changed that much even though everything was different.

At home everything was really messed up. Dad was worse than ever. Some days he wouldn't get out of bed, others he was full of energy but angry at the world. He had friends over to play poker, people I'd never seen around when Mom was alive. People I didn't want to be around. I started to stay over at Jenna's a lot, until her parents let me know I was overstaying my welcome. A week after my seventeenth birthday Dad sold the car. A couple of days later he started selling the furniture. He refused to answer any questions about where all the insurance money had gone, ranted and raved at me when I tried to push him, but I knew it was gambling. I've never been close to my father, not really, but I think that was when I started to really hate him. Two weeks later we were evicted from the house. He'd somehow managed to re-mortgage it, even though he had no job. He never made a single repayment and then acted like it was a complete shock when the eviction notice came. I knew what had happened. He would have ignored all the bank's letters, all the foreclosure stuff, until it was too late. What's really messed up is that he seemed almost relieved. After he'd ranted about banks and crooks for a few minutes, he dropped the notice on the kitchen table and put his hands in his pockets.

"Well, that's it, I suppose."

I stared at the notice and nodded. I had no idea if we could fight the order or not, but I knew he'd be no help either way. "Will there be anything left? If the house is sold and the bank is paid back?"

"Probably not." He said it like it had nothing to do with him.

"What are we going to do?"

He looked at me kind of absently, like I was someone he barely remem-

bered. "I'm going to stay with friends. It's not a good place for a young woman, so I think you should do the same. Stay with your friends, I mean. But that's up to you, Laura. Your mother and me, we gave you the best start we could. I wish we could have done more . . . I wish I could have done more, but losing your mom, it just about killed me. You're a good girl, and you're all grown up. I know you'll do just fine."

He went upstairs and packed a couple of bags. Then he called a cab. He was gone within an hour of that notice arriving and he didn't give me a dollar before he walked out the door. I went to Jenna's house, for a little while. Then I got myself a job and since then I've been on my own. When Jenna went to Northeastern for college, I followed her there. I never heard from my father again.

So that's why I can't call on my father for help. I have no idea where he is and even if I could find him, he would be useless in every way. The only person who can help me is me.

Hannah

ELEVEN

Hannah woke at five A.M. with a headache and a dry mouth. She climbed out of bed and padded downstairs in search of a glass of water. Howard the golden retriever lifted his head and she knelt to pat him.

"Good old boy, Howie," she said quietly. She filled a glass from the sink and drank, then filled it again and silently retreated to the bedroom. Howard got to his feet and followed her up the stairs and then into the bedroom.

"Really?" she whispered. He looked at her seriously, then settled down comfortably on the carpet and closed his eyes. Hannah sighed. "Fine." She got her laptop and sat on the floor beside him. There would be no more sleep tonight anyway, she might as well get some work done. She clicked and scrolled and when she could, she rested her left hand on Howie's soft fur, finding it surprisingly comforting.

She thought about Neil Prosper and Robert Parekh. If Parekh brought his monster charm to Charlotte, applied it to Neil Prosper, reassured him and gave him confidence, would Prosper change his mind about testifying? Something had kept him away all these years. Sean's theory about Jerome Pierce might be correct. She could email Pierce right now, let him know exactly where Prosper was. If Pierce was the intimidating type maybe he would do what was necessary . . . Hannah shifted uncomfortably and pushed her hand deeper into Howard's fur. She looked down at the dog.

"It doesn't feel right, does it, Howie?" she said.

She opened her browser, went to a site that allowed her to send untraceable, anonymous text messages, and prepared one, not to Pierce, but to Sophia Prosper. The dynamic between Neil Prosper and his sister was a hard one to read. On the one hand, they were clearly in touch, which suggested that they were close. And Sophia had lied for him, had tried to put them off searching for him. But was that to protect Neil, or was it to protect her family from the infamy of a connection to a murder trial? Camila had said she'd seen fear in Sophia, when Camila had pressed her. Assuming she'd been right about that, was it fear for Neil, or was it about self-preservation? Maybe it didn't matter.

Neil is talking to Dandridge's lawyers. You better stop him before I do.

Hannah hesitated, then sent the message.

Shit.

IT WAS NEARLY EIGHT A.M. BEFORE SHE HEARD MOVEMENT IN THE kitchen. She showered quickly and dressed and made her way downstairs. Morning in the Warner household was all business. She saw Abbie only briefly—the older woman had already showered and changed by the time Hannah came down—and she kissed Hannah on the cheek and said goodbye as she passed through the kitchen on the way out of the door to work. Sean made coffee, filled two travel mugs, and handed her a croissant he'd defrosted in the microwave. A minute later they were heading outside for the car.

"Sorry," Sean said. "I know that was a bit rushed. I don't want to lose time."

"No, it's fine," Hannah said. They walked to the car and Sean beeped the locks open. They dumped their bags in the trunk and climbed in.

"Nervous?" Sean asked.

"Why would I be?" She was so filled with nervous tension that she felt like a firework about to go off. It was all so much harder because she had to hide it, had to appear cool and calm and professional and together. But soon she'd be sitting across from the man who'd murdered her father and raped her mother and she'd have to pretend to be on his side.

"Most people are, their first time visiting a prisoner. But maybe you've done this before, in Maine?"

Hannah shook her head. "Not exactly." She'd never set foot inside a prison in her life. She sipped her coffee. "Do you visit prisoners a lot?"

"I don't know," Sean said, thinking. "I suppose. Last year, maybe ten, twelve times?"

"By yourself?"

"Sometimes. I came with Rob the first time, Jim Lehane the second. Often alone. It does depend on the prisoner. I haven't met Michael before, of course, but I know someone comes up to see him as often as possible."

Hannah spoke without thinking. "You call him Michael," she said. "I noticed that Professor Marshall does too. Does that mean . . . do you like him?" Sean gave her one of his sideways looks.

"It's not about liking him. I believe that he's innocent and does not belong in prison. Calling him by his first name—that's something we do with all our clients. You know, prison is dehumanizing. We try to build a relationship."

Hannah shook her head.

"What?"

"Nothing."

"What, Hannah?"

God, she was being stupid. Giving too much away. But it was so hard. He was such a smart, decent, likable guy. And yet . . .

"I guess I'm just surprised at how convinced everyone seems to be about Dandridge's innocence. Everyone is just completely onboard. It's a cause, not a case."

"Well, I—"

"This name thing is a symptom of the problem. Don't you think it's better to keep some professional distance? He's a client, he's not your buddy."

"I don't see that—"

"If you close your mind to every other possibility except innocence, you risk missing things. You stop seeing evidence that contradicts the narrative you have built up in your own head. That's not good."

"Okay, okay," Sean said mildly. "I agree. I can see the benefits of keeping an open mind to other arguments. We don't want to be sandbagged at trial."

"Right," Hannah said, subsiding.

Sean glanced at her. "Are you sure you're not nervous? It's all right if you are. Visiting a prison is intimidating at the best of times. Visiting someone like Dandridge, where there's so much on the line, is even more pressure. And look, he might not be . . . with the case coming up next week, I'm sure he's under a lot of stress. He might not be easy to be around. If things get difficult, just hang in there."

Hannah frowned. "What do you mean, difficult?"

"Just that . . . sometimes prisoners get a bit argumentative. He might press us on exactly where we are with the case. And we won't be able to answer everything. Everyone always wants certainty. The closer we get to trial the more afraid they get. Which is natural. But if they're our client, if they've come to the Project, they've probably already been badly disappointed by a defense attorney."

"Right."

He shot her another quick glance. "It's not that they don't trust *us*. I mean, they're always very grateful that we've taken their case and we work with them for months and years and we visit a lot so we build up a relationship. But when it comes to this period right before a trial, the client is always staring down the barrel of possible freedom, which is frightening in itself for most of them. Often they have no life or relationships left outside of prison, or they're looking at life imprisonment or the death sentence. And so everything starts to fray."

"Right," Hannah said again. If Dandridge was found guilty again, the worst he was looking at was life in prison. It was eight years since anyone had been sentenced to death in Virginia.

"You okay?" Sean asked.

"Yes, fine."

"Are you sure?" He looked at her more closely. "Did you get any sleep? How's your mom doing? You know, I meant what I said, don't let Rob run you ragged. If you need to see her, you need to see her. Some things are more important."

"I'm fine, Sean, honestly. I didn't sleep much because I was doing some research, that's all."

"Research on what?"

"On Jerome Pierce. The sheriff. You seemed to think that Prosper might be afraid of him. I guess I wanted to learn more about the guy." It was true that she'd been doing a little research, though she was, of course, lying about her motivation. The question in Hannah's mind was whether Pierce, like her, knew more about Dandridge than was admissible in court. Was he someone she could approach? Could he be an ally?

"Yes. Don't forget that he beat a confession out of Dandridge. He was definitely motivated. Three weeks had gone by with no arrest and no suspect. The local papers were full of it. Sarah Fitzhugh—well, she was this nice young mom. And the fact that she was raped and murdered in her own home while her kids were there. God. Everyone was scared and everyone wanted something done."

"So you're completely convinced that Pierce set up Dandridge?" Hannah asked quietly. "You don't think there's any chance at all that he killed Sarah?" She thought she knew what Sean was going to say, but he surprised her.

He frowned. "I don't know. I can't say that I absolutely one hundred percent believe that Dandridge is innocent. What I believe is that there is no evidence that he did it. So either he didn't do it and was set up by a police force that needed a scapegoat—and Lord knows we've seen that before—or he did do it and somehow the police found out but by some magical method they can't share it with any of the rest of us. Right now I personally think it's much more likely that he didn't do it and that's he's entirely innocent."

"Okay."

There was a silence for a moment before Sean broke it.

"So what did you find out?"

"Sorry?"

"About Jerome Pierce. Your research," Sean said.

"Oh," Hannah let out a shaky laugh. "Nothing. Social media stuff. Jerome Pierce, former high school football player. Married to Mindy Rawlings, former high school cheerleader. They had three children, all of whom are grown up now. Jerome is a member of a bowling league. Mindy has a popular hair salon. They go to church on Sunday. Just lovely, upstanding people. At least . . . at first glance."

Sean gave her a half-smile of sympathy. "Well, I guess we'll just have to try to unpick that a bit, won't we?"

"Right."

Sean kept talking, but Hannah couldn't find the words to maintain her side of the conversation and eventually they lapsed into silence. She stared out of the window and watched the countryside fly by, bringing her closer and closer to the Greensville prison and her meeting with the man who had everyone fooled.

LAURA

DIARY ENTRY #10

Wednesday, November 16, 1994, 10:30 p.m.

It's getting dark when the taxi pulls up outside Tom's family home. I can't see the house from the road. There's a six-foot-high wall made from cut limestone, and a gated entrance. Through the gate I can see a driveway winding its way around ornamental trees. The gate is closed. I think about walking away then and there, but I've come too far, I'm too desperate and angry and determined to let my fear stop me now. Still, when I step out of the car my legs feel weak. The taxi pulls away as I press the intercom button and I wish I could call it back. The intercom has a camera built in—you can see the lens. The sun has dipped below the horizon and it's almost dark, but a security light comes on as I wait, and I'm sure that whoever is in the house can see me clearly.

"Can I help you?" It's a woman's voice. Clipped. No southern drawl here. I take a breath.

"My name is Laura Rokeby. I'd like to speak to Mr. and Mrs. Spencer, please." I don't know who I'm talking to. If it's a housekeeper she might ask me if I have an appointment or what my business is, and if she does I'm planning on saying that I'm a friend of Tom's and I have something important to discuss. It might be Tom's mother. For all I know she might

already be calling the police. There's silence for a long, long time. Too long. Then there's a buzz and the gate swings open.

Just walking the driveway takes ten minutes. The house is enormous. I don't take much of it in. I concentrate on putting one foot in front of the other, on getting where I'm going. There are steps up to the front door and I count them as I climb. She opens the door before I have a chance to ring the bell or knock or anything. She's very beautiful, blond, patrician look-ing, elegantly dressed in loose tailored pants with a high waist and a silk blouse. She's clearly not the housekeeper. She looks me up and down and I feel like she has the kind of laser focus that can see right through me. She doesn't hesitate.

"Laura, won't you follow me, please?"

She waits until I've stepped inside before closing the front door, and then she leads the way across an enormous marble-floored hall. The click of her high heels echo across the room. I'm wearing hiking boots, jeans, a jacket over a heavy sweater. I feel like a peasant. I follow her into the most beautiful library I've ever seen. It's a full two stories, with a first-floor mezzanine so that you can reach the books. The bookcases are made out of a dark, polished wood. I think about the library in the island house. I'd loved it so much but compared to this place it would be a shack. There's a fire burning in the grate and two armchairs are set up for conversation, facing the fire. There's a glass of wine sitting on a table beside one chair. She takes that chair, points me to the other. She sips her wine and doesn't offer me anything to drink.

"I am Antonia Spencer," she says. "How may I help you, Laura?"

Her face is expressionless, her voice very cool. But I know the story that Michael has told her and I don't blame her for hating me. I'm sur-prised that I haven't had to beg to be allowed into her home.

"I knew Tom. We met this summer. We were together for five weeks. I know that sounds like very little time, but we fell in love. We were very happy. Michael Dandridge told you a bunch of lies about me. None of what

he told you was true. I'm sorry, I'm so sorry to tell you this, but the truth is that Michael murdered Tom. He admitted that to me. You have no reason to trust me, but if you give me ten minutes of your time, I'll tell you everything."

She looks at me. Her lips are tight. She was pale to begin with—she has the kind of skin that never sees the sun—but she's paler now. It's easier for me, probably, that Tom's dad isn't here, but I wish for her sake that he was. I can't imagine what it must be like to hear from a stranger that your only son has been murdered by someone you know and trust. She gets up and refills her wineglass from a bottle that is tucked away behind the bar. She returns to her chair, sips, and places her glass on the table. She folds her hands on her lap.

"Tell me," she says.

And I do. I tell her everything. I tell her about the little things and the big things. About how and why I fell in love, why I think Tom fell for me. The things we had in common—our love of books, our loneliness. I am too honest, maybe, but I am sure that only absolute truth will help me here. I cry. I haven't cried for so long but now it's hard to stop. I tell her about Tom and Michael fighting, and about the terrible night when he catches me on the boat. I tell her about his confession and his threats. I don't say anything about the baby. I'm not ready.

By the time I have finished she has filled and emptied her glass three times. Still she has offered me nothing. No water, no wine, no words of comfort. The expression on her face has barely changed while I have been speaking. There is silence. I fish a tissue from my pocket and wipe my face, try to pull myself together. Still there is silence. Eventually, in despera-tion, I say—"Is Tom's father here?"

"Stand up," she says to me.

The words feel like a slap and I flinch.

"Sorry?"

"I said, stand up."

I stand and she crosses over to me and I want to run away, but I hold my ground. She unzips my jacket, opens it wide and looks down at my round belly. After a minute she lets my jacket drop. She walks toward the desk at the far end of the room and I zip my jacket back up, wrap my arms around myself protectively. I start to shiver, despite the heat from the fire. She takes a checkbook from the desk, uncaps a pen, and looks at me.

"How much?" she says.

"What?"

"How much to be rid of you?"

She can't have understood me. I haven't explained properly. I'm too emotional, too messy. I try again. "Michael—" She cuts across me.

"I don't wish to discuss it further. I am, in fact, willing to pay you to ensure that this story is not told again, anywhere, at any time, to any person. Do you understand what I am saying to you, Laura? I will pay you, and you will be required to sign a nondisclosure agreement. If you breach that agreement, the consequences will be terrible."

I stand there for what must be minutes. I think that she doesn't believe me, that I need to try again. I try, for the thousandth time, to think of any proof I can lay before her to show her that Michael has lied. Surely if I can show proof of even a small lie, she will start to believe me? But then, as I look at the cool, remote expression on her face, I think of everything Tom ever told me about her (which was so, so little—she'd barely been in his life) and I begin to understand. She doesn't care. Not if Tom killed himself, not if he was murdered. She doesn't want a public scandal. Maybe she doesn't want conflict with the Dandridge family. I don't know what their business or social dealings might be. What I know for sure is that she doesn't want me and she doesn't want anything to do with Tom's baby.

I feel like I'm going to vomit, my vision darkens at the edges and I think I am going to fall. The feeling passes, and I am still standing. I think about Michael and what he said he would do to me. I think about my baby. I think about Tom. And then, very deliberately and very carefully, I sit back down on the armchair. And I tell her I want two million dollars. That *will pay for a home in a safe place, far from here. It will pay for health in-surance, and schools and music lessons and sports, and college too, when the time comes.*

"About the nondisclosure agreement," I say. "The agreement must be two-way. You must never speak to anyone about what we talked about to-night. Especially Michael Dandridge." I look her right in the eye. "If you do, the consequences for you must be terrible."

She agrees. And she adds a requirement of her own—that I will sign away any possible right to claim on Tom's estate, on the family trust. She makes me wait for an hour while she talks to her lawyer. He faxes her an agreement, we both sign. She makes me a copy of the agreement and she writes me a check. I walk away down the drive and call a cab from the gate. I go to a nice hotel and pay two hundred dollars for a room. They want a credit card number too, it's policy. I don't have a credit card. I'm so tired that I start to cry and the woman checking me in (she's already noticed my belly, I saw the glance) takes pity on me. I give her another hundred dollars, a deposit for incidentals, and she takes me to my room herself.

So here I am. I've ordered room service (a burger and fries, ice cream—comfort food) and it should be here soon. I'm wearing my pajamas and I'm wrapped in a soft hotel robe. Tomorrow morning I'll go straight to the bank and deposit that check. I guess it might take a few days to clear. That's okay. I already have my return ticket to Boston. I can get on the bus and tomor-row night I'll be back at my shitty apartment. I won't be there for long.

I think . . . I think everything's going to be okay. I'm going to leave all of this behind me. I'm going to take the money and build a life and I'm going to forget about Michael Dandridge and my father and everything bad that has ever happened. God help me, I'll even forget about Tom if it means I'll be a better person. I have to be better, for my baby. Everything I do from here on, everything, is going to be about being a good mother. My whole life will be about my child.

I'm finished with this diary. I'm done.

Hannah

TWELVE

The meeting room in Greensville Correctional Prison was window-less, deep inside a maze of a building, with grubby walls and furniture screwed to the floor. Almost exactly as Hannah had expected it to be, from a hundred movies and a hundred TV shows, actually, but no amount of television could have prepared her for the impact of being there. The smell of body odor, old linoleum, and disinfectant. The claustrophobia from the shitty air and from being so far underground. The simple intimidation of the security procedures—the guards had been so humorless, so filled with latent hostility. And on top of that she was still so much more nervous than she had expected to be. Somehow, with all her planning, she had never imagined that there would be a moment where she would be face-to-face with him.

"You okay?" Sean asked.

"Fine," she said. But she wasn't. She had to work hard to keep her turmoil from showing. "Will it take much longer?"

Sean shrugged. "Sometimes it's ten minutes, sometimes half an hour. There's nothing we can do but wait."

Fifteen minutes passed before they heard movement in the corridor, the door opened, and Michael Dandridge was shown into the room. He looked nothing at all like his mug shot, which was the only photograph Hannah had ever seen of him. The mug shot had been in black and white, and showed a thirty-five-year-old Dandridge, too thin, with a shaved head and a look of utter confusion in his eyes. Now he was forty-six years old. His head was shaved even tighter— he would have been largely bald if he hadn't shaved—and he'd put on some weight. He was taller than she'd imagined from the description in the diary. He wore glasses, little steel-rimmed glasses that might have given him the look of a college professor, if it wasn't for the orange prison jumpsuit. His wrists were in handcuffs behind his back as he entered but the guard removed them before leaving, and Dandridge shook Sean's hand, then turned and offered a hand to Hannah. She hesitated, barely a moment, but perhaps it had been noticeable, and then she found herself shaking his hand. She wanted to vomit. She wanted to lash out. For the first time in her life she found herself wishing for a weapon. A gun. A knife. She could use it too. She would be capable of it. Here was pure destruction. A psychopath who had killed her father, destroyed her mother, and even now was attaching himself like a leech to good people.

"Hello," he said. He had blue eyes, dark lashes, and an almost feminine mouth. She couldn't stop cataloguing his features, as if she could find the answers to all of her questions in his face. How was it possible that he should look so normal?

"I'm Sean." Sean paused and waited for Hannah to introduce herself. When she didn't, he continued. "This is Hannah. We've both been assigned to work on your case."

"It's good to meet you both," Dandridge said. "Thank you for your work." He took a seat on one side of the table and they sat opposite him. He rested both arms on the table and leaned forward. "Where's Rob? I haven't seen him in a while."

"He's tied up," Sean said. "With the hearing next week, he's been working on motions and preparing arguments. He wants to be here, but he also wants to do his best work for you."

"I get that," Dandridge said. "But I need to prepare too. I'm going to be in court next week, with Pierce and Engle and all of the rest of them out to get me. To get that needle in my arm." He tapped at his inner right elbow with two fingers of his left hand. The movement was sudden and unexpected and despite herself, Hannah flinched. Dandridge's eyes went to her briefly before returning to Sean. "I need to talk to Rob. Get my head straight before it all kicks off."

"I know," Sean said. "Rob knows that too. He's going to try to get down tomorrow, but worst case he's booked a video meeting. And you know we'll have at least an hour with you in Yorktown, pretrial."

Dandridge grumbled. "That video conferencing tech is a heap of shit. It works maybe a third of the time, if you're lucky. The rest of the time you get hooked up to the wrong meeting, or the audio goes out. And I don't trust the prison not to listen in, do you?"

Sean grimaced. "Maybe not."

"And fucking Yorktown. The last time I was there they broke my ribs. They gave me internal bleeding. I was lucky not to lose my goddamn liver. Going back there is going to make my PTSD worse, you know that? I don't know why Rob didn't get a change of venue. I mean, given everything . . . You know, even the feds saw that I was set up. How does it make sense to send me back to the same prosecutor and the same court system that sent me down in the first place? You tell me that."

There was no way to answer that question.

"We found Neil Prosper," Hannah said. She wanted to hurt him, even if it was only in some small way.

"Well, goddamn. You found Neil?"

"He changed his name and moved to North Carolina two days after you were arrested," Hannah said. "He hasn't been willing to talk to us. He won't answer our questions. He hasn't backed up your alibi."

Dandridge's expression darkened and he shook his head. "God-damnit. Goddamn. Pierce got to him. You can take that to the bank."

"Rob is thinking about subpoenaing him," Sean said.

Dandridge shook his head. "There's no point. Neil's not going to go up against Pierce for me. We never had that kind of friend-ship, not even back in the day. And now? After eleven years? I don't think so."

"We should at least try . . ." But Dandridge just kept shaking his head darkly and Sean let his voice trail off. There was silence for an uncomfortable moment.

"Well," Dandridge said in the end. "What else have you got for me?"

Sean shifted in his seat again. "Most of the arguments in court will be about pulling apart the old evidence that they used to convict you. It's really about pointing out to the court—to a new judge who will be very aware of the media glare—just how weak and unreliable that evidence is. And we'll be putting you on the stand to talk about the beating Pierce gave you, that will be new."

"What he did was beat me to a pulp. I was pissing blood for a month afterward. And I went cold turkey in their jail. No support. It's a goddamn miracle I didn't die." His expression darkened. "Maybe that's what they wanted. Wouldn't that have wrapped things up nice and neat? Junkie rapist dies in prison. So sad."

If she could have, Hannah would have curled her lip. So much for Angie Conroy's belief that Dandridge and Prosper didn't use heavy drugs. No one went cold turkey from weed and the occasional E tab.

"So we don't have photos to prove your injuries, unfortunately, but we do have the medical report from when you were transferred to Sussex I State Prison. That shows the fractured ribs beginning to heal, and at least records that you reported the other internal in-juries."

Dandridge leaned back again in his chair but he let his right arm rest against the table. He had a habit of doing that. Resting his right arm on the table, palm up, then cupping his left palm over the inside of his right elbow as if to protect it. "What I don't get is why we don't have anyone else ready to go on the record about how he beat them. There's no way I was the only one. Pierce knew what he was doing. His deputies didn't even blink when he hit me the first time."

"We're still working on that," Sean said. "There were two old formal complaints on the record apart from yours, but one of the complainants is dead and the other we're still trying to find."

The conversation continued, with Sean trying to sound upbeat and Dandridge complaining that they should be doing more. That any PI worth his salt would have found the other complainant now and if the Project was willing to spend some money they would get better results. One small part of Hannah's brain was still listening to that conversation, still cataloguing it. But the other part of her brain, the larger part, was utterly frozen. Dandridge had taken to opening and closing his right hand, like someone getting ready for a blood test, or a junkie preparing to find a vein. And every time he opened his right hand, she could see a thick, silvery scar, running diagonally across his palm.

"What happened to your hand?"

"What?" Dandridge said.

"Your hand. How did you get that scar?" Hannah's mouth was bone dry.

He looked confused for a second, then shrugged. "I was a kid. I was five. I think I put my hand through a window, but I don't really remember." He looked irritated. There was a moment's silence.

"Uh . . . can we talk again about Jerome Pierce and the interrogation?" Sean said. "Can you take me through who was in the room, before and after the beating? I'd like to know—"

"They fired the nanny," Hannah blurted out.

Dandridge stared at her. "What did you say?"

"I didn't . . . I didn't mean . . ." Hannah shook her head. She tried to push her chair back, but it was fixed to the floor. Her heart was racing painfully now, and her lungs felt tight. She couldn't take a deep breath.

"How did you know about my nanny?" Dandridge said. He was looking back and forth between Hannah and Sean, clearly expecting some sort of explanation.

"I didn't . . . I just assumed . . ." It was no good. Hannah stood up. "I have to go, I'm sorry."

Sean looked at her, openmouthed.

"I'm sorry," she said again, but insistent.

"If we call the guard, that's it. Mike will have to go back to his cell," Sean said.

"I think I'm going to be sick."

"That's all right," Dandridge said. "If Hannah's not well, she's not well." But he was staring at her, really taking her in. Shit. Hannah turned away, turned her back on him. Dandridge spoke to her one more time as the guard escorted them from the room. "Come back and visit any time, Hannah," he said. "Any time."

And then they were walking again down those endless gray corridors while Hannah blinked furiously against tears of confusion and anger, feeling sicker and sicker and then finally, finally, there was the door to the outside and she burst through it, took a few steps, and vomited on the gravel. Sean followed her out. She straightened and wiped her mouth. This made no sense. It was Tom who'd cut his hand. Not Michael Dandridge. Not Mike.

"Are you all right?" Sean sounded confused, concerned.

"Fine. I'm fine." But she still felt so sick. And hot. And her hands wouldn't stop shaking. He put a hand on her shoulder, turned her to face him.

"What's going on with you, Hannah? What was all that about his hand?"

Hannah shook her head. "I'm so sorry. I . . . it was nonsense. I just suddenly felt so dizzy in there. I don't know what happened. I think I'm sick. Maybe I ate something."

He knew she was lying. "Talk to me, Hannah. Whatever it is. Maybe I can help."

She very, very nearly did. For a moment she teetered on the edge of disaster, and then she pulled herself back. "I'm so sorry. I feel like an idiot. It was just . . . I think I just panicked in there. I was overwhelmed. A bit claustrophobic. I feel terrible that I ended the meeting early. I'm so sorry, Sean."

He didn't believe her. She could see it in his eyes. Oh, he was kind and he was solicitous, but they drove back to Charlottesville in near silence. They arrived just after one P.M. and she told him she needed an hour at home, to eat and shower and change before going into the office. He insisted on walking her to her door where they said a stilted goodbye. Hannah let herself into her apartment. She went straight to her bedside table and took out Laura's diary, that scrappy little notebook that meant so much. She flipped quickly through the pages until she found the entry from July, the one where her mother and Tom had kissed for the first time, the one where Laura had reached out and traced a thick silvery scar across the palm of Tom's right hand. Hannah knew every word of the diary by heart, but she had to see it in front of her, to see the words in ink on paper. She knew, for sure, that she had not made an error, that the words would be exactly as she remembered them, but until she saw them some small part of her could still hope.

She found the entry and let out an involuntary moan. It was all there. Undeniable. Hannah found her phone and dialed her mother's number. She let it ring and pressed her phone hard to her ear when it was answered.

"Mom," she said. There was no sound. "Mom?" she said again.

"Hannah? Is that you? When are you coming home?" Laura's voice was querulous, and thick with alcohol. Hannah put one shaking hand to her mouth. She tried to speak, and couldn't. And through the phone she heard the sound of something falling, clattering hard against the floor, and then soft weeping. Hannah pulled the phone away from her ear as if it had burned her. She stared at it for a moment, then switched it off and pushed it so hard across the bed that it fell onto the ground. She climbed fully clothed under the covers and curled up into a ball, pulling the duvet up under her chin and closing her eyes tightly against the pain.

Hannah

THIRTEEN

Hannah was still curled under her blankets an hour later when the apartment buzzer sounded. She climbed out of bed, feeling bruised and delicate, her skin aching as if she had the flu coming on. She pressed the button and heard Camila's voice.

"It's me. I have coffee. Can I come up?"

Hannah pressed the button again and sat back on the apartment bed and waited for the knock to come on the door. When Camila arrived she had a smile on her face, two coffee cups in one hand, a paper bag in the other.

"I came to see how you were doing. Sean told me you had a tough time at Greensville. I totally get it. I was completely weirded out myself the first few times I went. Are you hungry? I wasn't sure if you'd want this . . ." She waved the bag in the air. "How are you feeling?"

"Better," Hannah said. "Come in."

Camila went to the kitchenette, opened cupboard doors until she found plates. "I brought bagels. Do you feel well enough to eat?"

They sat at the little table. Hannah picked at her bagel while Camila talked about her latest family drama—one of her sisters had more boyfriends than their mother approved of and it was causing fireworks at home. Hannah let the monologue flow over her. This was what Camila did. She distracted you with chitchat, but her own clever brain never really stopped watching and analyzing.

"So Sean thinks you might have had a panic attack."

"Maybe," Hannah said slowly. "I don't know. It definitely threw me off balance. The prison. The pressure. The whole environment."

Camila nodded. "How do you feel now? If you're feeling better, want to walk with me to the office? If you're not up to it, that's okay. But if you are, I figured it would be nice to go in together."

They walked along in afternoon sunshine as other students streamed around them, going to class or the gym or coffee with friends. The normalcy of it was jarring. Hannah tried to tell herself that the scar meant nothing, changed nothing. It was just a coincidence, that was all. Maybe both men had had similar scars. That could happen. It didn't work. Nothing worked. A crack had opened in her mind and now other thoughts were seeping through. Questions she'd pushed aside over the years were now demanding her attention. She needed answers. She should make her excuses now, go back to Maine, talk to her mother. But could she be sure that Laura would tell her the truth?

"You know what's weird?" Camila asked, in her most conversational tone. "I filed some motions last week in a few different cases, just preliminary stuff, you know. Anyway, after the screwup with the Dandridge court filings I went and checked all of mine. Like I said, I figured, if the system glitched with Dandridge, no reason it wouldn't glitch with everything else, right? But guess what I found?"

"What?" Hannah said, dutifully. Maybe it was Dandridge she needed to talk to. The thought was frightening. Could she do that? Go back into the prison and confront him?

"Nothing! Everything's perfect. Nothing misfiled. All the document numbers line up perfectly."

"That's great." Hannah wasn't listening to Camila. She was thinking about how she could approach a conversation with Dandridge. How she could use the secrets she held to provoke him, to get to the truth.

"Mmm. It's good news for me, sure, but it's not great news for the Project, is it?"

"No?"

"Well, I think it's pretty clear that what happened with Dandridge was sabotage, right? It wasn't a computer glitch. Someone deliberately screwed with our files." That finally got Hannah's full attention.

"You think Pierce and his cronies hacked into our system?"

"Either that or it was an inside job." The words were delivered so lightly, so delicately, that it was almost possible to miss their intention. They hung in the air between the two women as they walked down the busy sidewalk, and Hannah, working hard to keep a cool facade, tried to figure out how best to respond. She wasn't capable of dealing with Camila this morning. She was far too distracted and conscious all the time of the looming deadline. It was now Friday, and the case was before the court on Monday. They were almost out of time.

Camila stopped short in the middle of the sidewalk. "Wait a minute." She put a hand on Hannah's arm. "Isn't that Hazel? Just over there?" She pointed to the other side of the road and waved her free hand high in the air. "Hazel! Hey, Hazel."

On the other side of the street Hazel Ellison, hat pulled low over her curls, cast a quick glance over her shoulder in their direction and then hurried in the other direction. Surprise froze Camila in place, then she exclaimed under her breath, tightened her grip on Hannah's arm, and tugged her across the road.

"Hazel," Camila called again, hurrying her steps. Hazel finally slowed, defeated, and turned to face them.

"Camila." Hazel's voice and face were tight. Her eyes flicked to Hannah's face, but showed no signs of recognition.

"You're the last person I expected to see today," Camila said, smiling tightly. "I thought you'd be in New York by now. Getting all set up for your big interview."

Hazel drew in a breath, as if she had just been slapped. "So it was you then? You were the one who set me up? Man, you're a good actor, Camila. I really thought you were pissed I was leaving."

Camila stood there, brow furrowed, looking utterly mystified.

"Don't give me that innocent thing." But Hazel looked unsure, and her eyes searched Camila's face, looking for confirmation of her suspicions.

"Hazel, I have no earthly idea of what you're talking about," Camila said.

Hazel blinked back tears of anger and disappointment. "There was no interview," she said. "I went to New York. The woman who was supposed to be interviewing me had never heard of me. I asked to speak to Gabe, the partner I'd worked with in the summer. He came down to see me. He had no idea what I was talking about. There never was any interview. Somebody played a hilarious, hilarious joke."

Camila drew in a horrified breath. "Oh my God," she said.

"It was awful," Hazel said. "I could see that Gabe thought I had . . . I don't know. Made it up somehow. That I was delusional, or hoping to . . . I don't know. I got out of there as fast as I could, but the story is already everywhere."

"I'm so, so sorry," Camila said. "Are you going to speak with Rob? Ask to come back on?"

Hazel shook her head, lifted her chin. "No point. He was so pissed at me and I can't blame him. I'm not going to humiliate myself." She wiped her eyes with the back of one hand. She hesitated. "It wasn't you, Camila? You didn't do this?"

"No. No way. I was really upset when you said you were leaving. And I know we haven't always been close, but I wouldn't do that to you, or to anyone."

"No. No, of course, you wouldn't. Sorry. I just keep thinking, who did I piss off this much, you know? Who hated me enough to do this? I mean, I thought maybe Rachel, in the office, but . . ."

"She wouldn't have the guts," Camila said quietly.

"Yeah." Hazel fished a Kleenex out of her pocket and blew her nose. "Look, I have to go. I'll see you around. And sorry. For what I said before." She hurried away, and Camila and Hannah stood and watched her go.

"Shit," Camila said quietly. "Poor Hazel. She was so embarrassed when she was the only one not to get an offer at the end of the summer. There was a rumor she'd been involved with that partner, Gabe, and it ended badly. You know stories like that are just so dangerous in law. Everyone knows everyone. People won't hire you in case you're trouble. So she had that following her around. And now she has *this*."

Hannah swallowed. "But she's rich, right? Didn't you say that, at the bar? Her family will look after her."

Camila flushed. "I was being a bitch, because I was angry. Hazel's parents are divorced. She lives with her mother. I don't even know if she's in touch with her dad."

"Oh," Hannah said.

"Yeah." Camila didn't move. "Funny how she thought it might have been Rachel though, right? I mean, yes, Rachel's jealous and she'd love to have taken Hazel's spot on the team. But I can't see it.

Rachel would never have the balls to pull it off. And Rachel didn't get Hazel's spot. You did."

Hannah gave her a look that said *back off,* and started walking on toward the office. Camila followed.

"So you agree?" Camila asked.

"What?"

"That it wasn't Rachel."

"I really don't know Rachel that well, but she doesn't seem like the type."

"No. No she doesn't. You might be, though."

Hannah stopped walking. "Excuse me?"

"I think you heard me. You're the kind of person who takes 'bold action.'" Camila drew air quotes for the last two words. "Isn't that what Rob said when he brought you on? That's what he said to me and Sean. That you were a doer. That you weren't afraid to be direct."

"What exactly are you accusing me of, Camila?"

"I'm not accusing you of anything. I'm asking you—did you fake a job offer to Hazel to get her off the team so there was room for you? And also—did you fuck with our filings? You came from out of nowhere, didn't you . . . with this transfer from Maine right into the heart of our team. So, who are you, Hannah?"

Hannah's fighting instinct finally kicked in. She stared the other girl down. "You've got to be kidding me. What is this about, really, Camila? Are you pissed that Parekh wanted me to chase down Prosper with Sean, instead of you? Because if that's your problem, I suggest you take it up with him, instead of making crazy swipes at me. I didn't have anything to do with Hazel's job offer, real or not. I've said hello to her, and bought her a coffee. That's the extent of our relationship."

Camila opened her mouth to stay something, but Hannah held

up a hand. "No," she said. "You don't get to talk right now. I don't know enough about Hazel to screw with her life so successfully, and I have no possible reason to do it. I'm here to volunteer, just like you. And yes, someone tried to embarrass her but what makes you think it has anything to do with the Project? It seems to me like someone out there doesn't like Hazel very much. What they did to her was personal. Designed to humiliate. I don't think it has anything to do with the Project at all. And as for the filings." Hannah made a scoffing noise. "Are you kidding me? You think I have the skills to get into the computer system and mess with a bunch of motions at the same time that they are being carefully edited by Jim . . . oh, and all while logged in under my student ID of course, and not get caught? Jesus, Camila. Get a grip."

Camila's expression was blank, giving nothing away.

"And for God's sake, why? If you honestly think there's a chance I did this, you must have a theory as to why?"

For the first time, doubt showed in Camila's eyes. "That's the one thing I can't figure out."

"WELL, HERE WE ARE," ROB PAREKH SAID. HE WAS IN HIS USUAL space, sitting at the top of the room on the edge of his desk. "All of our written motions are filed. Our expert witnesses are lined up. Today is about going through our pleadings and making sure every motion, every exhibit is in order and in the right place."

Hannah was standing on one side of the room, Camila on the other. They hadn't spoken for the rest of the walk into the office. Hannah had half-expected Camila to burst into loud accusations as soon as they reached the Project office but she'd said nothing. She couldn't be confident enough yet in her theories to want to share them with anyone else. Still, Hannah was now very aware that she was operating on borrowed time.

"What about Neil Prosper?" Sean asked.

"Jim tried calling him yesterday," Parekh said. "And we sent a process server to his house this morning. No luck. Looks like the family has decamped."

"Shit," Sean said, an expression of dismay on his face. "We should have stayed. We should have watched him, made sure he couldn't run again." He looked at Hannah, not with blame or suspicion but in a kind of wretched solidarity.

"The preliminary hearing won't take more than a day, two at the very most," Parekh said. "We'll do what we can to track him down. I'm almost encouraged that he's run. I was more afraid that we'd put him on the stand and he would lie. Now I feel like, if we get him there, we'll get the truth. That's encouraging." He sounded like a man trying to make the best out of a bad situation.

"Right, moving on. As you know we've been particularly concerned about Samuel Fitzhugh's potential evidence. The prosecution is likely to use him on Monday to establish their case. He was a compelling witness as a child; he could be even more convincing as an adult." Parekh paused, spread his hands wide. "Or not. We don't know because we haven't spoken with him. Jim and I have discussed it and we think the best chance of a positive outcome—and let's be clear here that our expectations are low. I don't want anyone getting their hopes up about this. But the best chance of a positive outcome is if a person close to Sam's age approaches him. We think we need to take some of the formality out of it. Two guys in suits showing up would likely send him running for the hills."

There was a general murmur of agreement from the team.

"So we'd like you, Sean, and you, Hannah, to go to Yorktown tomorrow and see if you can track Samuel down. See if he'll talk to you. Everyone else, the hearing is on Monday, so today is the last working day. I want you to take the weekend off. Let's go into Monday with our heads up and clear, ready to think on our feet. All right?" He clapped his hands and stood up and people started to move.

"Sean, Hannah, a moment please," Parekh said. They found a space in the corner of the room and Parekh lowered his voice, gave them a level gaze, his eyes very serious. clearly intended to convey serious intent. "Yorktown. Pierce is still the sheriff. I want you to keep a low profile. Don't take any risks. If Samuel doesn't want to talk to you, you walk away, got it? I want absolutely no trouble."

"Of course," Sean said.

"Right. I know you know that this matters. I know I don't need to ask you to do your best. Now, I want you both to take the rest of the night off. It's already late. Get some rest and start fresh in the morning."

Sean and Hannah picked up their coats and backpacks. Camila sat at her desk and watched them leave.

"You okay with this?" Sean asked.

"Fine," Hannah said.

They'd just stepped out in the cool, fresh air when Hannah's phone vibrated in her pocket. It was her mother.

"I need to take this, Sean." She stepped away, pressed her phone to her ear. "Mom? Hello?"

"Hannah, how are you?" Laura's voice was tired, a little gravelly and strained, but she'd obviously sobered up a little.

"I'm fine." Hannah emphasized the first word in the sentence. *I'm* fine. Did Laura realize she had answered the phone when Hannah'd called her just a couple of hours earlier? Was that the reason for this call? There was a long pause on the other end of the line and Hannah's grip on her phone tightened. She turned around on the path, looked back the way she had come. Sean was standing about fifteen yards back. He was on the phone too. "Mom, I can trust you, can't I?"

"Of course. Of course you can, darling," Laura said.

"I'm not talking about the drinking, Mom. I'm talking about everything else."

"I don't know what you mean."

"You've told me the truth, right?" Hannah said. She glanced over her shoulder. "Look, I need to ask you something. It's very important."

"All right."

"Everything you wrote in your diary. It's all true, right? You didn't take poetic license with anything?"

"Poetic license? For God's sake." Laura was offended. Hannah's instinct was to rush in, to apologize, to try to make it right. No. Not this time.

"The first time you kissed Tom, you held his hand. You traced a scar on his hand. It's in the diary."

"I . . . yes. I remember." The emotion in Laura's voice made Hannah hesitate.

"And you're sure that's how it happened?"

"I don't understand. What . . . ?"

"There's no way you could have mixed things up?" The thought of her mother ever touching Michael Dandridge with affection made Hannah nauseous.

"Hannah, this is crazy. What are you suggesting? You're talking about my diary? My diary from Bar Harbor?"

Hannah closed her eyes. She knew her mother. If she pushed her what would come next would be tears and angry reproaches and then there would be more drinking and self-destruction and pieces to pick up and nowhere in any of that would she find the truth.

"I have to go, Mom."

"No. You can't just go. Not after asking questions like that. What's this all about? What's going on?"

"I have to go. I'm sorry. I'll call you as soon as I can." Hannah hung up and silenced the phone, pushing it deep into her pocket. Sean was still waiting for her farther down the path, looking at his own phone, seemingly fully absorbed. Could he have overheard her conversation? She didn't think so.

"Everything okay?" he asked.

She forced a smile. "All good."

"Okay if I pick you up tomorrow around ten?"

"Sounds good," she said. She'd better call the car rental company and arrange for another car to be delivered to Yorktown. She would go with him that far, stay with him until he'd interviewed, or tried and failed to interview, Sam Fitzhugh, and then she was going to go straight to Greensville. Straight to Dandridge. Straight to the truth.

Hannah

FOURTEEN

SATURDAY, AUGUST 31, 2019

The next day Sean picked her up and they drove slowly out of Charlottesville. They didn't talk much and Hannah didn't mind the silence. She wrapped her arms around herself and suppressed a shiver.

"Cold?" Sean asked. It was warm out, at least eighty degrees. Hannah unwrapped her arms and took her phone out.

"I'm fine." Hannah just wanted the next steps over with. She started to review Samuel Fitzhugh's social media activity. He wasn't a prolific poster, more of a commenter, but there were some photographs. Enough so that she and Sean would have no trouble picking him out of the crowd. She waited until Sean stopped at a traffic light, then held up her phone so that Sean could see it. "Here," she said. Her screen showed a photo of Samuel, sandy blond hair a little grown out, baseball cap on backward and wearing a muscle shirt that he didn't quite fill out. He was posing goofily with three friends who were dressed much the same.

"Which one is he?" Sean asked.

"On the far left," Hannah said. "In the blue shirt." Sean took a closer look, nodded.

"Anything else on there that helps us?" he asked.

"There might be. There's a lot of chatter about tonight. There's a house party. Not at Sam's house, one of his friends. I can't figure out which one, though. And no one's giving out the address or anything."

Sean made a face. "It doesn't sound too promising."

"Yeah." Hannah thought about it for a moment, then put down her phone. She searched around in her bag for her little bag of makeup—then flipped down the passenger mirror and applied a thick layer of mascara and the slickest, reddest lipstick she owned. She pulled her hair out of its ponytail and flipped her head upside down for a second, tousling it so that it looked messy in that *just-got-out-of-bed-wanna-get-me-back-in-it* kind of way.

"What are you doing?" Sean said.

"What do you think I'm doing? I'm making a profile." Hannah unbuttoned the top two buttons on her shirt, then shimmied sideways in the car, holding her phone away so that she could take a selfie, with an exaggerated pout and a peace sign. She took a second one, this time laughing, from a higher angle but making sure she caught some cleavage, then straightened back up and buttoned her shirt.

She grabbed pictures from other sites. Pictures of other people's breakfasts, other people's coffees and sunsets and friends. She used them all, along with the two selfies she'd just taken, and created a profile on the site used most often by Sam and his friends. She used the laughing cleavage shot for her profile pic, then started liking and commenting on the boys' posts. Quickly, much faster than she'd expected, she had results. Two friend requests from two of the boys, and a few likes. Hannah shook her head, smiling a little. "Jesus. It's almost too easy."

Sean was shaking his head, half-smiling, but she could see that he wasn't relaxed. Something was bothering him.

"What?"

"What do you mean, what?"

"You think it's beneath me to use my feminine wiles?"

"Hannah, far be it from me to get between you and your feminine anything."

"Okay, but something's definitely on your mind."

He sighed, gave her one of his sideways glances. "I know you lied, Hannah." His hands clutched the steering wheel. "About your mom. There's no cancer trial at University Hospital."

"You checked up on me?" Hannah asked faintly. Shit. Shit shit shit. Not this. Not now.

"After what happened at Greensville, Camila had some crazy ideas. I thought they were out there. But . . . I called the hospital. They told me there's no cancer trial."

Hannah reached for words and found none. The silence went on too long.

"Maybe it's true that your mother's sick, I don't know, but she's not being treated here. You must have other reasons for transferring to UVA."

Hannah fought the urge to tell him everything. She might have, if it had been her story to tell. If she could have trusted him. But maybe she could tell him something. Some measure of the truth. "My mother is an alcoholic," she said flatly. "She's been an alcoholic all of my life, since I was a very small girl. She goes through stages where she has it together, stages where she falls apart. It's hard. Ever since I was a little girl, I've taken care of her. I needed to get away. I needed to be by myself. So I took the transfer."

Sean drew in a breath and let it out. "Is that the truth?" he asked.

"Yes." Oh God. She'd intended to lie, to cover herself, but . . . was there some truth to what she'd just said? Had she left Orono, at least in part, because she couldn't handle home anymore?

"Why the cancer story?"

"Because if I say cancer, people leave me alone. If I say I've left my alcoholic mother to fend for herself, people want to know more. And I don't want to talk about it."

He looked away. "Then I'm sorry. I should have respected your privacy. I'm sorry for pushing. It was a shitty thing to do."

Hannah nodded, swallowed her guilt, and they fell silent for a while. "I liked your mom," she said. "She seems . . . it seems like she loves you a lot."

"She's pretty great," Sean said quietly.

"My dad died too," Hannah said. "Before I was born. I never got to meet him."

Sean glanced at her. "That's rough, Hannah."

"Do you remember your dad?"

"Some. I have some really clear, specific memories. Like, on my tenth birthday he gave me this whole talk about how double-digit birthdays are really important—that was a good one. The day I knocked the TV off the table and broke the screen. Man, was he pissed. I won't forget that one in a hurry. And then other memories are a bit more confused—a kind of mishmash of lots of different days, you know, playing ball in the park down from our house, that kind of thing." He was smiling.

"That sounds nice." It was a while before Hannah spoke again. "Your mom, she doesn't seem angry about your dad dying. When she talks about him, she doesn't seem angry."

"Well, she used to be, for sure. For a few years. But I started to get into trouble in school, you know, and I guess she realized that I was pretty angry too. Maybe a small part of that was me realizing I was gay and not knowing how to handle it, but mostly it was that I was so angry about Dad. That's when she started talking to me more about everything. About how carrying that kind of anger around will poison your whole life. So we agreed to try to let it go, and for the most part we've been able to."

Hannah nodded. "That's good." It was impossible not to compare his life with her own. All her life she'd blamed their problems on her father's death and Laura's trauma. Things might have been different if they could have let some of their pain and anger go. Hannah shifted in her seat. It occurred to her that once things had been different. Before the diary, before she had found out the truth, the only person she'd been angry at was her mother.

"What about you? Your mom?"

"Not so much."

THEY STAYED AT ANGIE CONROY'S INN. SHE WELCOMED THEM warmly, and asked questions about the case that neither of them wanted to answer.

"Um, look, Angie, we really want to keep a low profile while we're here," Hannah said. "I'd appreciate it if you didn't mention to anyone that we're visiting."

"Of course," Angie said, managing to look offended. "We always respect our guests' privacy." She offered to help them with their bags, but they politely declined and climbed the stairs alone. Their bedrooms were adjoining, on the second floor.

"Meet you downstairs in ten minutes?" Sean asked. He was conciliatory, trying to make up for what he now saw as his insensitivity.

"Fine," Hannah said. The nicer he was, the worse she felt. They went to their rooms, dropped their bags. Hannah took a moment to use the bathroom and brush her teeth, reapply her lip gloss. Sean was waiting when she came downstairs.

"Where do you want to go?" he asked.

She shook her head. "I'm not sure. Camila and I went to the Fitzhugh apartment when we were here last." It suddenly struck her that there had been no warnings about Jerome Pierce for that trip. Had something happened to make Parekh more concerned this time around? Or was it simply that they were closer to the trial and tensions were rising? "Maybe we should drive by Samuel's grandparents' house—not to stop, I think, but just to find out where it is in case that's where we have to speak with him."

"Let's hope it doesn't come to that," Sean said. "I don't think that would go well."

"It's still worth knowing where it is," Hannah insisted. "We know that Sam will be coming from the house tonight when he goes out. If we can figure out where he's going, then maybe we'll be able to work out his route, and catch him along the way."

"I thought you were planning on crashing the party."

Hannah shrugged. "I think we should, if we have no other option. Assuming we can get the address. But it would be better—and safer—to talk to him away from his friends, I think."

Sean was busy with his phone. "Sam's grandparents' place is on Pulaski Street. It's a five-minute drive, but it will take us twenty minutes to walk. I think we should take the car."

"Okay."

Sean drove. They parked a little way down the street. The house was a two-story weatherboard home. It was pretty, even if the weatherboard was a little worse for wear and the grass overgrown. There was no wind that day and the American flag hanging from a flagpole outside the house was limp and sad looking. Hannah's phone buzzed. She woke the screen and checked social media, scanned the latest entries. "There's been a lot more chatter," she said. "It looks like the boys are planning on going to a bar before the party. Somewhere they can play pool?"

"They're all underage, aren't they?" Sean said. "I mean, if Sam's eighteen presumably his friends are around the same age."

"I guess they have fake IDs. Or maybe the bar turns a blind eye, if they need the money."

"I'd really rather not talk to him in a bar," Sean said. "That's very public." Hannah scanned through the messages.

"I don't think we're going to have much choice. He's already with friends, at someone's house. I doubt if he's going to go home before he goes out. The bar might be our best chance."

Sean grimaced. "Well, which one is it?"

"I don't know. They all know the place they're talking about, so no one feels the need to name it," Hannah said, frustrated.

"Well, let's just try to figure it out. It's Yorktown. How many bars can there be?" He pulled off to the side of the road and they went through the messages together, looking for references to any specifics that might help. There wasn't much, and in the end they decided that the reference to playing pool was all they had to go on. There was a bar, about five miles out of town, that advertised cheap beer, a three-hour happy hour, and pool tables. It sounded like the kind of place that attracted trouble and underage drinkers.

"We should go there now," Hannah said. "We'll find a table, get something to eat. Have a drink, settle in. We'll be there when Sam and his friends arrive." She wanted to get this over with.

Sean agreed that it sounded like the best plan, but she could see the tension in his face.

"It'll be all right," she said. "If he does come in, let me try to talk to him. If I can get him alone for a little while, I'll know pretty quickly whether or not there's any point in staying and talking to him. If he shuts me down, we get out of there right away, okay?"

"Okay," Sean said, reluctant but willing to go along. "That sounds like a plan."

THE BAR WAS CALLED THE THIRSTY BEAVER, AND IT WENT DOWN-hill from there. It wasn't much more than a large shack and a gravel parking lot one-third full with pickup trucks and a few beat-up sedans. Hannah and Sean went inside. There was a scattering of tables and chairs between the entrance doors and the bar, which took up the entire length of the far wall of the bar. There was a dance floor too, with a single, sad-looking disco ball. Most of the dance floor was taken up by three large pool tables and two of the tables were already in use—hard men in sleeveless shirts that exposed tattooed and muscled arms and covered generous beer bellies. Still, the place was less intimidating than the outside had led Hannah to expect. Most of the tables set out for dining were empty, but there were four couples seated and eating, and six or seven drinkers, comfortable enough to be regulars, were hanging out at the far end of the bar. The barmaid—she was in her thirties, with shiny dark hair tied back in a loose ponytail—looked up and smiled at Hannah.

"Get you?" she said.

"Are you still serving food?" Hannah asked. "Could we have a look at the menu?" The bartender gestured over her shoulder to a blackboard on the wall behind her.

"It's just what's there, sweetheart. We do burgers and fries, that's about it, but we do them well and we do them fast."

"Sounds good," Hannah said. She ordered a cheeseburger and fries and a bottle of Coors Light and Sean did the same. The bartender got them their beer and called their order into the kitchen. Hannah and Sean found a table and with no one else waiting on her, the barmaid made her way to the far end of the bar, where she leaned on the pitted wooden counter, dishcloth in hand, and spoke with the regulars.

SEAN AND HANNAH HAD FINISHED THEIR BURGERS AND ORDERED A second beer before Sam and two friends made their way inside. Sean saw them first—he touched Hannah's arm to get her attention

and they watched Sam and his friends for a moment. It was obvious that they had already been drinking; though they weren't drunk,
just lubricated in that louche, relaxed, bright-eyed way of the very
young at the beginning of a night out. They made their way over to
the last free pool table, then Sam came to the bar and bought three
bottles of beer. He had no trouble getting served, and he talked to
the barmaid like he knew her. By the time he returned to the pool
table his friends had already set up and started the first game. Sam
pulled over a stool and sat and watched, exchanging banter with his
friends. Hannah wasn't close enough to hear what was being said,
but the vibe between them all was friendly and relaxed.

"I'm not sure what to do," Hannah said. "Do I just go over there?"

"Maybe we should both go," Sean said.

Hannah shook her head. "I think, if the aim is to keep things
low-key and nonconfrontational, we'd better be as unintimidating
as possible." She stood up, straightened her shirt. "Wish me luck."
She didn't wait for Sean to naysay her. She walked across the bar.
Nelly Furtado was playing on the bar's speakers and the music gave
a lift to her feet, gave her hips a swing she hadn't intended. All three
boys looked up at her approach and there was a suggestion of appre-
ciation, a hint of anticipation.

"Hi," she said, directing her attention at Sam.

"Hi," he said. He looked surprised and pleased. He sat up a bit
straighter on his stool.

"You're Sam, aren't you?"

Surprise and a hint of confusion on his face. "Yes," he said.

"My name's Hannah. I'm a law student at the University of Virginia. I'm really sorry to interrupt your night with your friends. But
I wondered if you'd let me buy you a beer and talk to me for a few
minutes about the Michael Dandridge case."

He flinched—whatever he had expected from her it hadn't been that. She felt rather than saw his friends move closer. They'd either heard what she'd said or picked up on the change of energy.

"I promise I'm not here to make you uncomfortable, or change your mind about anything. I can't imagine what you and your family have been through." The horror of what he *had* been through struck her suddenly and she realized that despite her words she hadn't truly given thought or time or brain space to him. To what it must have been like to lose your mother in that brutal way, when you were just a little boy. It might have been the beer or it might have been the strain of the situation or the fact that he suddenly looked so young, but she found that her eyes were filling with tears. "I'm sorry . . ."

"It's okay," he said. "Yeah . . . I mean, we can get a drink."

"Are you sure? Thanks. Really. Thanks a lot." She felt the disapproval of Sam's friends as she turned away. She felt it in their silence, in the moment Sam took to reassure them before he followed her to the bar. She chose two stools a little away from the other drinkers.

"What can I get you?"

"Uh . . . one of these would be fine," he said. He held up his beer bottle, which was almost empty. Hannah thought briefly about the fact that he was underage and went ahead and bought the beers anyway.

"So look, Sam. I'm working with the Innocence Project. It's something I volunteer for, you know? The Project . . . they're pretty convinced about Dandridge's innocence." Hannah held up one hand. "I'm keeping more of an open mind. I want you to know that I'm not here with any kind of agenda. But my boss, the guy who runs the Project, he's convinced that Dandridge didn't kill your mom. That it was someone else. And he has some questions about the photo ID the police did with you. I guess . . . I was hoping to talk to you, to see if there's anything you want to say about that."

The bartender had delivered the beers and taken Hannah's money, but she lingered nearby, wiping a counter that was already clean, or at least as clean as it was going to get. Hannah caught the barmaid's eye and she wandered away. But Hannah didn't miss the fact that when the bartender reached the far end of the bar, she took out her phone and made a call.

Sam drank from his bottle of beer. In the photographs and chats online he had been all bravado and banter. Here in person he came across as much younger, less sure of himself.

"I don't know," he said. "You know the police don't want me speaking to you guys. Sheriff Pierce says I don't have to. My grandparents would be pissed if they knew you were here."

"I'm really sorry about that," Hannah said. "And Sheriff Pierce is right. You don't have to talk to anyone you don't want to talk to."

He cast her a sideways look. "You're not very pushy, are you? I thought you guys would be . . . I don't know. Pretty rabid about stuff."

"I care about what happened to your mom. And I want to know the truth. But I genuinely don't have an agenda beyond that. Look, Sam, I just transferred into Virginia. This case, the Project, everything is all new to me. Maybe if I'd been working for the Project for a year like some of my friends, I'd feel differently. But I haven't and I don't."

"Is he one of your friends?" Sam asked, nodding over her shoulder toward Sean. Hannah turned around. Sean looked back at them, smiled reassuringly.

"Yes," she said.

"How come he's not over here talking to me?"

She smiled. "I think we both thought we would have a better chance of you talking to me."

"Because you're pretty?" Sam said. He flushed when he said it, but he held his ground.

Hannah made a face. "Maybe. Or maybe it's just that I'm a girl. I don't know. It feels awkward now."

He laughed a little and she felt a bit easier.

"Sam, can I ask you, the photo ID . . . ?"

"Yeah." He looked down at the bar.

"Is that . . . did you really see the man who killed your mother that night?"

"What do you think?" There was doubt and reserve in his eyes.

She shook her head. "I don't know. I think, if I was seven and I woke at night, frightened, I'm not sure that I would be . . . I'm not sure I would remember too clearly, even if I did see something. I . . . it's every child's worst nightmare, to wake up to a stranger in the house. And then . . . you found your mom, didn't you?" Her voice was low, and full of sympathy. Their heads were closer together now as he leaned in.

"I found her. And you never forget. You never forget that. My grandparents tried to help. I saw a counselor for years, to help me come through it. But it fucks you up, you know?"

"Yes," she said.

There was a moment of awkward silence.

"The ID," he said, eventually.

"Yes?"

"I don't know if I want to talk about that. The police are very sure that Dandridge is the man who killed my mother. They warned me that you guys might try to talk to me. They worked really hard to get him. Anything I . . . talking to you feels like a betrayal."

"I understand that," Hannah said. She opened her mouth to

speak again, but Sam's eyes had turned from her—he was watching something that was happening behind her, his brow creased in sudden concern. Hannah turned. Sean wasn't alone anymore. There were three men surrounding his table—three of the guys who had been playing pool were suddenly crowding him.

"Do you know them?" Hannah asked.

"They're—"

Before Sam could continue one of the men grabbed Sean's arm and the other punched Sean full in the face. Sean's head snapped back and before he could respond—if he even could have responded after a hit like that—one of the others had taken his chair and lifted it so that Sean fell out of it and into a half-standing position. The first of the three then punched him in the stomach and as he doubled over, kneed him hard in the face. Sean's nose collapsed—from across the room Hannah saw it happen, saw the cartilage collapse and the blood burst from it.

"Oh Jesus," Hannah said. And she ran, slipped from her stool and ran across the room. Sean was already on the ground and they were kicking him and kicking him and he couldn't have been conscious because he wasn't doing anything to protect himself. It didn't occur to her to try to pull the men off. They were twice her size and twice her weight and she didn't have a hope of stopping them. All she could do was try to shield her friend. She threw herself on Sean, tried to curl herself around his head. She took a kick to her lower back that drove air from her body and replaced it with pain. Another to her arm and her side and again and again. And then one of them grabbed her hair and dragged her off Sean and across the room. She reached for his wrist. He caught her and half-threw her so that she fell back against a poker machine. He waved a finger in her face.

"Stay there, bitch."

He turned back and walked toward Sean, who was still taking a beating. Hannah scrambled to her feet and tried again to reach Sean. The man who had thrown her in the corner backhanded her across the face and she fell, this time to her knees. She crawled forward, crying, still trying to reach Sean.

"You're killing him. Stop it. Stop it. You're killing him."

A final deep, bruising kick to his stomach, and they stopped. No one held her back as she crawled the last few feet to Sean. He was . . . destroyed. His beautiful face. There was blood everywhere. His lip was split, his nose was off to one side and still spilling blood. She wanted to lift his head into her lap but she was afraid to. What if he had a neck injury? She put her hands to his face.

"Sean," she said. She was aware of tears slipping down her face. "Sean." Her hands came away bloody. He made a choking sound and she panicked. She turned him on his side, moved him into the recovery position, leaned over him. "Sean." He was breathing, she could hear it. His eyes flickered open. "I'm here. I'm here," she said. She took out her phone and dialed 911, keeping her hand on him all the time. He shifted, moved to sit up.

"No. Don't move. Stay where you are." She was aware of the men still behind her. Watching. What were they waiting for? The operator answered and she asked for an ambulance. She was interrupted by a voice that came from behind her.

"What's all this?" The voice was loud and authoritative and when she turned she saw a man in a sheriff's uniform, flanked by two deputies. The three men who had attacked Sean still stood there, showing no fear, as if they were innocent bystanders.

"These men attacked my friend," Hannah said, pointing to them from her position on the ground. "All three of them. It was completely unprovoked."

"Is that true?" the sheriff asked, turning to the men.

"No, sir," said mullet man. "He was drunk, on something, causing trouble. Giving Marie trouble." He gestured toward the bartender. Mullet man's knuckles were stained with Sean's blood. The bartender was standing behind the bar, arms folded and face sullen. "I think he's on PCP. I had to punch him hard just to stop him coming forward and then he just kept coming at me."

"Are you shitting me?" Hannah said. "Are you fucking shitting me? On PCP? You jumped him. He was minding his own business and you beat the shit out of him. What is wrong with you?"

The sheriff shook his head. "That's not very ladylike language. I don't think your daddy would be pleased to hear you speaking like that." He turned to the barmaid. "Marie?"

The bartender shrugged. "Happened just like Carl said it did."

"You bitch," Hannah said. She was breathing hard. She wanted to stand up. She felt way too vulnerable there on the floor, but she had one protective hand on Sean and she couldn't leave him. She cast about, looking for support and finding none. People were staring, sure, but she could tell by their faces that no one was going to get involved. Sam was there, looking shocked and scared, standing far away from the scene.

"You keep talking like that, young lady, and we'll have to bring you in too," Pierce said. He made a gesture to his officers, who stepped forward.

Sean pushed himself up to sitting. One of his eyes was already swollen closed. He was cradling one hand to his chest.

"Sean?"

He tried to focus on her, couldn't. "Hannah? Let's get out of here." His voice was thick, and he had to swallow twice to finish the sentence.

"I don't think so," the sheriff said. "We're taking you in. Carl here will be pressing charges, won't you, Carl?"

"I sure will."

The officers stepped around Hannah, grabbed Sean under his arms and heaved him to his feet. Sean groaned, turned his head, and vomited. One of the officers swore in disgust as some of the vomit splattered on his shoes.

"Get him out of here," the sheriff said.

Hannah stood up. "You can't do this. He needs to go to the hospital. You can't do this." But the officers were already dragging Sean toward the door. He cast one look over his shoulder as they took him through the doorway, and Hannah's last glimpse of him was of that frightened, battered face. Sean, who was so good. Sean, who was so warm and so clever. Fury boiled up inside her. She stepped up to the sheriff, chin raised high.

"I know who you are," she said. "You think this bullshit is going to scare us off? You have no idea." Her hand was in his face, pointing, aggressive. She laughed, laughed in his face, though she was crying too. "You have no idea who you're dealing with."

Initially Pierce stared down at her, a look of sneering amusement painted on his face. But as she continued to rant at him the amusement disappeared and his expression changed to something vicious. He stepped forward, looming over her, and despite herself, Hannah took a step back. She was absolutely sure that he was going to hit her. Then she felt someone grab her arm and pull her away.

"Come on, Hannah," said Sam. "Come on."

Sean's car keys had fallen onto the floor. She shook Sam off and bent to pick them up.

Pierce looked between Hannah and Sam and back again. "You should know better, Samuel, than to spend time with the likes of these people. Your grandfather is on the way to pick you up. I hope you have an explanation ready for him." Pierce turned on his heel and walked for the door.

"You get Sean a doctor," Hannah said. "You get him a fucking doctor, you hear me?" The door closed behind him and Hannah collapsed in on herself, sobbing. Sam moved his hand on her arm, stepped forward as if to comfort her.

"Hannah, I'm so sorry, I—"

She wrenched her arm from his grasp. "No," she said. "No. Fuck you." She stepped back, away from him. Every face in the bar was looking at her, and none of them were friendly. "I'm going to make you all pay," she said. "Every single one of you." The threat felt empty. She picked up her bag and coat from the back of the chair she had sat on when she'd eaten dinner with Sean just an hour before, and she turned and made for the door.

Hannah

FIFTEEN

Hannah burst out of the bar and into the parking lot. She saw the brake lights of a police car as it disappeared into the distance. Her hands were shaking as she fumbled with her phone. Her mind was blank . . . who could help her at eleven P.M. on a Friday night? She rang the number of the Project offices but no one answered. She didn't have Rob Parekh's cell number, but she did have Camila's. She tried Camila's number once, twice, then a third time. No answer. Shit. She was crying for real now. She hadn't cried in years and years and now she couldn't stop. She heard the doors open behind her and turned to see Sam coming out with his friends. They stood and stared at each other for a moment, and then Hannah turned away, started walking fast toward the highway. She couldn't drive; she'd had two beers and she wasn't stupid enough to give Pierce an excuse to pull her over. She would have to leave the car. She called an Uber—she was tapping the accept ride button and standing at the entrance to the bar's parking lot when a truck swept by. She got a glimpse of Sam's face, pale and strained, staring at her from the passenger seat, and then they were gone. It took ten minutes for the car to arrive. She spent those minutes calling Camila's phone number and sending group emails from her phone to the entire Project team, begging for someone, anyone, to call her as soon as they got the messages. She thought about the men who had attacked Sean in the bar. They were still inside. If they came out, if they saw her standing there alone, what would they do? When the car finally arrived, she all but threw herself into the backseat and answered the driver in monosyllables. She wanted to go back to the inn, as quickly as possible. Beyond that she didn't want to talk.

She had reached the inn when her phone finally rang. A number she didn't recognize.

"Yes, hello?" Hannah said.

"Hannah, it's Robert Parekh. I got your email. Are you all right?" He sounded calm, measured.

"Yes. No. It's not me, it's Sean. We were at a bar. I was talking to Samuel Fitzhugh. These three guys jumped Sean. They kicked the shit out of him. And then the police came—one of them was Jerome Pierce—and they arrested Sean. The guys who jumped him said Sean started it and everyone in the bar went along with the story. It was a setup."

"Samuel Fitzhugh was part of a setup?"

"What? No . . . I don't know."

"All right. That doesn't matter for now. What matters is getting Sean medical attention. And bail as soon as we can get him in front of a magistrate. I'll take care of that, and I'll see if I can track his mom down. What about you? Where are you now? Are you safe?"

"I'm at the inn. I had to get an Uber—Sean's car is still at the bar."

"But you're all right?"

"Yes. Yes, I'm fine." She was shaking, actually. Her whole body was shaking so hard and she couldn't tell if it was from cold or from fear.

"Okay," he said. "Stay inside. Lock your door. I'll call you back as soon as I know more."

Hannah went inside. She used her key to unlock the front door and climbed the stairs to her room. She got into bed, fully dressed, and pulled the bedclothes over herself, hoping that if she could get warm, she could stop shaking, slow her body down, and start thinking again. But it got worse before it got better. The roaring in her ears, the spinning of the room. She closed her eyes tightly, pushed her fists against her forehead, and tried to concentrate only on her breathing. She breathed in and out, in and out, focusing on that until finally, slowing, the shaking started to ease and she came back to herself. Slowly, she sat up, looked about for her phone, and found it in the sheets. She checked it. No missed calls, but it had been an hour since she spoke to Parekh. An hour? How was that possible.

She dialed his number. He answered immediately.

"Hannah?"

"I'm sorry. I just wanted to know if you had been able to help Sean."

"He's being held at the police station over on Goodwin Neck Road," Parekh said. "I've got a doctor on his way there now, but he's driving over from Norfolk so it's going to take him another fifteen minutes or so to get there. First bail hearing will be at nine A.M. in the morning and you can bet your ass that Sean will have the best representation in the county there with him."

"You're coming down?" Hannah said.

He paused, and when he answered his voice was dry. "While I appreciate your confidence in me, Hannah, given that the bail hearing is in the morning, I think we need someone there for Sean who is already familiar with the local judges. Particularly when we know that Pierce and Engle will resort to dirty tricks. There's no time for me to do any research."

"I didn't mean . . ." Hannah put a hand to her forehead. She still felt stupid, as if her brain was on strike.

"No, that's fine," he said. "Look, I need to keep this line clear. Sean's mom is going to call me back."

"That's fine," Hannah said. "Of course."

He hung up. Hannah lay back on the bed, feeling lost and utterly useless. She forced her brain to focus, tried to think about what, if anything, she could do to help Sean, and came up with nothing. She became aware of the pain in her lower back, in her arms and side. She got up and went to the bathroom, examined the purple bruising that was beginning to appear, and turned away. Sean was so much worse off. There would be no sleep tonight and there was no one else she could call for support or comfort. She couldn't call Laura right now, but even before all of this, had she ever been able to call Laura when she was in trouble? Coming to Charlottesville, living this crazy life, none of it was normal or safe or right . . . but had her life ever been any of those things?

Thinking about that right now would make her crazy. Better to work, if she could. Hannah sat at the desk in her room and started by making notes on her conversation with Sam Fitzhugh. Then she wrote a detailed account of everything that had happened at the bar. As she worked she kept thinking of that early morning in Sean's mother's house, when she'd come so close to emailing Pierce and setting him on Neil Prosper. She'd thought she was on the same side as Pierce, had built up an internal image of the kind of person he might be. A dedicated cop, someone who cared deeply. A driven man who maybe crossed a few lines but only in the pursuit of a just outcome. The reality was starkly different. Hannah put her pen down and started to pace the room. She'd been so sure of herself and now the ground was moving under her feet. What else had she been wrong about?

Hannah started shivering again, so she climbed back into bed.

She set her alarm, closed her eyes, and tried to sleep. It wouldn't come. Finally, just after five A.M., Hannah went downstairs. There was a coffee machine in the reception area. She switched it on, waited for it to brew, then with her coat on and a blanket around her shoulders, she went to sit on the steps of the porch and wait for the sun to come up.

It was very, very quiet outside. No traffic sounds, only the occasional screech of a distant barn owl, which, thankfully, moved on. Hannah was lost in her thoughts and it took her a minute to realize she wasn't alone. As her eyes adjusted to the darkness she realized that what looked like a tree trunk was a tree trunk and something else. There was a man there, leaning against the tree and watching her.

"Jesus." Hannah jumped to her feet, dropping her coffee mug, which bounced two steps before breaking in half. She backed toward the house.

"Hannah, wait. It's just me."

She didn't recognize the voice and kept retreating. It was only when the figure took a few steps forward and the porch light fell on his face that she recognized him—Sam Fitzhugh, wearing the same jeans and boots as earlier in the night, but now with a dark jacket to keep him warm.

"What are you doing here?" Hannah kept her distance.

"I'm sorry. I didn't mean to frighten you. I just . . . wanted to talk. What happened in the bar, to your friend. I can't believe that happened."

Hannah just shook her head.

"And I didn't do anything to help. I guess that made you think that I was part of it, but I'm telling you I wasn't. I would never do anything like that. I wanted you to know that."

"Right." She had no energy for his self-recriminations. She had enough of her own to deal with. She turned to go.

"Wait," he said. He climbed the steps to the porch and she was suddenly aware that he might be young, but he was much stronger and taller than she was. She folded her arms across her stomach. Sam glanced around as if he was afraid that they would be overheard, then he lowered his voice.

"No one knows I'm here. My grandparents . . . my grandfather would kill me. I biked over, so they wouldn't hear the car."

Hannah frowned and he hurried on.

"I've decided to tell you the truth. I don't know, I still don't know if it's the right thing to do. I don't know if Dandridge is guilty or if Pierce and everyone, if they were just looking for a scapegoat. But I do trust you, Hannah. I figured I'd tell you what happened and leave it up to you what to do with it." He paused, as if waiting for her permission to continue. Hannah managed a stiff nod.

"I never saw Dandridge that night," Sam said, his words tumbling over each other. "I did wake up, when my baby sister was crying, and I went looking for my mother. I found her, in bed, and she was dead. I pulled my sister out of her crib and I went next door, to our neighbors. They took us in and they called the cops. I never saw Dandridge or anyone else."

"How did the photo identification come about?" Hannah's mouth had gone dry; her tongue made a clicking sound when she spoke.

"Sheriff Pierce came to the house, a few weeks later. He sat me down with my grandfather and told me that I could help to send the man who murdered my mother to jail. They said they knew for sure that he had done it, that he had even confessed, but that the law and the courts were very complicated, and it would help if I could say I had seen him at the house that night. Pierce had the photo array with him and he showed me which one was Dandridge, so that when I did the formal ID at the station later, I would know which man to choose. Pierce told me exactly what to say when they did that video interview and I said it."

"You lied," Hannah said and her voice was barely more than a breath on the wind.

He nodded. "I lied."

Hannah closed her eyes.

"You don't understand," Sam said. "Sheriff Pierce was . . . look, he was my hero when I was a kid. My dad wasn't around much. He never really came home again, after my mom died. He just did one tour after another and he visited friends in between and there was always some excuse and then he just stopped bothering with the excuses. And my grandparents, they did their best but they're old school, you know? I had one really good friend, my best friend, Teddy Rawlings, and his home life was screwed up too. His dad used to beat the shit out of him, his mom, his sisters. But Sheriff Pierce was Teddy's uncle. So Teddy's dad was an asshole and mine was never around and Sheriff Pierce basically adopted us. Took us to all our Little League games. Made sure no one messed with us. Pierce and his wife, they've got this big old house out on Lafayette Road. They have a pool and a huge yard and Mindy Pierce, she liked having kids around, so Teddy was always there, playing with his cousins and I was right there with him. Sheriff Pierce treated us all like one big family. He used to give money to Teddy's mom, and if things got too hard at home, he'd step in. We just worshipped him, you know? And I believed everything he told me about my mom and the investigation too."

"So . . . what changed?"

"I don't know if I can tell you. I don't know if you'll believe me."

"Sam . . . come on." Hannah shifted her weight, started to stand.

"No. Okay. Just wait."

She sat back down.

"Okay. Look. Teddy's dad was scary, all right? He was really violent, and things were getting worse. Teddy was afraid, so he went to his uncle Jerome and he asked for help. And a few weeks later Teddy's dad died in a car accident. The cops said he was drunk and drove his car into a tree. It happened late at night, no one else was around. His car went up in flames and he died. Sheriff Pierce dealt with the investigation and it was ruled an accidental death. But then, at the funeral, Sheriff Pierce came up to Teddy and made it very clear that Teddy owed him a very big favor."

"Jesus," Hannah said. "Pierce killed him?"

Sam nodded. He was very pale, very tired looking in the moonlight. "We were actually okay with it, you know? We were only kids. Teddy was just relieved that his father wasn't going to beat his mom up anymore. Or hurt his sisters." Sam's expression had darkened. "But then, a few weeks later, Teddy found out that Sheriff Pierce had taken out a life insurance policy on Teddy's father, in his mom's name. I guess he used a dodgy broker, or leaned on someone to get the paperwork filed because Teddy's mother didn't know a thing about the policy until after Teddy's dad died and the insurance company got in touch with her. Again, we thought it was a good thing, you know? Sheriff Pierce, looking out for Teddy's mom. But it turned out he wanted the money for himself. Told Teddy's mom it was payback for all the years he'd been helping her out. He forced her to hand the money over to him. There wasn't a thing she could do about it. You give him what Sheriff Pierce wants and you don't ever get in his way. If you get in his way he comes after you."

"What do you mean, he comes after you?"

Sam's face was screwed up in his efforts to explain. "It took me and Teddy a long time to really get it. I mean, taking the insurance money was the first crack in the halo, obviously. But you have to understand. We were boys. We really loved him. So we made excuses, pretended not to see the small things we saw. It was only as we got older that we started to hear the rumors and we could see for ourselves how it really works. Sheriff Pierce runs this town and everyone in it. You talk back to him, and your daughter gets pulled over, maybe there's a little bit of pot in her car. Or your house is suddenly broken into three times in a row and the cops can't do anything for you. He leans on people, you see? And he's got something on everyone. He keeps a filing cabinet in his workshop. It's where he keeps all his blackmail material. I'm pretty sure he's even got something on the prosecutor, Jackson Engle. Or maybe Engle just likes the way Pierce does things. Doesn't really matter. Either way, they're a team."

"How do you know?" Hannah said.

"What, about Engle?"

"About the filing cabinet? About the blackmail."

Sam shrugged again. "Teddy figured it out. He spent a lot of time in that house. Sheriff Pierce likes to drink. He likes to brag. Teddy hates him now, you know? He got out of Yorktown as soon as he could, got a scholarship and went to college in New York. Columbia. I don't think he's ever coming back." Sam looked sad, and lost, and despite everything Hannah felt a pull of sympathy for him.

"What about you, Sam? What are you going to do?"

"I . . . do you want me to talk to someone? Do you want me to talk to your boss? About the photo ID, I mean. About Michael Dandridge?" he asked.

Hannah shook her head and pressed the palms of her hands to

her forehead. She closed her eyes and listened to her own breathing. What should she do? Here was clear evidence that Dandridge had been set up for the Fitzhugh murder. Could she honestly say that she still believed with absolute, unshaken certainty that Michael Dandridge had killed her father? And if she couldn't say that, if she didn't believe that, what did that mean? She had the horrible, sickening feeling that she'd been on the wrong side. Should she bring this information to Robert Parekh? But if she was jumping to conclusions, if the scar on Michael Dandridge's hand was some crazy coincidence, she would have betrayed her mother, betrayed her dead father, for nothing.

"Hannah?"

"No," she said. Sam looked uncertain.

"I think you should leave it with me. Give me a little bit of time. I want to make sure . . . let's make sure than Dandridge really is innocent. If he is, then you come forward. If he isn't, then you say nothing at all. Does that sound okay to you?"

He nodded, wilting with relief. She understood his feelings. He didn't really want to speak up, didn't want to be exposed as a liar in the newspapers or invite trouble with his grandparents or the police.

"My grandparents are taking me and my little sister Rosie away," he said. "They have a cabin, up in the woods. My grandfather is afraid that you'll keep coming, or that there'll be too many journalists sniffing around, with the preliminary hearing next week. We're going to the cabin and we're going to stay there until things blow over."

"The DA doesn't want you in town next week? For the hearing, I mean?"

"Well, yeah. That's what they're saying. But the plan is that my grandfather is going to come with me back to town for just long enough for me to give evidence. Then we'll go back to the cabin. And now . . . I can't . . . I don't know what to do."

"Right," Hannah said. "Well, I'll phone you. As soon as I can. I just need a day or two."

"No phones," he said. "There's no service. Do you have a pen, and some paper?"

"I . . . I can get some."

"The address won't do you much good. But I can draw you a map. If you need me, in the end, you can come get me."

Hannah went back into the house. There was a notepad and some pencils sitting on one of the side tables. The notepaper had a little printed drawing of the inn as its header. She took the pad and a pencil outside. Sam quickly wrote out instructions, drew a little map, then ripped the sheet off and handed it to her along with the notebook and pen.

"There," he said. "If you need me."

"And you won't change your mind?" Hannah said.

He shook his head solemnly. She could see the fear in his eyes, but she thought that he meant it. His nerves made him rattle on.

"I wish I'd said something before now. Because if Dandridge didn't kill my mother, then someone else did. What if he rapes or kills some other woman? What if he already has?"

SAM LEFT, AND HANNAH RETREATED INTO THE HOUSE. SHE TOOK A long, hot shower and got dressed in jeans, boots, a T-shirt, and a cardigan that she'd probably have to shed later when the day warmed up. She needed it though. If she had had armor she would have worn that instead. She waited in her room for the sun to come up. The police station wouldn't open until nine. Every minute that ticked by hurt, but she couldn't leave Yorktown without seeing Sean, without making sure that he was okay. She stood up and paced the room. Something was nagging at her. Something Sam had said had snatched at another snippet of memory. He'd talked about Rawlings. His friend Teddy Rawlings. Pierce's nephew. Why was that name familiar to her?

Hannah took out her computer, started going back through her notes. Mindy Rawlings. That was it. When she'd researched Jerome Pierce she'd found that he was married to Mindy Rawlings, former cheerleader and his high school sweetheart. Okay, so that was all it was. Hannah sat back, but she didn't feel satisfied. There was no relief from her mental itch. She ran a search through all of her documents for the name Rawlings and came up with one more hit. From her notes about her conversation with Angie Conroy. Angie had told them that on the night of the murder she had gone to Neil Prosper's house and she had hung out there. She said that they had ordered pizza and the pizza had been delivered by Derek Rawlings. She also said that Rawlings died ten months later in a car accident. So that must mean that he was the same man. Derek Rawlings, pizza delivery guy, was also Teddy Rawlings's dad, wife beater, and possible murder victim of Jerome Pierce. A coincidence, that was all.

But . . . wasn't there something else? Something from her very first meeting at the Project? Jim Lehane had been giving them a recap of the case, and he had said that Sarah and Samuel Fitzhugh had had dinner . . . Hannah was almost sure he had said they'd had pizza. Hannah pushed her laptop aside and started to pace around the room again. What did this mean? If Derek Rawlings had delivered pizza to both Dandridge and Prosper and the Fitzhugh home that same evening, that must mean *something*? But what? Could Rawlings have killed Sarah? Could Pierce have known that Rawlings was the murderer, and so killed him not to help out his terrified nephew, but for reasons of his own? Derek Rawlings was Jerome Pierce's brother-in-law, after all, his wife's brother. If Rawlings was found out, if people knew he was a rapist and a murderer . . .

Hannah paced on. Was this possible? Oh God. Was Dandridge really innocent? Could she have stumbled across the answer or was she putting two and two together and coming up with twenty? But it had always struck her as unusual that Pierce should go to such lengths to convict Dandridge. Yes, he would have been under pressure to arrest someone, to get a conviction, but he seemed so established a part of the Yorktown community—he had been sheriff for fifteen years by the time of the murder—surely he hadn't been at any real risk of losing his job. The risks he had taken to put Dandridge away would have to be motivated by something more personal. She'd told herself all along that that was because Pierce knew for sure Dandridge was guilty and his own personal code forced him to take extreme action. One meeting with the man had been enough for her to realize how off base she'd been with that theory. Pierce was not driven by any kind of moral code. He was someone driven by self-interest.

Okay, say she was right. Say Rawlings had delivered pizza to Sarah and Samuel that night. He had seen they were alone and later, much later, he had come back, broken into the house, and raped and murdered her. Say Pierce had somehow figured out that Rawlings was the murderer and had been afraid the truth would get out. That would cause a scandal. Jerome Pierce's brother-in-law, a rapist and a murderer. What would that scandal do to a family living in a small community? So what would Pierce do? Well, what if he decided to cover it up? Rawlings knew that Prosper and Dandridge were home alone that night, doing drugs. Pierce knew that Dandridge had a record. The police said that anonymous calls had led them to Dandridge. But everyone at the Project had assumed that those calls were entirely made up. What if they were right about that? Pierce could have chosen Dandridge as a scapegoat because he'd known—through Rawlings—where Dandridge was that night, and he'd known he was a drug user with a record, albeit a minor one.

Hannah's mind was spinning faster now. Putting everything together. It all made sense, in a crazy kind of way. Maybe. But she had no proof. And even if she had it, she still had to decide whether or not to use it. Innocent of the Fitzhugh murder did not mean he was innocent of everything.

Hannah

SIXTEEN

SUNDAY, SEPTEMBER 1, 2019

At eight-thirty A.M. Hannah went downstairs and checked out. Angie was at the desk. She took in Hannah's jacket, the bag over her shoulder.

"No breakfast this morning?" Angie asked.

"No, thank you," Hannah said.

"I can make an omelet if you like? I have beautiful fresh spinach and some really special cheese." She offered a warm hostess smile.

"No. Thank you. I'm sure it would be great."

"No problem," Angie said, but she managed to look hurt and Hannah suppressed a flare of sharp irritation. Angie led the way to the small reception desk, took out a receipt book. "Is your friend checking out too?"

Hannah hesitated. Maybe she should be getting Sean's things, checking them out and taking them with her. Did she have the right to go into his room, to pack his personal stuff?

"He'll check out later," she said.

"Oh, okay." Angie gave her a curious look, but she produced Hannah's invoice quickly enough. Hannah handed over her credit card, said goodbye, and stepped outside into the chill morning air. The sun was up now, somewhere behind the clouds, but the mist was still thick on the ground. It would burn off soon enough. The police station was only five minutes away.

There was a woman waiting on the steps of the station as Hannah approached on the opposite side of the road. She was dressed in a dark gray suit and conservative heels and she was looking at her phone. A car pulled in in front of the station and parked, and Abigail Warner got out. Hannah froze. Abbie went to greet the woman in the gray suit and exchanged hugs. Gray suit must be Sean's lawyer. After a minute or two of tense conversation, the lawyer disappeared into the station, leaving Abigail standing alone on the steps, waiting. Hannah told herself she should cross over and speak to Abbie. At the very least she could answer any questions about what exactly had happened the night before. But Hannah couldn't make her legs move. Instead she retreated. She'd passed an open coffee shop, a couple of doors down. She went in, ordered a coffee and a bagel, sat at the window, and watched.

Ten minutes later the lawyer emerged from the police station, followed closely by a limping Sean. Abigail rushed forward as best she could, throwing her arms around Sean. They held each other, hugging hard for what seemed like minutes, before Abbie led him to the car, holding on tight to him all the way. Moments later the car swept past, probably going directly to the closest hospital. As the car went by Hannah thought she caught a glimpse of Sean's face, thought maybe he saw her too, before he was gone. Hannah pressed her head into her hands. She felt sick with guilt and apprehension.

After everything that had happened it was impossible to imagine going back to the apartment, to her place in the Project, and resuming her attempts to damage the case from the inside. She'd seen both sides of this war now, out in the cold light of day. Maybe Robert Parekh was not a paragon of virtue, but he wasn't the dark side either. Up until the events of the night before she'd seen the

Project as the establishment; seen them as self-satisfied and self-congratulatory and far too sure of themselves. That was wrong. What they were was brave. What they were up against was so much more dangerous than she'd ever imagined.

Hannah had never gotten around to arranging for a rental car. She'd have to take Sean's—she could deliver it back to Charlottesville for him afterward and pick up her own from there. She would swing by the inn too, once she had the car, and collect Sean's things. If Sean had gone straight to the hospital, probably no one was thinking about the stuff he'd left behind at the inn. So she should pick it up. Maybe he'd see that as an invasion of his privacy, but she didn't want any of his stuff left here, in this town, where Pierce or his goons might come and pick over it. And while she was waiting for the taxi she would call Greensville prison. It was a Sunday. Not the easiest day to arrange a visit, maybe, but Dandridge's preliminary hearing was so close now. The prison would surely not deny him a visit from his lawyer.

In the end everything went as planned and she was with him by lunchtime. The room was the same. Dandridge was, inevitably, wearing the same orange jumpsuit, the same glasses. They sat in the same seats. The only thing that had changed was that Sean wasn't sitting there too. She felt his absence.

"All alone this time?"

"I have some questions for you. Some background questions." Hannah tried to sound businesslike, focused. She had a pen and a notebook ready to go.

"Where's Rob? Did you tell him I wanted him here?"

"He's busy." Hannah couldn't bring herself to say more. How long would it take before he saw through her? Not long, probably, not if she started asking her questions. There was no truly convincing way to make him believe that questions about Bar Harbor, about her mother, had any connection to the Fitzhugh case, and she wasn't even sure she wanted to try. But she couldn't figure out another way to begin.

"I want to see him. Okay? I mean, I'm grateful and all, but I am his client. He needs to come and see me."

Hannah said nothing and Dandridge fell silent. His eyes narrowed as he looked at her. She could almost feel his scrutiny.

"You said you want background. Is this for tomorrow's hearing?"

"That's right."

"Don't you think we're a little late in the day for you to come looking for background? I mean . . ." He held out his arms in an expansive gesture and Hannah looked at the floor. She didn't want to see the scar again.

"Have you spent all of your adult life in Virginia?"

"Uh . . . I guess. Yes."

"You never traveled overseas?"

Dandridge shook his head. "With my parents, as a kid. We went to Europe a few times."

"Okay, and as an adult, before your arrest, did you vacation anywhere in the United States?"

"I mean, sure." He was looking at her as if she was an idiot.

"Where, exactly?"

"Well, all over. Skiing in Lake Tahoe most winters was a thing. I went to LA a few times with friends. Sailing—"

"Did you ever visit Mount Desert Island? In Maine?"

He didn't look defensive, or wary. Not yet. "Yes," he said, slowly. "Why?"

"You had a friend who died there in suspicious circumstances. Can you tell me more about that?"

Dandridge's brow was furrowed. He leaned forward, his arms

resting on the table. "Are you talking about Tom? Tom Spencer? There was nothing suspicious about his death. The poor guy drowned. He was drunk. He hit his head."

"Tell me about your hand." She was trying to keep him off balance without pissing him off too much. It wasn't an easy line to walk.

"What?"

"The scar on your hand. Can you tell me again how you got it?"

"I told you. I fell and put my hand through a window when I was five."

"Okay. Let's go back to Tom Spencer."

"What's this all about?"

Hannah just looked at him, and after a moment Dandridge snorted, and said, "There's nothing more to tell. Tom has nothing to do with any of this. He was dead years before Sarah Fitzhugh was killed. It's not relevant. Are you suggesting the DA is going to try to drag his death into this somehow?"

"That summer in Maine. Did anyone else spend time with you or Tom close to the time of his death? Did either of you have a girlfriend, for example?"

Dandridge stared at her. He said nothing and he stared at her. "Hannah," he said, after a long silence.

"Sorry?"

"What did you say your last name is?"

She thought about lying, but there was no point. "It's Rokeby," she said.

"Oh, my God. You're Laura's daughter."

Hannah nodded. She was trying desperately to read him.

"Of course you are. Jesus. I can't . . . How did you find out about me? Laura didn't send you. No way *she* sent you."

"She told me enough. I figured out the rest," Hannah said.

"Oh, God. Hannah. I've thought about you. I've thought about you a lot. I've thought about meeting you. Not in here, but . . ."

Hannah swallowed hard. She let her eyes travel around his face, taking in his features, the shape of his eyes, his mouth. "You're my father," she said, flatly.

"I never thought she'd tell you, not Laura. I should have come to visit or written to you, but then I was in here and I—"

"You were my mother's boyfriend in Maine that summer," she said, cutting him off.

"Well, we were together. It wasn't serious."

"And she didn't have a relationship with Tom Spencer?"

Dandridge didn't respond. Just sat there, brow furrowed, looking at her.

"Well?"

"What did she tell you?" he asked.

"It doesn't matter what she told me. I'm here and I'm asking you for the truth. Okay? If you're my father, then I think you owe me the truth, if nothing else." Her voice was low and quiet. Was it weird that she felt so calm? Her eyes were dry. She felt emptied out.

"Laura never had a relationship with Tom. Tom was *my* friend. He had a girlfriend in Virginia he was very serious about. Laura and I, we had our thing. There was nothing with Tom, not ever."

"Tell me about his death."

Dandridge shook his head. "I don't . . . what do you think happened? We were drinking one night, messing around, playing music. I went to bed. Honestly? Laura was pissing me off. I'm sorry. Maybe I shouldn't say that. But . . ." He let his voice trail off as he laughed awkwardly. "I mean, she's *your* mother. You know the deal."

"Yes," Hannah said, quietly.

"So we had an argument and she called a cab and went back to the hotel. Tom was alone when he went down to the jetty. I don't know why he went down so late. We thought later maybe he forgot something and went to get it—the cops found the book he was reading in the galley of the boat the next day. It could have been something that stupid. The wood on the jetty was slippery as hell. The cops thought he just lost his footing. He hit his head on the way into the water and he drowned. The postmortem—"

"The postmortem?" Hannah interrupted. "There was a postmortem?"

"Well, yeah. Any sudden death like that, there's always a postmortem. And it showed that he'd hit his head but also that he'd inhaled water. They found some of his blood on the edge of the jetty where he hit his head on the way into the water. He'd either been conscious but disoriented or unconscious but still breathing, when he went in. Either way, the coroner said it was an accident."

Shit. Hannah wanted to press her face into her hands, to block out the world so that she could think. But he was there and so she couldn't do that. She clutched her pen and tried not to let her uncertainty and her need for answers show on her face.

"Why are you here?" Dandridge said, suddenly. "Does Rob know you're my . . . does he know the history?"

Hannah just shook her head. The man sitting opposite her bore no resemblance at all to the monster in her mother's diary but that didn't make him a good or trustworthy person. Still, there were questions she needed to ask him.

"For years I thought Tom Spencer was my father," she said. "His family paid my mother money to look after me, after his death. They must have believed it too. If you really are my father, then my mother lied to the Spencer family and you let her do it. Why?"

He flushed. He was silent for a long time, obviously floundering, searching for words. "Shit, Hannah. I was twenty-one and I was stupid. That's the truth. My dad had just lost a lot of money on a bad investment. I was broke and I was pissed and I was looking for a way . . . I didn't want to lose everything, you know? And Laura and I had already moved on from each other. We were over by the time she told me she was pregnant. Look, truth is, I didn't take it very well. I didn't step up the way I should have."

Hannah took a breath. "Whose idea was it to scam the Spencer family?"

He was very still. "I don't know what to tell you."

"Tell me the truth."

His flush was deeper. An uneven, splotchy, almost purple that made him look old and sick. The reality of the fact that he'd spent the past eleven years in jail hit her hard.

"It was Laura. But I went along with it. When she realized my family didn't have any money, or at least not the kind of money that she wanted, she thought about Tom. He was dead. His family were shaken up . . . Laura thought that she could say that she was pregnant with Tom's baby. If I backed her up, they'd have no reason not to believe her. And she figured they'd pay to be rid of her, as long as she wasn't too expensive."

"What about DNA? Why didn't they ask for a test? For proof?"

"They probably would have, if it wasn't for me. I went to Tom's dad. Laura wrote me a script. I told him that Tom had been with a girl in Maine, that the girl had been head over heels for him, that she was a sweet, poor girl from a religious family. He was very upset. He didn't want Tom's girlfriend or her family or anyone else in Virginia to know about it. I told him that Laura didn't want to cause any trouble. She just wanted to take care of her baby."

"Jesus."

"It sounds bad. It is bad, I know. It's something I'm really not proud of. But I was young and stupid." Hannah said nothing and after a moment Dandridge continued. "My relationship with my family was a mess. My dad knew I was using drugs. He wasn't happy. He'd already threatened to cut me off. I didn't want to go to him and tell him I'd gotten a girl pregnant. I was scared. I didn't want my life to change."

"So the Spencers paid my mother off."

"Yes."

"And you took a share too, right?" There was no way he'd lie like that just to take care of Laura and a baby he clearly didn't want.

He widened his eyes and spread his hands "Not much. Really, Hannah, not much. I wanted most of the money to be there for you, to keep you safe. Look, I know this all sounds terrible, but you have to understand. Thomas and Toni Spencer, the whole family, they are loaded. I mean *loaded*. The money they paid Laura they didn't miss for a second."

"Their son was dead. They were grieving. You knew it and you took advantage." Jesus. This was her father. This is what she came from. And her mother. That diary. That goddamn diary. It had been a lie. Every last word of it.

Dandridge was nodding. "Okay," he said. "Okay. I can't argue with that. But I've been in prison for eleven years. I think, if I deserved punishment for what I did, I've had it and then some."

She believed him. God help her. Maybe she was a fool . . . no, *clearly* she was a fool. Laura had lied to her and manipulated her for years and she'd allowed it. Why? Oh God, why? Hadn't some part of her known that things didn't quite add up? She'd been so young when she'd found the diary—discovering it, now that she thought about it, in a box of old papers that Laura had asked her to sort out. Young, but old enough to know what her mother was. So why hadn't she seen the truth? Because . . . because there'd been a busy little part of her mind that brushed away doubts, directed her attention away from inconsistencies, reassured her that Laura's behavior—

her neediness, her manipulation, her sporadic outbursts and destructiveness and selfishness—all of it was understandable and excusable, seen through the light of the diary. But only because a part of her had wanted to believe it. That was the worst of it. She, who had so prided herself on her clear-sightedness. She had been the most deluded of all.

"I didn't kill Sarah Fitzhugh. I never knew her, never met her, never touched her. I would never hurt a woman, or any person. I've never even been in a bar fight. I need to know that you believe me, Hannah. I know I don't have the right to ask a thing of you. But . . . you're not going to get into all this with Rob, right? I mean, it's not relevant." He looked genuinely worried. Maybe he thought Parekh would kick him to the curb if he knew he was a fraudster.

"I believe you," she said. Then she laughed, a little bitterly. "But I believed my mother too. For years and years. So what do I know?"

His lips parted and he drew in a shaky breath. "Why did you come here? Did you come here to help me?" His eyes narrowed, suddenly suspicious. Hannah stood.

"I came here to see for myself who you are." She made for the door, knocked for the guard. He came quickly.

"Are you going to help me? Are you going to talk to Rob?" Dandridge said, raising his voice to be heard over the unlocking of the door, her quiet conversation with the guard. "Will I see you again?"

She turned back and looked at him one last time.

"I don't know. I haven't decided yet."

IN THE PRISON PARKING LOT HANNAH GOT INTO SEAN'S CAR AND set off in the direction of Charlottesville. She had nowhere else to go. She drove for ten minutes before pulling over. She got out of the car, stood at the side of the road, and dialed her mother's number. Laura answered right away, and her voice was warm, and loving.

"Hannah, baby, I—"

"You fucking lied to me, *Mom*."

Laura drew in a breath in a sudden, sharp inhalation.

"You lied to me. All of it. All of it was bullshit."

There were tears. Immediately, there were tears, of course. And despite her fury there was still a part of Hannah that heard her mother gasp for breath, heard her weep, and wanted to apologize, to comfort. Hannah imagined a steel-toed boot inside her head, stomping down on that feeling and crushing it forever.

"You manipulated me," she said. "You trained me like a goddamn dog. Every time you clicked your fingers, I jumped."

Laura sobbed into the phone. But Hannah imagined her mother, standing in the house in Orono, holding her phone, dry eyed, sobbing violently but feeling nothing, just faking it all. It was such an ugly image and for a moment she felt doubt. Memories flooded her. Laura's arms around her, a soft hand holding hers, a shared smile, laughter. But the memories were too few and they were drowned out by others. A slap, right across the face, when she was very young. Days when she was clung to, nights when she was left alone and afraid. Awkward attempts at friendship destroyed by Laura's interference. Alcohol binges that always seemed to happen at key moments, like school sports days or holiday concerts. A screaming fight in the parking lot with Hannah's favorite teacher, another relationship fractured. Hannah and Laura were close, so close, because Laura had made damn sure that Hannah never had a chance to have anyone else.

Hannah gripped her phone hard for a moment, and then in one swift motion she threw it away as hard as she could. It flew out of her hand and landed twenty feet away in the dirt of a newly plowed field. Hannah climbed back into the car. Her hands were shaking. She turned on the engine, gripped the steering wheel, and drove.

Hannah

SEVENTEEN

Hannah went to the apartment in Charlottesville. Where else did she have to go? She climbed into bed. Time passed. Hours, perhaps. She lost track. The buzzer rang, twice, three times. She ignored it. Ten minutes later there was a loud, insistent knocking on the door. Slowly, her limbs stiff and uncooperative, Hannah climbed out of bed. She opened the door. Sean was standing there, one arm holding his side, his face a mass of bruises. Hannah stood and looked at him stupidly for a moment, unable to think or speak, then she stood aside and let him in. He sat on the armchair, lowering himself gingerly, clearly in pain. She sat on the little couch and pulled a blanket down from the bed and wrapped it around herself. She felt raw and far too vulnerable.

"Are you okay?" Hannah shook her head, tried to clear her jumbled thoughts. "Sorry. Obviously you're not okay. I didn't expect to see you. Not for a while at least. Definitely not today." She looked at the windows. It was dark outside. What time was it anyway?

"Mom's pretty pissed. She wanted me to stay home." His voice was gravelly, exhausted.

"I thought you'd be in the hospital."

He shook his head. "It's not that bad. Four fractured ribs. Stitches." He put his hand to his mouth and then his cheek. He had stitches for his split lit, more just under his left eye. "They gave me painkillers. It's not too bad."

"You should be in bed."

"No," he said. His expression was fierce.

"No?"

"They did what they did for a reason, Hannah. To get us away from Sam Fitzhugh, sure, but also to punish us. To shut us up and shut us down. The hearing is tomorrow."

"How did you know I was here? In Charlottesville?" She didn't want to talk about the hearing. She wasn't ready.

Sean shook his head. "I have a tracker on my car. But that's not the point."

"You have a tracker on your car? Really?"

"Jesus, Hannah. People track their goddamn iPads. I don't want to talk about that. I want to talk about Sam. How far did you get with him? Had he told you anything before they jumped me?"

She would have to tell him. Oh God. There was no way around it.

"He told me the truth. He lied about the photo ID because Pierce and his grandfather asked him to."

"Are you serious? He told you that? At the bar?"

"Afterward. He came to find me at the inn this morning, really early. God, it feels like that was days ago now. He was upset about what Pierce did to you."

Sean stared at her. "But wait a minute. You've talked to Rob since then, right? He told me you talked to him. You never mentioned this."

"That was before Sam found me."

"Hannah, don't you lie to me. You haven't told anyone about this, have you? You haven't called anyone, not Rob, not Jim. No one."

She thought, briefly, about claiming a lost phone, and abandoned the idea. There was no point to it. She shook her head.

"Why not?"

It felt like minutes before she could speak. Minutes, while they sat in silence and she tried to force herself to meet his gaze and find the words.

"My mother used to know Dandridge when she was young. She told me that he killed my father, murdered him, and raped her and that no one ever found out. She told me that her only comfort was that Dandridge was in prison for another murder. That he was being punished for what he had done, even if the truth never came out."

There was silence for a long moment, then Sean swore quietly. "*Jesus.*"

"That's why I came to Virginia," Hannah said. "I came because I knew, with all your work, that there was a chance that he would be released. I thought that the knowledge that Michael Dandridge was free again would destroy her. She's never been strong, you know. But it wasn't true. None of it was true."

"You came to stop us."

Hannah swallowed. "Yes."

"It was all you," Sean said. "The files. The motions that were messed up. You did that. And poor Hazel. Jesus. That job in New York. Camila tried to tell me. You set Hazel up, didn't you? So that you could take her place."

"Yes," Hannah said.

"Oh my God, Hannah."

"There's more I need to tell you." Quickly, she filled him in on her theory about Derek Rawlings. That he may have been the real murderer in the Fitzhugh case and the motivation behind Jerome Pierce's actions in setting Dandridge up.

"I don't know what I can do with all of that," Sean said. "It's too late. There's no proof. Parekh can't just go into court and start throwing accusations around. Pierce is still a serving police officer."

"I know."

Sean's face was tight with anger. "Is Sam Fitzhugh willing to give evidence?"

"Yes," Hannah said. "But he's fragile, I think. He's not stupid. He knows he'd be stepping out onto the edge if he does. His grandparents would be horrified, and the whole town would turn against him. He knows that not only would he be accusing Pierce, he'd be admitting his own complicity in the thing. He was a child at the time but his grandfather wasn't. If nothing else, press coverage could be brutal."

"Okay. Okay. I get all that. But he's willing to do it?"

Hannah hesitated. "He said he trusted me. He said he would do it if I said so. But his grandfather has taken him away. Up to some cabin they have in the hills and there's no cell service, no nothing. So I'll need to drive there. To go and get him. He drew me a map." A thought struck Hannah suddenly. She looked around the room, spotted her backpack, stood and scrabbled through it until she found the piece of paper folded and shoved deep into the front pocket. She breathed a sigh of relief.

"Give it to me," Sean said.

"What?"

"Give me the map."

"You're not going up there."

"What, you're volunteering?" he said, his tone bitter and mocking.

"I can go . . ." She was uncertain.

"Is that a joke? Do you think I'm stupid? You're never getting near our witnesses or this case ever again."

"Okay. Okay, but, Sean, listen to me. It might not be safe. Sam's grandfather has guns and he sounds pretty extreme and he really didn't want Sam talking to us. I don't think you should go up there. It's not a good idea."

There was silence for a moment. When Sean spoke again his voice was low and tense. "It isn't your job to try to protect me. You're not my mother, and you're not my keeper. Give me the map."

Hannah drew a deep, shuddering breath. She handed him the map. He took it from her roughly.

"Do you remember we talked about the murder rule, back in the car, that time when we were going to interview Prosper?"

Hannah swallowed. "Yes."

"You said then that we should all be responsible for the consequences of our actions, if those consequences could be reasonably foreseen." He stood up. "These consequences weren't just foreseeable. They were completely predictable. You didn't give a shit if Michael was guilty or innocent. You were angry and hurt, and you wanted to make someone pay for whatever shit you've been through."

Hannah hung her head. It was true. Every word he said was true.

"You're not a lawyer, Hannah, not even close. You're . . ." Sean took a breath, cutting himself off instead of finishing the sentence. He stood and walked to the door. "Did it ever occur to you that this is not just about Michael Dandridge? Pierce and his cronies, Jackson Engle, all of them, how many other innocent people have they sent to prison? Did you ever think about that? Jesus, your own theory is that Pierce murdered his brother-in-law. If you see shit like that in the world, Hannah, you stop it. It's simple. You just . . . you just stop it, all right?"

He left, slamming the door shut behind him. Hannah got back into bed, pulled the covers over her, turned off the lights, and stared into the darkness.

Sean

EIGHTEEN

MONDAY, SEPTEMBER 2, 2019

Sean called Rob Parekh before he did anything else. Parekh had been good, after the beating and arrest in Yorktown. He'd been concerned, without a doubt, and he'd acted quickly, calling in favors from one of the best defense attorneys in Richmond, finding a doctor who would go to the police station, and putting enough pressure on the deputies that they'd let her see and treat Sean. He'd called Sean's mother, filled her in, supported her. But Parekh had been professional too. The concern had felt genuine, but it also felt one step removed, which was much easier to handle than the overwhelming panic and upset of his mother. Sean didn't know what to do with those feelings. His mother was usually so put together. Now she couldn't leave him alone. A hand on his shoulder, a kiss on his head, as if to reassure herself that he was still there. Every time she looked at Sean tears came into her eyes. The whole thing was horribly uncomfortable.

Sean got it. Of course he understood. She had been terrified that he would die in that police station. It wasn't as if her fear was irrational. The beating he'd taken in the bar had broken his nose, split his lip, shaken a couple of teeth loose, and fractured ribs. Every minute he'd been in that jail cell he'd been waiting for Pierce or one of his deputies to come and finish the job. But in all of the time he'd been in that cell, sitting on the bunk propped up against the wall, struggling to breathe against the pain, he hadn't been afraid. He had been so filled with utter fury that there had been no room for fear. It was a brand-new emotion to him, that anger, but he still felt it now. It filled him up, fueled him so that he ignored the painkillers the doctors had prescribed. Sean welcomed the pain. It kept him sharp. He couldn't do what his mother seemed to want him to do, which was retreat and grieve. He had to fight.

When the tracker app on his phone had beeped to let him know that his car was on the move without him, he'd assumed it was Hannah. He'd tried calling her, more than once. His phone kept going to voice mail. When the car had come to a stop at her apartment block in Charlottesville, that had given him an excuse to get up and go, to do something. He had been climbing the walls with nervous energy and had wanted to talk to Hannah about exactly what had been said by Sam Fitzhugh. It had seemed like Hannah was making a connection with him at the bar, before everything went wrong.

After Hannah told him the truth he'd left her apartment, gone to his own, and called Robert Parekh. He'd been so pissed off and so distracted that he'd forgotten to ask for his keys back, and had driven his mother's little car, leaving his own at Hannah's apartment.

"Christ," Parekh had blurted out, showing more emotion in that moment than he had at any time during the aftermath of Sean's assault. "I can't believe this. I can't believe I let her in. I thought I was clever, looking out for dirty tricks from the other side, but I missed everything. I'm off my game. I didn't see the new trial coming and I sure as hell didn't see who Hannah really was."

"I don't know that anyone could have . . . although . . . ."

"What?"

"Camila was suspicious. I told her she was nuts."

"Jesus. We should all listen to Camila more."

"Yes." Sean was confused about his response to Hannah's confession. He was furious at her betrayal, but he couldn't seem to *feel* it. Maybe there was so much anger already inside him that he didn't have room for more emotion. Or maybe it was the shame and contrition that she so obviously felt. She'd seemed broken. What kind of mother would send her daughter on a quest like this? The whole thing seemed insane and completely messed up.

"Right now we only have her word about any of this. We don't even know for sure that Fitzhugh came and spoke with her. We'll have to find another way to approach Fitzhugh and sound him out."

"I'll go," Sean said. "I can drive up there in the morning, before court. Get him to Yorktown before court's in session so you can talk to him. At least that way you'll have an opportunity to adjust your strategy if you need to."

Parekh had been silent for a moment. Long enough for Sean to know that he was tempted by the offer. "No," said Parekh in the end. "It's not a good idea. We don't know what kind of welcome you would get, but we can be pretty sure it wouldn't be a warm one. And Sam might take careful handling. We can't afford to blow this, Sean. Getting him onboard is our best chance of winning this case. I'm not feeling confident right now. I think we have to change our strategy. Let's just get through the hearing tomorrow. Accept that Michael is likely to be indicted again and we're not going to be able to prevent it. We can approach Sam again carefully, get him lined up for the trial."

Sean had agreed. There was no point in arguing with Parekh when he had his mind made up, but Sean knew before he hung up the phone that he was going. Sam Fitzhugh was their best chance of freeing Michael Dandridge, and their best chance of bringing Jerome Pierce down. Delaying things for months and months until the full trial was way too risky. It would just give Pierce more time to do whatever. Blackmail, lean on people—what sort of pressure could be brought to bear on Sam in that period of time? Not to mention, if Hannah was right, Pierce wouldn't hold back from making people disappear.

So Sean went to bed but he set an alarm for seven A.M. When he woke he took a careful shower and studied Hannah's map while eating a banana, very slowly, and then took more painkillers. He spent some time trying to plot the route out on his maps app. He would be able to find the Fitzhugh cabin without too much difficulty, even if he did lose internet service. He had an hour's drive ahead of him before he got into the hills, so when he got into the car he put on some music, settled back, grimaced at the pain in his ribs and side, and thought about what he would say to Sam Fitzhugh.

Sean turned off the main route just after eight A.M. The road dipped into a valley before it started its climb upward. Initially the road was in good shape—it was wide enough for comfortable two-way traffic, it was well marked, and every so often he passed a home, set well back off the road—but he lost his signal after the first half an hour. Sean was more relieved than concerned. He had already missed three calls from his mother. He had no intention of speaking with her until he was back at home, or at least in Yorktown, with Parekh and the others, and this little adventure behind him. He took a turn marked on the map and the road narrowed abruptly to a single lane that twisted its way through thick forest. The engine of his mother's little Hyundai whined as he leaned on the accelerator to push up the steep hills. At one point he came over a hill to find that the road curved sharply to the left without warning, and in front of him was a sheer drop. Sean was going too fast to take the turn. He hit the brakes and the car slid forward before stopping a breathing distance from the cliff's edge. The drop must have been a hundred feet. More.

After that Sean drove more slowly, leaning forward and with hands clammy on the steering wheel. A scribbled note on the side of the map told him to watch out for a red mailbox at the turnoff for the cabin. He nearly missed it—it was half hidden in the bushes—but he spotted it in time and took the turn. At every turn he took, the road deteriorated—the drive that led to the cabin was just dirt. At some point someone must have laid down gravel; he could see the remnants, but most of it was buried under dried mud and leaves and other debris. He gave a silent thank you that it hadn't rained recently—the car could never have handled the track if it was wet.

Sean came upon the cabin through a sudden break in the trees. It was a small log structure with a wraparound porch. There was a generous clearing in front and to the left of the cabin, and there was a stream too, a little way down and farther to the left. It should have been a pretty place, but it wasn't. Maybe it was the early morning sun, only weakly filtering through the trees, but the cabin looked brooding. Not the kind of image you'd see on a vacation home listing, that was for sure. Sean stopped the car well back from the cabin and turned off the engine. There were signs of life—smoke rose from the cabin's chimney—but . . . and it only just occurred to him—how was he supposed to contact Sam without attracting the attention of Sam's grandparents? Shit. What could he do? Lurk out here and hope that Sam wandered out for some early morning fishing? That seemed both pointless and stupid. There was just as much chance that one of Sam's grandparents would emerge, and maybe run him off before he had a chance to even let Sam know he was there.

Sean got out of the car and walked toward the cabin. He mounted the steps of the porch and knocked firmly on the screen door. There were two rocking chairs on the porch, hand carved by the looks of them, and an untidy bundle of fishing rods, waders, tackle boxes, and jackets piled off to the right. Footsteps approached from inside and Sean gathered himself. The door opened. The man standing just inside the cabin was Jerome Pierce, in full uniform, gun in holster, a cup of coffee in his hand.

Sean took an instinctive step backward. Jerome Pierce's first response was a jaw drop; his second was to look past Sean, out into the clearing, as if to check to see whether Sean was alone. Seeing that the clearing was empty he turned his attention back to Sean, shook his head in mock regret.

"You people never give up. I thought you'd have learned your lesson."

That single step backward was the only backward step Sean took. Fury rose up inside him, and he stepped forward instead, getting right into Pierce's space. Pierce was the bigger man; Sean didn't care. He wanted to provoke him, wanted a fight, the satisfaction of landing one decent punch on this preening asshole.

"And what lesson would that be?" Pierce stood for everything he hated about the world and the fact that he could stand there in complete confidence, a sneer on his face and a threat in his words, was so stomach-churningly offensive that Sean couldn't take it.

"You don't belong here," Pierce said. "Why don't you go back to your little college and tell your professors that you need to be taught some manners. No one invited you here. This is private property."

"It's not your private property though, is it?" Sean said. "Were you invited here?"

Pierce smiled. "Oh, Sam Senior and I go way back. I've got something of a standing invitation, you might say." He took a sip from his coffee. "The family have made a complaint about you. Harassment. I'm going to give you thirty seconds to get in your little piece of shit car, and get off this mountain. Otherwise you're going to find yourself back in a cell by lunchtime."

Sean's anger sharpened to the point of hysteria. "You are so sure of yourself, old man," Sean said. "You think you're high up on the hill and you're untouchable. You're so far gone you can't even see it when someone's coming for you. You're so far gone you can't even see when they're at your gate."

That got to Pierce. "What the fuck are you talking about?"

"I'm talking about Rawlings," Sean said. "I'm talking about your wife's brother. Mindy's poor dead brother. Did you think we wouldn't figure it out?" Sean shook his head mockingly. He felt an almost manic excitement. Provoking Pierce was crazy, but in that moment it was also exhilarating. "All it took was to get to know you a little, you see. Once we figured out that Jerome Pierce only ever acts in his own self-interest, it didn't take us too long to figure out the rest."

It was a bluff, only a bluff, and it might have fallen humiliatingly flat, but it didn't. Fear flared briefly in Pierce's eyes followed by a murderous rage. The coffee cup was abandoned, and suddenly his hand was on Sean's neck, grasping and pushing him at the same time. Sean pushed back, harder, and then Pierce was stumbling backward, but his hand was moving in the direction of his holster. At that moment Sam Fitzhugh came out of the cabin at a near run. He put his body in between Pierce and Sean and tried his best to bundle Sean away from the cabin.

"Jesus. What are you doing? What are you doing here?" he said, with a fearful look over his shoulder at Pierce. Half-pushing, half-pulling, he moved Sean down the porch steps and away from the cabin and Sean allowed it as pain flared again in his ribs.

"Hannah sent me," Sean said.

"Oh my God," Sam said. "You have to go. You have to go right now." He tried to push Sean toward his car but this time Sean planted his feet firmly.

"No," he said.

Sam looked at him with an expression that was almost comical in its shock and fear. "You have to go. You don't know . . . he's dangerous. It's not safe."

Sean laughed. He was still riding that high. "What's he going to do, Sam? Kill me in broad daylight with your entire family here to witness it?" They turned at the same time to look back toward the cabin. Pierce was standing on the porch, staring at them, holding his body in a way that suggested he might take a run at them at any moment. And Sam's grandparents were both there, standing in silent condemnation. Oh shit. Was that Sam's sister? A small figure had emerged from the cabin. She had curly dark hair and a frightened little face. She grabbed at her grandmother's hand and the old woman turned and ushered the little girl back into the house, closing the door firmly behind them. Sudden fear gave a lurch at the base of Sean's stomach, momentarily breaking through his hysteria. It occurred to him that he might very well die here, if Pierce chose to take out his gun. And maybe, just maybe the Fitzhughs would stand back and watch it happen.

"I'm not leaving without you, Sam," Sean said. "Not if you told the truth when you spoke to Hannah. We need you."

"It wasn't supposed to be like this," Sam said. "You weren't supposed to just come here, right out in the open."

"But that's just it," Sean said. "It all has to be in the open. Everything has to be exposed and seen and everyone has to know, otherwise how will things ever get better?"

Sam wasn't listening. He was very afraid. Sean could see it in his eyes and his own fear grew. What did Sam know about Pierce that he didn't? But he couldn't go. Couldn't force himself to get in the car and retreat.

"Sam, Pierce knows who really killed your mother. He's always known."

Sam's eyes flew back to Sean's and locked on.

"It was Derek Rawlings. His brother-in-law. Pierce set Dandridge up to protect Rawlings."

Sam aged right before him. The fear in his eyes fell away and was replaced by . . . something. Sadness. Disgust. Regret. Suddenly there was nothing boylike about him at all. "How do you know?" he asked.

"Hannah figured it out," he said. She had. My God, she had. And all by herself. "We haven't proved it, not yet, but I believe it."

Sam nodded slowly. Out of the corner of his eye Sean saw movement on the cabin porch. Pierce wasn't going to allow them any more time.

"We have to go, Sam. We have to go now."

"Okay," Sam said.

"Really?"

And Sam nodded.

"Just start walking, slowly," Sean said. "Act like you're walking me to the car to get rid of me." The walk was only thirty feet or so, but it felt like it took an hour. As soon as they turned away Sean felt an itch between his shoulder blades, had to fight the urge to look back. But they made it to the car and Sam climbed into the passenger seat and Sean had the car started and moving before anyone on the porch could react. They lost sight of the cabin almost immediately and Sean drove too fast down the track, the little car bouncing and jolting. Sam braced himself against the door but didn't suggest that they slow down. When they reached the end of the drive and turned left down the narrow, winding road that would take them off the mountain, Sean and Sam let out a simultaneous, audible sigh of relief, looked at each other, and suddenly they were laughing.

"Oh my God," Sam said. "I'm sorry. None of this is funny, but I was so scared."

"I wasn't," Sean said. "Not until the last minute. I think I lost my mind for a moment."

"He's so . . . he scares the shit out of me."

"Is Pierce really friends with your grandfather?" Sean asked.

"Since my mom died. Not before. But since then, yeah. They go fishing sometimes. And Granddad won't hear a word said against him. He's put him on this pedestal. Like Pierce is this lone guy fighting for justice against the system. Granddad just doesn't want to hear about anything else."

Sean drove for a moment, concentrating on the road. Driving down the mountain required even more concentration than driving up had. The steep slopes combined with loose stones on the road meant that the car slipped and skidded a little.

"Thank you for doing this," he said, eventually. "It's brave of you." But Sam was distracted. He turned in his seat and looked back up the track. Sean's eyes went to his rearview mirror but he saw only dust. "What is it?"

"I thought I saw . . . *shit.*"

And then Sean saw it. A black Dodge Ram coming up fast behind them. "Who is it?" he said, knowing the answer.

"That's Pierce," Sam said. "That's his truck. It was parked behind the cabin. That's why you didn't see it." He turned back to face front. "You have to drive faster."

"I can't," Sean said. "I won't be able to control the car." But he put his foot to the accelerator all the same. Their speed increased but his control slipped away and he had to slow again. The truck was nearly on top of them in moments, crowding them and nudging the little car. Sean and Sam were silent, Sean was doing everything he could to keep control of the car, to keep it on the road. Then the truck fell back by about fifteen feet. Still too close, but no longer crowding or nudging. Sam glanced back.

"Has he stopped? Maybe he just wanted to scare us."

Sean shook his head grimly. He was thinking about the precipice that lurked somewhere up ahead; he tried to remember how long it had taken him to reach the cabin after he had passed it. "Does Pierce know this road well?" he asked.

"I guess so," Sam said. "He's been up here, fishing, with my grandfather."

Sean shook his head. He was trying to think about what he could do. He couldn't just stop driving. There was nothing to stop Pierce coming after them with a gun. On this lonely road they would be easy targets. Jesus, with a truck like that Pierce could tow the little car down one of the firebreaks, come back later to dispose of them more permanently. Was this his imagination getting away from him? But Sam was afraid too, that was very clear. And Pierce was a killer. Sean knew it in his bones. So he kept driving.

"There's a cliff, just up ahead," said Sean. "Can you remember where, exactly?"

Sam turned to him. "I . . . I think so."

"Can you tell me when we're getting close? I'm going to speed up. Try to get past it before . . . before he can do anything."

"You think he's going to push us over the edge."

"I think he might try."

Sam turned his attention back to the road. Sean could hear his breathing even with the rattle of stones against the car and the noise of the engines.

"We're close," Sam said, tightly.

It was a bad place to speed up. The slope was steep and the road in terrible condition. Sean gripped the steering wheel hard and put his foot to the accelerator, but even before the car could respond the truck engine behind them was roaring and the car jerked forward as the truck made contact, ramming them once, then again. The car skidded and slid and nearly hit a tree but Sean managed to get it back on the road and then the truck hit again. The car was now careening down the hill, far too fast. Every time Sean came close to regaining control the truck hit them again.

"It's right there," Sam said. "The cliff is right there."

The road ran straight ahead, downward, and at the bottom of the slope only a few saplings stood between them and the drop. Sean hit the brakes, turned into his skid, and waited for the almighty jerk as Pierce's truck hit them again. It didn't happen. Instead they heard a car horn blaring from behind them. Sam turned.

"It's Granddad! He's coming behind Pierce."

The horn blared again and again and Pierce dropped back and Sean finally, finally managed to control the car and leaned hard on the brakes, trying to make the turn. The car was skidding sideways by the time they hit the bottom of the slope, but it had slowed enough that when he leaned on the accelerator again he was able to pull the car forward out of the skid. They avoided the cliff's edge, and the little car rattled most of the way around the corner before hitting a bump and coming off the road and to a complete stop. Sam and Sean turned at the same time to see what was happening behind them.

Jerome Pierce's black truck came to a stop well back from the edge of the cliff. A moment later the red truck pulled in just behind it and Sam's grandfather climbed out. With speed and strength that Sean wouldn't have expected, given his age, Sam Senior stalked toward Pierce's truck, opened the driver's door, and, grabbing Pierce by the collar of his shirt, pulled him out of the car. The next minute the two men were pushing and shoving, gesticulating.

"Jesus," said Sam. "Go, Granddad." They watched for a moment, still in shock, then Sam reached for the door handle. "I need to go and help him," he said.

"No," said Sean. "We have to go, right now."

Sam stared at him.

"Think about it. If we go, there's a good chance Pierce will follow. Your granddad is giving us a head start. And if Pierce thinks there's a chance we're going to get away, he can't do anything too terrible here or he'll go to prison for it. If we get out of the car and go back, then there's nothing to stop him from pulling the gun on all three of us. We need to go, Sam."

"You go. I'm going back."

"Sam, please." Sean glanced over his shoulder. "Look," he said. Pierce had left Samuel Senior standing in the dirt and was climbing back into his truck. "We have to go. We have to go now."

Sam hesitated for one more minute, then nodded. Sean drove, expecting all the time that Pierce's truck would catch them on the road, that the whole wretched process would start all over again. But they didn't see him again and were left to wonder if Sam Senior had managed to stop him, or if he'd called off the chase. The idea of the latter was less reassuring than it should have been.

"He could call ahead," Sam said, when they finally reached the main route and felt safe enough to talk again. "To Yorktown, I mean. He knows that's where we're headed."

"He could," Sean said. "But two can play that game. We're going to change cars before we get there." He picked up his phone, spirits soaring. They were in this game now, and they were going to win it.

Hannah

NINETEEN

Hannah did sleep, eventually. She'd fallen asleep sometime after three A.M. and she woke with the sun streaming in through the windows. Slowly, still a little disoriented, she climbed out of bed and went to the shower. Sometime after midnight she had begun to hatch a plan. She tested the idea in the hard light of day. It was still deeply risky and probably incredibly stupid, but really, she didn't have a choice.

Hannah left Charlottesville at eight A.M. and reached Yorktown at ten. She drove down Ballard Street, away from the courthouse and out through town toward Lafayette Road, where Sam Fitzhugh had said the family home of Sheriff Jerome Pierce was located. She stopped at the hardware store along the way, asked directions, and bought herself a crowbar. They had pay-as-you-go phones behind the cash register and she bought one of those too. Lafayette Road was a short, pretty, tree-lined avenue with beautiful homes. Sam hadn't mentioned the exact address, so Hannah parked the car, put on her best smile, and knocked on the door of the very first house on the street. An older man—salt-and-pepper hair, handsome—came to the door.

"Help you?" he asked.

"I'm so sorry to bother you. My mom asked me to drop something off at the Pierce house? I was sure I wrote down the address

but now I can't find it. I know it's on Lafayette Road but I can't remember..."

He didn't wait for her to finish, just directed her to number
129 and told her to be sure to tell Mindy hello from him. Hannah
smiled her thanks and returned to her car. She drove down the road,
found the house, and drove on a little before parking and returning.
She pulled her clothes out of her backpack, replaced them with the
crowbar, put the backpack on her back, and set off in the direction
of the house. Her hands were shaking. She didn't allow herself to
slow or hesitate or even think too much about what she was going
to do. When she reached number 129 she stepped over the low fence
and walked into the property, hugging the fence line between 129
and number 131. She watched the house. Jerome Pierce would be at
the courthouse. His children were grown and moved away, but his
wife might be there, watching. There were no cars in the driveway,
no sign of movement in the house. Hannah kept walking. Sam had
mentioned a workshop. There was a garage, to the front of the property that she'd already passed, but that didn't feel right. She kept
going around the back and spotted it. A small building at the rear,
off to the left of the pool, that looked like a purpose-built studio. It
had a pitched roof and weatherboard siding, like a mini-version of
the main house. This had to be Jerome Pierce's man cave, the place
where he sat and plotted and admired his good work.

Hannah tried the door but it was locked. She tried the crowbar,
but the dead bolt wouldn't give. Okay. Fine. Hannah took a chair
from a nearby patio, put it alongside the building, stood on it, and
used her crowbar to break the window. One good strike and it shat-
tered. She used the crowbar to clear the glass as best she could, then
climbed inside, cutting her left hand a little in the process. She left a
smear of blood behind her.

The shed was expensively decorated, with a custom-built desk and bookshelves along one side of the room, a small wood-burning stove, and a beer fridge. The other side of the room was lined by three large, metal filing cabinets. Hannah had to climb over the cabinets to enter the room. Hannah glanced uneasily toward the door, very aware that if someone came through it suddenly she wouldn't have time to climb back out the way she had come. She looked around for cameras, didn't see any, and tried to slow her breathing. She'd gotten this far.

The filing cabinets were unmarked, unlabeled. The drawers were locked, but these at least were no match for the crowbar. She popped the second drawer of the first cabinet and pulled it out. She really didn't know what she had expected to find. Sam had said blackmail material, which might be anything and nothing. A fever dream of his friend Teddy, even. Inside the drawer she found a mix of police case files and plain manila folders, each one neatly labeled with a case name and number, or on the plain manila folders, a name alone. Hannah took a random selection to the desk, sat down, and started to read.

The police folders seemed to be copies of old case files. She leafed through a couple, saw copies of investigative reports and witness statements, police forms, but nothing that struck her as unusual. The manila folders were different. The first one she opened was marked with the name *Carole Anne Saunders* and contained handwritten notes and photographs. According to the file, Carole Anne was a married mother of three who lived on Nelson Road. Carole Anne was a member of the Yorktown School Board. She had also been having an affair with the high school principal for at least eight months, and the photographs were there to prove it. Hannah closed the file, turned it over in her hands, and looked again at the filing cabinets. This file, the Saunders file, was an old one. The information in it was out of date. Maybe Carole Anne Saunders had moved on, left her husband, left Yorktown. Or maybe she still lived here, still sat on her place of minor power on the school board. Maybe Pierce had already used this information to lean on Saunders for whatever small favors she was in a position to deliver or maybe he held it over her head. None of that mattered to Hannah. The point was that Teddy and Sam had been right. Pierce used these cabinets to store the information he stockpiled against his enemies and, pre-sumably, given his character, his friends. She had come here looking for evidence of that blackmail. Something that could take him down.

Hannah abandoned the files on the desk and returned to the cabinet. Everything appeared to be filed alphabetically. She hunted through until she got to E and looked for a file marked Jackson, Engle. Bingo. She pulled it out, then went back and went through the D's and the F's. She found a copy of the Sarah Fitzhugh police file, and a manila folder with Michael Dandridge's name on it. She put both in her backpack along with the crowbar, and made for the door. At the last minute she scooped up the Carole Anne Saunders file and took that with her too. She'd trash it at the first opportunity. She wished she could light a bonfire with the contents of those filing cabinets. Was there a file in there on Sophia Prosper? Her husband? How many other lives had been blighted by Jerome Pierce? Hannah went straight back to her car, unlocked her door with shaking hands, swung her backpack inside, and drove away. She pulled in outside the York Pub, where she'd had crab cakes with Camila only a few short days ago. She felt safer here, with people coming and going, than she would parked down a quiet side alley.

She opened Dandridge's file first. More handwritten notes, re-cording the life Dandridge had been leading at the time of his arrest, his known associates, his drug habit, the fact that he was cut off from his once-wealthy family who had, according to the file, lost money in a real-estate investment. There was information about Prosper in the file, but it was all general stuff—again, where he lived, who he spent time with. Nothing that would prove Pierce had leaned on him or why. Damn. Damn damn damn. Hannah blinked back tears of frustration.

She turned to the police file. It was bigger, heavier, more complete. She opened it out on the passenger seat and started to go through it. The contents were largely familiar to her. Photographs of Sarah Fitzhugh, which she quickly put aside. Dandridge's mug shot, various witness statements, and long police forms. She was nearly at the back of the file when she found it. A small plastic evidence bag, sealed, with a second bag inside that appeared to contain a number of dark hairs. Hannah stopped, puzzled. A single strand of hair had been found in the Fitzhugh case, but that had been sent off for testing. What then, was this? She looked at it more closely. The evidence bag wasn't marked with the name Sarah Fitzhugh. The label said "L. Cantrell—Victory Hill" and the case number was different.

Victory Hill. Victory Hill. This was evidence from that other case she had found during her research, the home incursion and attempted rape that had been interrupted by the return of the victim's husband. The case she had thought so similar to the Sarah Fitzhugh case. But the newspaper reports on the Victory Hill case said that no DNA evidence had been found. So why was hair evidence from that case sitting in a copy of the Sarah Fitzhugh case file in Jerome Pierce's home office?

Hannah

TWENTY

By the time Hannah made it to the courtroom court was well in session. She pushed her way through the double doors and quietly took a seat off to the side. The courtroom was bright and modern and absolutely packed with members of the public and press. There were uniformed deputies, there to keep order. There was Robert Parekh, impeccably dressed and looking utterly confident, sitting at the defense bench, Jim Lehane at his side. And her father, of course. Michael Dandridge. Perhaps he felt the weight of her gaze because he turned and looked at her, gave her a slow nod of recognition. She nodded at him in return, then looked away. Sam was sitting in the witness box, looking scared and uncomfortable. Hannah looked for Jerome Pierce. He was leaning against the wall at the back of the courtroom, in full uniform, arms crossed and scowling.

"Mr. Parekh, if you're ready to proceed," said Judge Burrell. She was younger looking than Hannah had expected, in her thirties. The judge had dark circles under her eyes, like she hadn't had enough sleep, but her eyes were sharp and she was clearly paying attention.

Parekh stood. "Sam, we've talked about the earlier part of the night, about your last hours with your mother. She put you to bed at around seven P.M. Now, I have to ask you, what woke you up, later that night?"

"My sister was crying. She didn't usually. She was a pretty quiet baby, and anyway, Mom just picked her up if she cried. Often Mom would bring her in the bed with her, and they'd sleep like that until morning. So I wasn't used to hearing her crying at night. That night though, in my memory, she cried for a long time." Sam's voice was steady and quiet. His eyes were fixed on a scene somewhere far away. "I was scared," he said. "Before I even got out of bed. Maybe it was just Rosie crying, or maybe it was something else. But I remember being afraid. I wanted to stay under my covers, where I was warm, and safe. But Rosie kept crying and crying. So I got out of bed. I . . . I walked along the corridor to my mother's room. The door was shut. I remember that because it was unusual. Usually Mom left her door a little bit open, in case I needed her. That night it was closed. I opened the door and went inside. The lights in the bedroom were turned off but the light in the hall behind me spilled through."

Sam stopped and swallowed. There was absolute silence in the courtroom. Every eye was on him, and every voice was silenced. There was something very soft, very tender in his face when he spoke about his mother bringing Rosie into bed with her, and Hannah found herself blinking back tears. An image of Sarah Fitzhugh as a living, breathing woman struck Hannah forcefully, followed by a pang of guilt. She'd been angry with Parekh and the rest for failing to think about the victims in the cases they'd brought, but had she ever thought of Sarah as anything more than a pawn on a chessboard?

"I didn't realize. Not at first. I could see my mom's body lying on the bed, but she was in shadow. I went to her and put my hand on her arm, tried to wake her. She didn't move, didn't react. I tried again, and she still didn't move. I saw that she was staring at the ceiling."

Sam fell silent, and Parekh said, very gently—"You were just a little boy, Sam. It must have been terribly frightening."

Sam nodded, a single awkward jerk of his head. "I went to my sister. She was standing up and crying in her crib. I picked her up and carried her out of the room. I went down the hall toward our front door. The door was open. I was so afraid. But I was more afraid to stay. I took Rosie next door to Mr. and Mrs. Stamford. I knocked on the door again and again and Mrs. Stamford opened it and took us in. She called the police."

Sam still wasn't looking at Parekh, but rather off into the distance.

"Thank you, Sam," Parekh. "Now, I know this is very difficult for you to talk about, and if you need a little time, I can ask the judge if we can take a short break."

Hannah saw Burrell give a slight nod. Her face was sympathetic.

"But if you're okay to continue, Sam, I'd like to talk about the most important part of your testimony today, something you haven't touched on yet. When you left your own bedroom at the back of the apartment, and walked along the hall to your mother's room, what did you see?"

Sam blinked. "I saw the hallway. The light on. And my mother's door, shut."

"And you didn't see any other person in the house?"

Sam shook his head. "No."

"It was just you, your mother, and little Rosie, is that right?"

"Yes," said Sam.

"Sam, the prosecution has argued that your evidence in the original trial should be entered into the record here today. Can you tell us what evidence you gave in the original trial that is different from what you are telling us here today?"

"Yes," Sam said firmly. "When I was seven I gave a statement that said I was hiding in my room and I saw a man dressed in jeans and a black windbreaker."

"And did you later identify this man as Michael Dandridge?"

"I did."

The courtroom was utterly silent. Hannah kept expecting the prosecutor to object, but he was sitting very still. Parekh waited to ensure that the question had the maximum dramatic effect.

"Why did you do that, Sam?" he said, into the silence.

"Because Sheriff Pierce came to my house. He explained to me that he knew for sure that Michael Dandridge had killed my mother, but that the kind of evidence he had wasn't the kind of evidence that the courts would allow. He told me that Mr. Dandridge had attacked other women before and that they'd been trying to catch him for a long time, but that he was very sneaky. Very good at not getting caught. He told me I could make sure that my mother's killer went to prison and that I could protect all those other moms out there from Mr. Dandridge. He showed me Mr. Dandridge's photograph. He gave me a copy, actually, told me to keep it and be sure I looked at it every day."

This time the murmur around the courtroom was considerably louder. Hannah wanted to turn and look at Pierce, but at the same time she couldn't take her eyes off Sam. He was being so brave.

"And you believed him?" Parekh asked.

"I did."

"But you don't believe him now?" Parekh asked.

"I don't," Sam said firmly.

"And why is that, Sam?"

"Because I don't believe good cops use seven-year-old boys to fabricate evidence. As far as I know, the only evidence against Mr. Dandridge is my identification and his confession, which everyone knows was beaten out of him."

"Objection, Judge. Facts not in evidence." The prosecutor made his objection lazily, confidently, from his seated position.

"Sustained," the judge said.

"Well, we'll come back to that," said Parekh. "But for now, Sam, let me just ask one more time for clarity. Did you see Michael Dandridge in your home on the night of your mother's murder?"

"I did not."

"And had you ever seen him in your home or at any time?"

"No. The first time I saw Mr. Dandridge was when Sheriff Pierce handed me his photograph. The first time I saw him in person was in court." Sam turned to Dandridge. "I'm very sorry, Mr. Dandridge."

Dandridge's head was bowed as if he couldn't bear the weight of hope that was upon him, but he looked up at Sam's words, and nodded.

"Thank you, Sam," Parekh said. He took his seat, and Engle rose to cross-examine.

"Mr. Fitzhugh, did you speak to the defense team before taking the stand today?" Engle asked briskly.

"Yes," Sam said.

"And did they ask you to change your testimony?"

"They asked me to tell the truth."

"Do you know who killed your mother?" Engle asked.

"I . . . no . . ."

"You didn't see some other man that night, creeping out of your mother's room?"

"No." Sam was flushed now, angry.

"So you're telling the court now that you don't know if Mr. Dandridge here murdered your mother. The very best evidence you have to offer, which contradicts your previous sworn testimony, is that Mr. Dandridge may have committed the crime, or he may not have, but either way, you have no light to shed on the matter."

Sam sat there, lips tight, eyes angry, and said nothing.

"What age are you?" Engle asked.

"I'm eighteen," Sam said.

"Eighteen years old," Engle said. "So eleven years have passed since the first trial, and you say now you lied in that trial. And during those eleven years you never once thought about coming forward to tell what you now say is the truth?"

"I believed Sheriff Pierce when he said that Mr. Dandridge had killed my mother. I know it was wrong to lie and I'm sorry. But I was very young. And who could I have come forward to? Sheriff Pierce was still the sheriff."

"Nevertheless," Engle said. "You had options. A smart, educated young man like yourself. It never occurred to you to go to the police in Richmond, for example?"

Sam hesitated and Engle pressed on.

"In fact this *new* evidence of yours, it only occurred to you after you had a series of meetings with the defense team. Isn't *that* correct?"

"You're making it sound—"

"And isn't it the case, Mr. Fitzhugh, that Mr. Dandridge is from a wealthy Virginia family?"

Sam, angry, shook his head. "I don't know. I don't see what that has to do with anything."

As Jackson Engle's questioning of Sam continued Hannah stood quietly and made her way down the side of the courtroom to the defense table. She crouched down and, leaning around Jim Lehane, touched Robert Parekh's arm to get his attention. He jumped, looked at her like she was something that had crawled out from under a rock.

"Ask for a recess. I have evidence I need to share with you," she whispered.

He recoiled. "Hannah. You can't be here. You need to leave, right now." He tried to return his attention to the front of the court but she tightened her grasp on his wrist.

"Listen to me. Ask the judge for a short recess. I have evidence. Just give me five minutes to explain."

She could see that he didn't trust her. But either he felt like he had nothing to lose or it suited him to request a recess at that time. When Engle finally released a distraught Sam from the witness box, Parekh stood and requested five minutes. The judge wasn't happy, Engle objected, Parekh pushed harder.

"Two minutes, then, Mr. Parekh. Use them wisely because there will be no more unscheduled breaks. The court has a full day."

Parekh tried to usher Hannah into a side room. She held back.

"Michael has to come too," she said.

Parekh hesitated, but really there was no reason to refuse her request, and he could surely tell by the look in her eyes that she wouldn't yield on it. So he made the arrangements and Dandridge too was escorted to a side room. Lehane, Sean, and Camila followed.

"What's all this about?" Parekh had his arms folded.

"I have evidence that Pierce knew who really killed Sarah Fitzhugh. That he framed Michael for his own reasons."

Parekh glanced at Sean. "This is your theory about Derek Rawlings again. What's the evidence? Rawlings is long dead."

"There was hair evidence taken from another crime. Another home invasion and attempted rape. That evidence was hidden by Jerome Pierce because he didn't want anyone to know that his brother-in-law was a rapist and murderer. I believe that that hair will match the hair taken from the Sarah Fitzhugh murder and prove that Rawlings committed both crimes."

"Where did you get this evidence?" Parekh snapped. "And how do you think we're going to prove it came from Rawlings?"

There was a knock on the door to the side room. The bailiff, calling them back to court.

"Look, there's no time to explain everything," Hannah said.

"You'll have to trust me. Has Pierce already given evidence? Call him to the stand again and let me cross-examine."

Parekh shook his head, eyes wide in disbelief. "I'm not going to do that. Are you crazy? Apart from the *minor* fact that you told Sean you've been working against us for the past week, you're not even qualified. You're a student, for God's sake."

Hannah was very conscious of Dandridge's eyes on her. "I'm a third year," she said. "I'm enrolled and in good standing at Virginia Law. The third-year practice rule says that I may, in the presence of a supervising lawyer, appear in any court in any criminal matter on behalf of any person if the person on whose behalf I am appearing consents." She turned to Dandridge. "You have to consent. If you say no, it's all over." Hannah was surprised that her voice sounded steady. Inside she was jittery and uncertain.

Parekh was still shaking his head. Hannah turned to Dandridge.

"Please. What possible motive would I have to cross-examine Pierce in an open courtroom, other than to help? I can't hurt you."

"That's just not true," Parekh cut in. He took a step forward, putting himself between Hannah and Dandridge, cutting her off. "She can hurt you. Deliberately or not. She doesn't have the experience."

There was another knock at the door. They were running out of time.

"Please. Please, Michael. You have to trust me."

"Hannah." Parekh turned to her, trying for patience. "I haven't seen this evidence you're talking about. I have no idea if it has any value or if you're just plain making things up. I'm not going to risk my case by putting you . . . Look, we can discuss this tonight. You can lay it all out for me. We can take it to trial."

"No," Hannah said firmly. "That's not an option. You know Pierce. Give him time and he'll find a way to make it all go away."

There was yet another knock on the door, this one louder. She had to push him. She had the strongest feeling that she had one chance to make things right. If she let this chance slip through her fingers everything could get much, much worse. She *had* to make Parekh listen to her. Maybe she'd been unfair about him, back in that conversation she'd had with Sean's mother. Maybe he was running the Project for all the right reasons. But he was still a human being with his own private motivations, and the Robert Parekh that she had observed was a man who loved to win, no matter the cost.

"Look, the evidence I have, I stole it from Jerome Pierce's home. An hour ago. When he gets out of here this evening and finds out that it's gone, he's going to move heaven and earth to find me. There's nothing he won't do to stop this information from coming to light. If you let this chance go by, it will not come again."

Parekh looked appalled. "Jesus Christ. You did what? You broke in?"

"When you took me onboard, you said you were taking me on because I was the kind of person who did things other people wouldn't do. That I'd go the extra mile, think outside the box, whatever. Well, now I've gone and done it. I've got the evidence you need to turn this case around and you're too afraid to use it. I'm telling you. Let me do this and it's all over. Let me do this and Michael goes free. If you don't . . . well, I don't know what's going to happen. But I know Pierce and Engle are awfully good at making problems go away. Do you want to win this thing, or don't you?"

Parekh wavered just for a moment, but Hannah could see he was going to refuse her and her heart sank.

"Let her do it," Dandridge said.

Parekh turned on him.

"Let her do it, Rob. I trust her. And it's my case, after all. My life."

There was yet another knock on the door, more insistent this time. Parekh held her gaze for a long moment, then he threw his hands up.

"Why not? If nothing else, you'll have grounds for an appeal for incompetent counsel, right?" He spun away, thrust open the door, and before Hannah quite knew what was happening, he was back in the courtroom, asking the judge for permission to call Pierce again, asking that Hannah be allowed to question him. It took some persuasion for the judge to agree. It helped that Jackson Engle seemed more bemused than concerned. He turned to look her over. The judge was watching her too. Hannah took a breath, closed her hands into fists to stop them from shaking.

"I hope you know what the fuck you're doing," Parekh hissed at her as he returned to his seat.

Jerome Pierce took the stand. His pale eyes met hers and she had to shake off a feeling of impending doom. Christ, he was intimidating. Oh God, this was actually going to happen. She'd talked herself into this situation. Now she had to deliver. It was harder even than she had imagined, standing alone in the middle of the courtroom with every eye on her. She wanted just one more quiet moment alone, to order her thoughts and strengthen her nerve, but there was no more time. It was now or never.

Before entering the courtroom Hannah had placed the evidence bag from the Sarah Fitzhugh file in Pierce's garage inside another clear plastic bag, to protect any fingerprint evidence there might be. She took that bag from her backpack and carried it across to Pierce, placing it in front of him.

"Sheriff Pierce, can you tell me what this is?" she said, her voice clear and loud and carrying across a suddenly hushed courtroom. He looked at the evidence bag and back at her. He searched for words and found none.

Engle jumped to his feet. "Judge, this is a preliminary hearing, not a trial. This is not the time for the defense to try to enter new evidence."

Hannah turned to Burrell. She made sure that she was very calm, very professional, and very clear when she responded. She also made sure that she pitched her voice loud enough that the journalists at the back could hear her. "I'd ask the court for a little leeway, Your Honor. I'm afraid we have come across evidence of a decade-long cover-up by the sheriff. The evidence already put before the court today in an effort to indict our client is a deliberate attempt to mislead you. I'm not trying to enter new evidence, just to demonstrate that the evidence already put before you is false."

Burrell looked over Hannah's head to Robert Parekh. Hannah resisted the temptation to turn to him too and kept her eyes on the judge. After a moment, Burrell said—"A little leeway, Ms. Rokeby, but let's not get carried away. And I hope you're going to back those very strong words up with very strong evidence. We don't malign the character of long-serving police officers in the courtroom without good reason."

Hannah inclined her head and turned back to Pierce. "Sheriff Pierce, do you recognize that evidence bag?"

He cleared his throat. "I do not."

"Okay, let's go back a bit. Do you recall a break-in and attempted rape of a woman named Lana Cantrell in Victory Hill in 2009?" Hannah raised her voice again for the benefit of the gallery. "Lana was at home alone with her baby late at night. A man broke into her home and attacked her. Luckily, Lana's husband came home unexpectedly from a business trip and interrupted the attack. According to the police report the attacker escaped and left no DNA evidence behind. Do you recall that case?"

"I do," Pierce said gravely. "Not all of the detail. It was a long time ago, but I recall the case." God he was good. He came across like an upstanding guy. The kind of serious, measured, feeling person you'd want to have running your town's law enforcement. Hannah thought about that moment in the bar after Sean had been beaten to a pulp. *Now, Pierce. Now you get what's due.*

"Do you recall then that your crime scene officers did in fact recover hair evidence from the Lana Cantrell case?"

"No, I don't. As you said, there was no DNA evidence in that case."

"You don't recall that hair evidence was recovered from the scene in the ordinary way and logged into evidence by an officer named Nicola Pandy?"

"I . . . no. I don't recall." For the first time, Pierce looked uncertain.

"You don't recall going to Officer Pandy and threatening her? Officer Pandy's grandson had a record for pot possession. You don't recall going to her, taking that evidence bag from her, that bag which contains the hair evidence recovered from the Cantrell scene, and then threatening Officer Pandy? Warning her if she told anyone about what you had done, that next time you arrested her grandson, it would be for intention to supply and it would be heroin?"

"Absolutely not."

"So if I were to call Officer Pandy to the stand and she were to testify to that effect, she would be lying?" Hannah waved a hand vaguely in the direction of the courtroom, as if she had Nicola Pandy right there, ready to go. In fact Pandy was retired and living in Florida. Hannah had spoken to her on the phone. Pandy had no family in Virginia these days. She would be willing to testify, she said, but travel wasn't easy for her with her various health problems, and she certainly couldn't have gotten to Yorktown with an hour's notice. Pierce didn't know any of that though. His eyes swept the courtroom, looking for a woman he hadn't seen in person for over seven years. And the judge saw him do it, even as he denied everything.

"She would be lying, yes," Pierce said firmly.

Hannah picked up the bag and carried it to the evidence clerk. "Judge, we'd like to admit this into evidence please. It is hair evidence taken from the Lana Cantrell case. The chain of evidence is written on the bag. It tells you who collected the evidence and the person to whom they passed it. The name of the crime scene officer who collected the evidence is written on the bag. Nicola Pandy. Officer Pandy doesn't work for the state of Virginia anymore. She is willing to testify because her grandson and all of her family have left Virginia and are therefore no longer in danger from Sheriff Pierce."

Jackson Engle stood. "Objection, Judge. We have no information as to where this evidence came from. Anyone can throw some hair in a baggy and write a name on the front. This is hardly credible. And Ms. Rokeby seems to have forgotten that she is here to question the witness, not to testify herself. And even if Ms. Rokeby *was* a witness, which she is not, she has no direct knowledge of any of this. This is all hearsay."

"Actually," Hannah said. "I recovered this evidence myself just over an hour ago when I broke into Sheriff Pierce's private office in his home here in Yorktown. Sheriff Pierce maintains a collection of duplicate police files and what appears to be voluminous blackmail material in that office, including a duplicate of the Sarah Fitzhugh file. That's where I found this evidence."

Pandemonium broke out in the courtroom. The public gallery burst into conversation. Engle jumped to his feet again and called out objections. The judge called for order. Eventually, more perhaps because people wanted to see what would happen next than for any other reason, the courtroom quieted.

"Judge, this supposed evidence was obtained by the most egregious breach of Sheriff Pierce's constitutional rights and should be excluded on that basis. It's not admissible."

But Hannah was ready. "*Burdeau v. McDowell,* Judge. I am not a member of law enforcement. I'm a private citizen. And I just have a few more questions."

The judge hesitated. Her eyes were on Jerome Pierce. Hannah got the distinct impression that the allegation that Pierce was a blackmailer hadn't come as a complete surprise to the judge, but she came down on Hannah's side. "Proceed, Ms. Rokeby, but carefully please. These are very serious allegations."

The courtroom settled again into tense, anticipatory silence. Hannah was painfully aware that every person in the courtroom was focused on her and on what she might say next. This was so difficult and Jackson Engle was right. She was essentially trying to testify through Pierce. Her eyes went to Michael Dandridge. Her father. God. What kind of man was he really? Not the monster of her mother's fairy tale, but not an angel either. None of that had been real. From now on she would look at life with eyes wide open. Right now Michael looked flushed and agitated. Excited and scared at the same time. His freedom in her hands. It was too much.

"Isn't it the case, Sheriff Pierce, that you knew that your brother-in-law, Derek Rawlings, was the man who committed both crimes? The rape and murder of Sarah Fitzhugh and the attempted rape of Lana Cantrell? That you covered up for Derek Rawlings after the murder of Sarah Fitzhugh because he *was* your brother-in-law and you did not want the social embarrassment that would follow if he were exposed?"

"Absolutely not," Pierce said. He was red-faced with fury and frustration and he was sweating hard.

"Isn't it the case that you arrested Michael Dandridge for the murder of Sarah Fitzhugh as part of that cover-up, and that you beat him up during your interrogation to force him to confess?"

"No. No way."

"And isn't it the case that after Derek Rawlings tried to rape Lana Cantrell, you stole and hid the hair evidence from that case to make sure that it wasn't tested? You couldn't allow the hair to be tested because you knew it would match the hair recovered from the Fitzhugh murder, and if that was discovered, your whole setup against our client might well collapse."

"You are full of shit," Pierce said. Spittle flew from his mouth. "This is unacceptable. I don't have to take this."

Hannah turned to Burrell. "Judge, I spoke to Teddy Rawlings. Teddy is Derek Rawlings's son." Thank God for social media. She'd found Teddy online. Sam had mentioned he'd gone to Columbia University and that had been enough to track him down. She'd messaged him and then called him after speaking with Nicola Pandy. "Teddy believes his father was guilty of Sarah's murder. He is willing to have his DNA taken, for the purpose of familial DNA testing. I believe that the test will show that the hair that was taken from Sarah's scene was that of Derek Rawlings, and that it will match the hair from the Cantrell scene also."

Engle finally took to his feet. He looked utterly shaken and Hannah wondered again what was in that manila folder with his name on it. She hadn't had time to look at it.

"Judge, this is all well and good, but we are in obvious hearsay territory here. If Ms. Pandy wishes to give evidence in this case, then she should give evidence. We cannot rely on Ms. Rokeby's word. She has, after all, just confessed to breaking into the property of a law enforcement officer. And we still have no chain of title for this so-called hair evidence, even should DNA testing proceed."

Parekh stood too, keen to take back control of his case, and the attorneys argued the law around admissibility until the judge called a halt. The tiredness that had been in her face when Hannah had entered the courtroom had disappeared. She looked sharp and focused, like someone who had sensed an opportunity and wasn't about to let it go past.

"Let's not lose track of what we're doing here. This is a preliminary hearing, not a trial," she said. "Right now, I'm not satisfied that there is sufficient evidence against the defendant for this case to proceed. The eyewitness has withdrawn his testimony. There is also serious doubt about the credibility of the evidence that Sheriff Pierce has put forward regarding Mr. Dandridge's confession. Right now, unless you have something else, Mr. Engle, I'm inclined to dismiss the charges."

She looked at Engle, waiting for his response, and Hannah held her breath. Engle looked at Pierce, who was still sitting and sweating in the witness box. Pierce looked like a trapped animal. It occurred to Hannah that he was probably armed. She noticed that the bailiff, a huge man, at least six foot four and built like a UFC fighter, had taken up a position close by.

Engle had nothing. Burrell knocked her gavel lightly. "I'm dismissing the charges in this case at this time. I am not satisfied that there is probable cause here. Mr. Dandridge, you are free to go."

Michael didn't move. He looked from Hannah to Parekh and back again, as if he couldn't believe what was happening. Parekh clapped a reassuring hand on his shoulder. Pierce stood up to leave. His eyes—red-rimmed and furious—went to Hannah and she knew that he would be coming for her.

Judge Burrell raised a hand. "No, Sheriff Pierce, I'd like you to stay for a moment, please." She turned to her bailiff. "Marcus, can you clear the courtroom, please?"

IT TOOK TEN MINUTES OR SO, BUT THE COURTROOM EMPTIED OUT. Even Michael left, disappearing through a side door with Sean and Camila. Soon it was just the judge and her staff, the bailiff and the deputies, the attorneys, Pierce, and Hannah.

Burrell stared at Jackson Engle with narrowed eyes. "Given the serious nature of the allegations made by Ms. Rokeby, Jackson, I assume that you are going to investigate without delay." It wasn't a question, precisely, and Engle looked back at the judge blankly. "For example, I would assume that you will shortly apply to me for a warrant to search Sheriff Pierce's home for duplicate police files and blackmail material?"

"Judge—" Pierce tried to interrupt. The bailiff stepped closer to him. Burrell held up a hand to silence Pierce.

"I assume too that you will be applying for a warrant to arrest Sheriff Pierce so that he can be questioned about the allegations?"

"I . . . yes."

"Very well." Burrell turned to her clerk who handed her a sheet of paper. The judge bent her head to it, started writing, and without lifting her head from her work, said—"Marcus?"

The bailiff leaned into the witness box and, putting one meaty hand on Pierce's forearm to restrain him, quickly unclipped Pierce's holster and removed his gun. Pierce reacted like a jack-in-the-box. He burst from his chair and turned and tried to reach for the bailiff, swearing. But the bailiff—Marcus—shoved Pierce back into a sitting position with relative ease. Pierce sat staring up at him while Marcus hovered over him and there was an air of barely restrained violence between them.

Burrell signed the sheet of paper in front of her with a flourish. She held it out to Jackson Engle. "Here you are, Jackson. The deputies here will assist you in taking Sheriff Pierce into custody."

Hannah held her breath. There was a moment when things hovered. Burrell sat with her arm still extended. The deputies, who were technically under Pierce's command, after all, and only seconded to the court for security purposes, hesitated, unsure of themselves. And Pierce seemed like he might tackle the bailiff at any moment. And then Engle nodded heavily and took the warrant, bowing to the inevitable. The deputies followed his lead and took Pierce into custody. And just like that, it was done.

LATER, HANNAH AND ROBERT PAREKH WERE ALONE IN THE EMPTY courtroom. "I knew there was something," he said. "From the beginning I knew. I should have sent you away, but I was curious. You were a mystery that I wanted to solve." He had a mocking, amused look on his face, but it was directed inward. "Serves me right that you were a mole." The amusement turned into a grin. "But if I hadn't brought you in we'd never have ended up here, would we?"

"I don't know. I think, maybe, if I hadn't been distracting everyone . . ."

"Bullshit." He regarded her. "What are you going to do next? Not go back to Maine, I think."

Hannah said nothing. She hadn't thought about what might come after. The decisions she would have to make.

"Come back to the Project," Parekh said. "Finish out the year. You have talent, Hannah. And more than that, you're a fighter. I told you I need people who are willing to go the extra mile." He laughed. "Jesus, if that's ever you . . ."

"I . . ."

"Remember the Nia Jones case? You brought that to me, and it's waiting for you. There's still work to be done. So think about it, okay?"

The idea appealed to her. She didn't want to go back to Maine. But she didn't know what she wanted. She felt more adrift than ever. But it wasn't that easy. And besides, there were complications.

"I'm not a student," Hannah said abruptly.

He stared at her. "What?"

"I mean, I'm enrolled at U Maine, but not at Virginia. I only found out about the appeal in Michael's case a few weeks ago. There was no way I could get a transfer so late in the year. I tried, but it wasn't going to happen. Then I figured, I didn't really need to be a student. I just needed to look like one so I could get into the Project. So I paid someone to hack into the system at UVA and enter my name. They got me a student number and an email address and I had an ID made up."

Parekh looked completely thrown. "Are you serious?"

"I don't know how long it would have worked. I didn't try to attend classes. I didn't want to risk getting caught. I just needed some time at the Project."

Parekh was shaking his head. "Hannah, you've just . . . we've just told the court you're enrolled at Virginia Law. That's the only reason you were allowed to question Pierce. Christ. If this was known, you'd be disbarred before you were ever admitted. You'd never be a lawyer."

Now that it was all over Hannah felt only a sinking, drifting feeling. Whether or not she could return to school, whether or not she would ever be a lawyer, none of it seemed to matter. "I know. It seemed like it might be worth it."

He was lost for words. He just stood there, thinking, for a long moment. "Do you plan on going back to Maine to graduate?"

"I suppose that's up to you. You could report me."

He started packing up his papers again and was silent for a time. "Maybe some things are better left unsaid, for everyone's sake. With all the fallout from this, there'll be enough headlines. Maybe no one will think to look too closely at you."

It surprised Hannah that Parekh was being so generous, but she thought it wasn't likely she would get away with everything. There had been journalists in the courtroom. What had happened would be reported and she'd been front and center to all the drama. Someone was bound to ask an awkward question. She'd need more luck than she'd ever had in her life to get away with this, to be able to return quietly to Maine, without repercussions. If that was even what she wanted. "What happens next?" she asked. "With Pierce, I mean."

"Burrell will make some phone calls. Engle won't have this investigation long. This has been too public. They'll have to do it right." Parekh had put the last of his papers into his bag. He glanced around the courtroom, as if committing it to memory, and turned to go.

"Robert."

He turned back.

"Why do you do it? What's in it for you?"

"Why do I do what? The Project, you mean?"

She nodded.

He sighed, like it was a question he had been asked too many times. "Because it has to be done. Because if you see something like this, and you can fix it, then it's your mess to clean up. We're talking about basic maintenance, Hannah. That's what we're doing. Our work is necessary, basic, bare minimum maintenance of the system. If we don't do it, the house falls down around us. You asked what I get out of it? That's the answer. A house I can live in. Somewhere safe to sleep at the end of the day."

She let him go, but she thought about what he'd said for a long time.

Hannah

TWENTY-ONE

Hannah let herself quietly into the little house in Orono, Maine. Laura was waiting for her, by arrangement.

"Hannah."

"Mom."

Laura was standing near the fireplace, her hand on the back of the armchair. She was beautifully dressed in tailored wool trousers and a silk blouse, her hair smooth and shiny. Hannah, in her travel-stained jeans and T-shirt, felt a familiar sense of inadequacy.

"I hope you are ready to apologize," Laura said stiffly. "I don't know what got into you, down there in Virginia. I don't know how I'll ever forgive you."

"Michael Dandridge is my father," Hannah said quietly. She'd been anticipating this confrontation for days, had seen it, in her mind's eye, painted in colors of high drama. But now that the moment had arrived, she felt curiously flat. Laura, on the other hand, was almost quivering with tension and pent-up energy. She must have known exactly what was coming, but she blanched as if Hannah had slapped her, and took a half-step backward. Hannah drew on reserves of strength that felt almost depleted and continued. "You wrote that diary for me, to keep me in line. I'd started high school, I was getting older, I was beginning to see through you, wasn't I? But I was still sad, still lonely. So you gave me a fairy tale. A story I could cling to. Something that would explain you and excuse you. And my God, it worked, didn't it? I just ate it up."

Suddenly, Laura was fighting back tears. She held up a hand to Hannah and wheezed as she tried to take a breath. Her face tightened again in fear as she tried and failed to draw another breath.

"Hannah . . ." It was a gasp more than it was a word.

"Stop it, Mom," Hannah said flatly.

It took a minute for Laura to realize that this time Hannah wasn't going to run to the rescue. She dropped the outstretched hand, straightened up, and her expression changed to one of injured innocence. "How could you ever think that of me? That I could do that to you? How could you accuse me, after everything I've been through . . ."

Hannah saw the calculation in her mother's eyes and wondered how she could ever have been blind to it.

"It's not true," Laura continued. "Not true. Whoever told you all of this is lying to you. Manipulating you."

"You told me that my father was a murderer and a rapist. You let me go to Virginia to do everything I could to keep him in prison. That's sick. You're a sick person."

"I *never* lied to you. Michael Dandridge is *not* your father."

"Jesus, Mom. Give it up. He's a free man. You must know that by now. A DNA test would take a few weeks. What are you going to do when I come to you with the results?"

Laura shook her head in seeming distress. "If you did do a test it would only prove that I've been telling the truth. But . . . if by the smallest chance . . . I mean . . . I don't think so, but the rape . . ."

Hannah felt sick. "Jesus, Mom."

Laura looked back at her, mutinous.

"Why do you hate him so much? Because he left you? Or because he wasn't as rich as you thought he was when you hooked up with him?"

Laura just shook her head.

"How much punishment would have been enough? You sent him to prison for eleven years. You almost got him killed."

"I had nothing to do with him going to prison!" Laura flared up. "What happened in Virginia had nothing to do with me."

"Bullshit. I checked the files. The cops were looking for a scapegoat, sure, but they chose Michael for a reason. Those anonymous calls. Michael's lawyers thought the cops made them up. But I've checked. Those calls came from Orono. They came from here. They came from you."

For the longest moment Laura said nothing. Then she straightened up, and all the distress fell out of her expression. She smoothed her hair back from her face. "You can't prove any of this," she said.

All the breath went out of Hannah's lungs. She stood still for a moment, then forced herself to move, to walk toward her bedroom. She pulled a suitcase out from under her bed and started packing, throwing in clothes and books as fast as she could. Laura stood in the door and watched.

"I'm going to tell the Spencers the truth," Hannah said. "I'll take that DNA test and prove that you lied to them. They'll come after you with their expensive lawyers."

Laura's expression didn't change. "If they come after me, they'll come after your precious father too. He's the one who betrayed their trust. Don't you think he's suffered enough?"

Hannah ground her teeth and kept packing.

"Where will you go?" Laura asked.

"None of your business."

Laura smiled. "I wouldn't be quite so confident, if I were you.

You forget that I control the money. You walk out of that door and I cut you off."

Hannah closed the suitcase. There was an empty backpack at the bottom of her closet. She took her college folders from her desk, put them in the backpack, and filled up the rest of the space with pajamas and underwear. That would have to do. She put the backpack on her back.

"I did terrible things, Mom, but I can't blame you for that. That's on me. I'm not a child. I have to take responsibility for my own decisions, for my mistakes. I'm not going to be like you, see? Blaming everyone else, hating everyone else. But I'm done. I'm done with you." As she spoke Hannah felt the last connection between them, a tight cord of pain, snap. She took a breath, and the air felt cleaner.

"Dandridge has nothing," Laura said, her voice shrill. "You get that? His family's broke and he's a bum. You think I set the sheriff on him for no reason? He tried to get more money out of me. We made a deal and he went back on it. He would have taken food from his own daughter's mouth. I did it for you, Hannah. I did it all for you."

Hannah settled the backpack on her back. She tightened the straps and, pulling her suitcase behind her, pushed past her mother and out into the hall. She went to the door and then outside to her car. Sean was there, waiting. Camila too. They had proved to be far better, more forgiving friends than she deserved. Sean helped her to lift her bags into the trunk.

"Okay?" he asked quietly.

"Okay."

Laura stood at the door of the house. Hannah half-expected her to scream something as they left, but she stayed silent, watching with hooded eyes. Hannah felt a wrench of emotion, a pull of regret. Maybe some part of her still wanted the fight. If they were fighting, then it wasn't over. Sean was waiting for her to get into the car. Hannah hesitated, then turned and walked back to the house. Laura's face brightened in anticipation. Hannah stared at her, trying, by sheer force of will, to look past the shiny exterior and see, clearly and finally, what her mother was.

"You can have the money," Hannah said. "But you can't have me."

Laura's face fell. Hannah turned and walked back to the car. She climbed in and Sean started the engine. They drove. Hannah cried quietly for a while. They didn't talk. Every now and then Sean would take his hand from the steering wheel and squeeze hers. Eventually Hannah stopped crying. She looked out of the window and watched the countryside go by. She wiped away the last of her tears. She was smiling.

Acknowledgments

I owe enormous thanks to many people who helped me to write the book I wanted to write.

First, to Shane Salerno, my agent, who pushes me exactly how I needed to be pushed, makes space for me when I need to take a breath, and advocates for me in a way I haven't been able to advocate for myself. Shane, I hope you know how grateful I am. Thank you.

To my editors, Anna Valdinger, Emily Krump, Phoebe Morgan, and Julia Elliott, thank you for your support and encouragement, your confidence, and your always excellent taste and guidance.

Thank you so much to booksellers all over the world, who have worked so hard in such difficult circumstances over the past two years. Thank you for giving so much to preserve our industry.

Thank you to everyone on the sales and marketing teams at the publishing houses I've been lucky enough to work with, who somehow make a space in a loud and busy world for my books. Thank you in particular to Alice Wood, marketing genius and travel buddy extraordinaire. Thank you to Sara Foster, who read an early draft and, as always, provided a friendly ear.

Thank you to the readers, in particular those who read one and come back for more and then tell me about it. You make my dreams come true.

Last, but never least, thank you to my family: to Kenny, Freya, and Oisin. Thank you for the title suggestions, the log lines, the jokes, and the love. I'll never know how I got this lucky.

About the Author

Dervla McTiernan is the internationally bestselling author of *The Rúin, The Scholar,* and *The Good Turn.* After twelve years working as a lawyer, she moved from Ireland to Australia and turned her hand to writing. Dervla is a member of the Sisters in Crime and Crime Writers Association, and lives in Perth, Australia, with her husband and two children.